The Death of a
Disco Dancer

D1310850

The Death of a Disco Dancer

David Clark

Provo, Utah

Published by Zarahemla Books
869 East 2680 North
Provo, UT 84604
info@zarahemlabooks.com
ZarahemlaBooks.com

For Robin

"To everything there is a season,
and a time to every purpose under the heaven:

A time to be born, and a time to die;
a time to plant, and a time to pluck up that which is planted;

A time to kill, and a time to heal;
a time to break down, and a time to build up;

A time to weep, and a time to laugh;
a time to mourn, and a time to dance."
—*Ecclesiastes 3:1–4*

"Humiliation is the beginning of sanctification."
—*John Donne, Sermon at St. Paul's Cathedral, Christmas Day, 1625*

Playlist

prologue

Last Dance

3:49 p.m. Tuesday, August 18, 1981

My hair, brown and bushy, was parted down the middle, feathered back, Officer Poncherello style.

I was sporting new button-fly 501s. They'd only been washed twice and were still blackish blue, slightly stiff. The jeans were snug around the waist and crotch, but not too terribly tight—part of my new junior high wardrobe. The grocery bag–colored tag above the right back pocket read W27 L30, subtly pronouncing to those with a view of my behind that I was tall and lean—but not skinny.

A silver and blue vinyl Velcro wallet stamped with a yellow lightning bolt was tucked in my left back pocket, protected from the jostle of the crowded room by a red plastic comb, handle slightly peeking over the pocket's edge. Wallet contents: one yellow Mesa Public Library card, one newly minted white plastic Mangas Coloradas Junior High student ID card, seven dollars, a stick of Big Red, and a ticket stub from *Clash of the Titans*.

On top, I was wearing a cream-colored, terrycloth collared Kensington shirt. Two horizontal velour stripes—royal blue and burgundy—sat just below pectoral level. All three buttons were unfastened, seventh-grade style. As I walked, I lifted my arms slightly out from my sides in what I hoped was a subtle attempt to air out the beads of sweat threatening to give me pit stains.

On my feet were Wally Waffle Trainers, royal blue with a gold Nike swoosh and standard-issue white athletic socks. They, too, were starting to feel damp. A wad of grape Hubba Bubba was plastered among four waffle treads, slightly sticking to the cafeteria floor, annoying me as I shuffled and shifted my weight.

And, underneath it all, was Gregory's jockstrap, practically shrink-wrapped over my goods, like battle armor—for "containment," he said—and the extra-large Band-Aids beginning to peel off of my otherwise bare, river-stone-smooth butt cheeks.

I aimlessly took a few steps to my right, beside what was usually a stand offering lukewarm slices of pizza for fifty cents, which in the darkness and throbbing beat of the music and pulsing lights ricocheting off the disco ball in the center of the cafeteria managed to look almost decorative. And that was the moment I learned the first advanced equation of my fledgling junior high career:

$$\left(\frac{LD \ + \ KR}{JS} \right) \ x \ JGL^2 \ = \ \textit{Prepubescent Apocalypse}$$

Where:

LD = last dance at the eleventh annual Mangas Coloradas Junior High School "Hello Dance"

KR = Kenny Rogers crooning about being the knight in shining armor of some lady named "Lady"

JS = jockstrap

JGL = Jenny Gillette's lips, lacquered with a fresh coat of bubble-gum-scented Kissing Potion roll-on lip gloss—gleaming beneath the reflection of the disco ball hanging from the cafeteria ceiling of Mangas Coloradas Junior High

1

Don't Leave Me This Way

The back of my mother's auburn bob blocked my view of Ben-G standing in the open crack of our enormous red front door. The only part of him I could see was his new Adidas Superstars, slightly shuffling as he spoke.

I had been upstairs in my room, finally calmed down and staring out the window.

Grounded again.

Jericho Croshaw, T. J. McKay, Curtis Walker, and Ben-G—Jericho's younger brother—were up the street, armed with Nerf footballs, hunting the stray cats that live in the orange groves.

When the doorbell rang, I knew it was for me. I peeked out of my room and crept to the top of the staircase.

Mom told him I wasn't allowed to go swimming.

"Sorry, he's on restriction," she said solemnly.

Dad calls it "grounded."

Grounded is better.

"Grounded" made it sound like I was an F-15 that got rolled back into the hangar because of bad weather. "On restriction" made it sound like I was chained to a steel post, like Megiddo, the Croshaws' psychotic German Shepherd.

There was nothing I could do, so I stayed quiet and went back to my room.

She had completely overreacted.

A Quarterback Sack should really not have been that big of a deal—*definitely* not worthy of grounding. Punching or kicking? Both worthy of grounding. I expected to be grounded for premeditated, malicious violence (which a Quarterback Sack is *not*).

Swearing? Maybe. It would depend on the situation—which word you used, the way you said it, the way you used it. "Aaggh! I spilled the *damn* Spaghetti-Os!" Not worthy of grounding. Especially since wiping up a slimy pile of overcooked circular noodles in sticky red sauce would be punishment enough. It would be like wiping up brains at a homicide scene. Disgusting and completely ruin your appetite. The poor guy that has to clean up the crime scene is definitely saying *damn*—a lot.

If used as an adjective, there's really no way *damn* should ever get you grounded. *Damn* as a verb, though—at my house that got you grounded every time.

Case in point. After we saw the Suns play the Bullets, Gregory's favorite basketball player was Mitch Kupchak. Why? I'm pretty sure it had something to do with his baseball coach.

Gregory's baseball coach, Dale Throckborden, a stock broker that still lived on the fumes of glory provided by a season playing class B ball in Keokuk, Iowa, was big—very big—on cup checks. Just before he turned in the lineup card, Coach Throckborden would line the team up on the first-base line, just outside the dugout, and then walk down the line, aluminum baseball bat in hand. Clutching the barrel of the bat in his right hand and loosely holding the rubber-gripped bat stem between the index finger and thumb of his left hand—like a pool shark lining up his cue stick—he would jab the handle of the bat between each boy's legs, one after the other. For those boys wearing correctly positioned cups, the tap of metal on hard plastic gave an affirmative, painless reply. For those boys who forgot to wear their cups, knee-buckling agony told the sad story of dressing out too hastily. No member of Dale Throckborden's E. F. Hutton Sidewinders ever forgot to wear a cup more than once.

Mom was suspicious. She thought Coach Throckborden was way too interested in the testicular well-being of thirteen-year old boys.

"Bob, will you look at what he's doing? He's doing it again! It's like he takes a sadistic pleasure in it. He's a *pervert!*"

I wasn't even sure what that really meant, but I knew it meant she thought Coach Throckborden was a weirdo.

"No, he's not, Linda. All the boys have to wear cups, and he has to vouch for them to the umpire before the game. How else should he check to see if they're wearing them?"

"How about just asking the boys?"

No response from Dad. Silence signaled surrender. Mom won.

Since the Suns-Bullets game and Gregory's infatuation with Mitch Kupchak began, every so often, but not too often, when you'd be walking past him, he'd hold out his hand to give you a casual five as he passed by. And, just as you'd raise your hand to slap him the five, out of nowhere he'd smack your gems with his other hand and say, "Hi, I'm Mitch Cup-check. Nice to meet you." The initial shock and the lingering nausea, like a migraine in your nut pouch, left you powerless to retaliate for at least fifteen minutes.

After a couple of times, I fell for it again. And when I say "fell for it," I mean that the last time it happened, Gregory had sworn he'd never do it again. I dropped to my knees. Crumpled up on the floor and cradling my sack, I shouted, "*Damn* you to *hell,* Gregory!"

Damn as a verb. Mom heard it. I was instantly grounded.

According to Mom, only God could damn someone, and trying to do what only God Himself could do was blasphemous and made a mockery of sacred things. Apparently, possible permanent damage to my ability to fulfill His commandment to multiply and replenish the earth was not nearly as serious. Gregory got off *again* with a lecture along the lines of "showing some respect for your younger brother's privates."

Thankfully, he never actually tried to do that.

But the reason I was grounded *this* particular time was the Quarterback Sack. And a well-executed Quarterback Sack does not *necessarily* have to involve swearing. Maybe grunting and growling, but not swearing. In fact, the best Quarterback Sacks involve no words at all. They're sneak attacks.

Fifteen minutes before Ben-G showed up, my eight-year-old sister Maggie (aka, Terry Bradshaw, Ron Jaworski, Phil Simms, Jim Hart, Steve Bartkowski, Vince Ferragamo, Billy Kilmer, or whatever other quarterback was facing the Dallas Cowboys that week) had been skipping through the family room. I was lying in wait behind the maroon corduroy recliner that Dad sat in to read his four daily newspapers. Crouched in a four-point stance, I waited for just the right moment to spring to my feet, attacking silently, without warning—like an Israeli commando at Entebbe.

What exactly does that look like? Well, I'll put it this way. After Entebbe, Ben-G and Jericho's dad, Brother Croshaw, was beside himself. He said the Israelis were bad asses.

It was all he could talk about for three weeks.

"I'm sorry boys," he'd say whenever the topic came up—which it generally did when he was around. "I'm generally not one to curse or swear, but there is really no other way to describe them." Brother Croshaw was one of those guys that no matter how hard he tried to be poetic, descriptive, or eloquent about something, he somehow got worse and even coarser, the harder he tried.

"You know those Israelis at Entebbe were all Sayeret Matkal?" he'd ask too intensely, veins bulging in his neck and forehead and attempting to impress us with a guttural Hebrew pronunciation—which was so ridiculous that we knew it had to be wrong. It sounded like he was summoning a loogey. "That's Israeli special forces. They're just like Joshua's boys who took down Jericho with nothing more than a hooker's red hankie and a marching band. These guys are just the same—except now they have planes and Uzis. You can tell your mommies and daddies on me boys, but there's no other way to say it—they're Bad. Asses. That's right. *Bad asses*," he'd repeated for emphasis.

As Maggie skipped through the room, she glanced toward the TV, which was still blaring Grandma Carter's string of game shows. Grandma's spot on the couch was empty, but her red, white, and green hand-crocheted afghan, unraveling at the corners, was lying neatly folded in her place.

Just as Maggie made momentary eye contact with Paul Lynde in the center Hollywood Square, I pounced from my position behind the maroon corduroy recliner on her right.

My left shoulder caught her square in the small of her back. On impact, a whiplashing shockwave pulsed across her short brunette Mom-like bob. I wrapped my arms around her waist and dropped her to the baby blue family-room shagro-turf (that's what Gregory called it).

It was a textbook Quarterback Sack from the blind side. I rose to my feet, tilted my head back, and raised my arms like Rocky Balboa. Maggie bawled and wailed. I suppressed the urge to do a Mark Gastineau, caveman-inspired celebration dance and triumphantly point to Jenny Gillette in the imaginary bleachers.

Instead, I dropped my arms and provided a play-by-play recap in my best Howard Cosellian staccato twang:

"And num-bah se-ven-ty two—Too Tall Jones—the all pa-ro de-fen-sive end for the Da-llas Cowboys sacks Bi-lllee Kilmah again! This time in bone ca-rushing faa-shun!"

"I'M NOT BILLY KILMER!!!" Maggie shrieked.

Mom made it out of the kitchen and into the family room in record time.

"I just wanted to play with my Barbie Electric Piano!" Maggie wailed, practically foaming at the mouth.

Seeing Maggie on the floor sobbing and drooling set Mom off. I got a serious lecture—the standard just-you-wait-until-your-father-gets-home warning and, more ominously, banishment to my room to work on memorizing the Articles of Faith.

When I protested, she called me mister.

"Don't you sass *me*, mister!"

It was a clear indication that she would've used a wooden spoon, spatula, hairbrush, or other household item with a handle on my buttocks, if only one had been in reach.

Perched in my room, peering out the window, the Articles of

Faith opened on my nightstand in case Mom came up to check, I watched Ben-G rejoin Jericho, T. J. and Curtis up the street on the edge of the orange groves. They were squatting to see if there were any cats below the lowest hanging orange-tree branches.

I watched as T. J. locked in on what appeared to be an abnormally large Morris-the-Cat look-alike about ten yards away. The cat arched its back and hissed. T. J. cocked and chucked his maroon and gold ASU Nerf football. Morris leaped effortlessly up and over the fence behind the orange trees. T. J. missed by a mile.

T. J. threw like a grown woman—which is about ten times worse than throwing like a girl. There's hope for a girl. There's no hope for a grown woman.

"Holy crap, Tammy Jane! How could you miss?!" I could hear Ben-G hollering.

His effeminate shot put/wrist flick is the reason we called him Tammy Jane. We just knew he'd throw that way the rest of his life. It's probably one of the latent defects he passed along to his posterity.

Jericho, first born of Ezekiel Croshaw—the kid named in honor of the Israelites' pious, bloodless first battle in the land of Canaan—swaggered up beside T. J. Mimicking Tweety Bird, he yelled, "I tawt I taw a puddy!"

He paused and then added, "And I'm *not even* talking about the cat!"

Jericho Croshaw had the foulest mouth of any fourteen year old I knew. He couldn't let it go. He was one of those kids that could have been pretty funny, but he never knew when to stop. So mostly what he said was either too late to the conversation, stupid, or gross.

Stuck in my room, I started fantasizing that I would be imprisoned unfairly for eternity like Nelson Mandela or the Count of Monte Cristo—stuck memorizing the Articles of Faith until I was an old man and could finally, for once in my life, remember that "evangelists" came *after* "prophets, pastors and teachers," and could, at long last, properly pronounce "paradisiacal glory." At the moment, it seemed pretty likely that my emancipation would not happen until after the "literal gathering of Israel" had literally taken place.

And that's when I first caught sight of Arvil Cooley spasmodically lurching up our front walkway.

"Linda!"

"Linda!"

"LINDA!!"

2

The Boss

Linda is my mom.

Besides taking care of Grandma Carter, her main jobs were as follows:

(1) Forcing me to do my chores
(2) Forcing me to be nice to my sisters
(3) Forcing me to drink milk with every meal
(4) Forcing me to practice the piano
(5) Forcing me to memorize the Articles of Faith

Bob is my dad. He was a doctor.

His main jobs were as follows:

(1) Going to work
(2) Being the bishop
(3) Making sure that we listened to Mom
(4) Making sure that Grandma Carter didn't make Mom go crazy

Dad's favorite lines were:

"What did Mom say?"

"Did Mom say you could?"

"Ask Mom."

"Sounds fine to me, but you should check with Mom first."

"Your Mom won't appreciate that kind of behavior."

For the right situation, he was also known to say:

"Ask not what your mother can do for you, but what you can do for your mother" (used when we pestered Mom).

"Fools mock, but they shall mourn" (usually used in response to complaints about Church, bad behavior in Church, or anything even remotely related to Church).

"Count your blessings, it could be worse—a lot worse" (used in response to virtually any expression of self-pity).

"The mortgage on this house doesn't get paid with good times" (the standard explanation for denying our requests for money; also a frequent response to expressions of ingratitude).

"Be careful, or I'll write you a prescription for some alone time in your bedroom" (used in an attempt to be tough and clever at the same time).

"Calm down and take a mulligan" (used when one of us—usually Lisa—had a bout of hysteria brought on by the unfairness of life as a teenager).

Dad may have been the "breadwinner"—that's the term Sister Nelson, the Relief Society president, liked to use when speaking adoringly of the ward's husbands (which, by the way, Mom hated—she said it marginalized *her* contributions—"as if we'd all starve without him," she'd scoff)—but Mom was definitely the Boss. If you wanted permission for anything—going swimming, spending the night at the Croshaws, leaving the dinner table early, riding your bike to Circle K to get a Grape Fanta, staying up late to watch Johnny Carson, whatever—Mom was the sole arbiter of permission requests.

The funny thing was, most people looked at Dad and saw a tall, fit, friendly, "handsome man" (as Grandma Carter described him, even though she couldn't remember who he was—"is that handsome man going to bring in the mail today?") who also happened to be a doctor and the bishop, too. So they automatically thought he was some kind of overachieving puppeteer who controlled every aspect of every life that was close to him. They automatically assumed that he ran the place.

Not so. Dad was the faithful drone. Mom was the queen bee. It was Mom—not Dad—who was the sun of our family solar system. We all orbited around her. One way or another, every one of us could trace every mood, feeling, or attitude back to Mom somehow. She was our life force—and she was in charge. Dad knew it, Mom knew it, and we knew it too. Even

Grandma Carter, who didn't really know anything in those days, knew it.

I think Mom found it kind of funny when all of these people who knew Dad as a doctor or a bishop would come up to her and gush about how her husband was just "the greatest," a "godsend," or "such a talented man." I'm pretty sure she always thought he was all those things too—at least most of the time—but she also knew the real Dad. The guy who didn't know how to change a tire, turn on the oven, ride a motorcycle, or use the electric can opener and never really was quite sure how to identify an Allen wrench. But despite the fact that he was totally uninterested in nearly all of the standard chest-thumping activities of the neighborhood alpha males—yard work, muscle-car makeovers, garage chatter, chrome rims and mud tires, boats, dirt bikes, or any other activity that required a pickup truck or pulling a trailer behind a pick-up truck—I think she secretly believed he was an Atticus Finch–type. A gentle, idealistic, high-minded albeit seemingly prissy Man with a capital M, that could absolutely kick your butt, even though he never would.

Dad totally deferred to Mom. He worshipped her. And after Dad would miss dinner for the third time in the same week—even after his assurances two hours earlier that he would positively, without a doubt, no question about it, most assuredly, darling, be home on time, but he wasn't, because of some last minute call from some teenager who couldn't wait a minute longer to confess the misdeeds of his adventures in dating—and Mom would be standing at the sink helping one of us learn the finer points of using S.O.S. pads on the petrified tomato sauce, ricotta cheese, and crumbled ground beef and other lasagna remnants that the extra twenty minutes at 400 degrees waiting in vain for Dad cemented into the rounded corners of the glass casserole dish, and he would come up from behind silently, index finger on his lips making the "shh!" sign to those of us that could see him come into the kitchen and then would give her a slightly risqué pat on the butt, a kiss on the neck, and a sincere "Sorry, babe" in her ear, and even though she would arch her back at the touch of his lips like an anxious cat and say, "Stop it, Bob!" in an annoyed tone, I knew she was mostly faking and she worshipped him too.

3

Stretchin' Out

Arvil Cooley, our eighty-two-year-old neighbor down the street, the eyes of Shady Grove Estates and one of General Pershing's World War I Doughboys, was huffing and puffing, starting and stopping, gasping and coughing up our front walk way. From my bedroom window it looked like he was playing a game of red light/green light.

Green light!

Arvil lunged forward three steps.

Red light!

Arvil jerked to a stop, yelled "Linda!" and then panted like an English Bulldog.

Green light!

More staggering.

Red light!

More panting and gasping. More, *"Linda!"*

Wobbling toward the front entryway in his shiny white sneakers, canary yellow Sansabelts pulled up past his belly button, and cream-colored Castro barbershop shirt, he stretched out both arms to brace himself as he at last reached the promised land of our over-sized red door. Then, grabbing the brass knocker—more to balance himself than to knock—he banged it down, hoarsely and breathlessly gasping, *"LINDA!"* all the while.

I left the window seat of my bedroom, raced down the stairs, and got to the door just as Mom (who hadn't heard a thing at this point, other than the persistent knocking) casually approached and unlocked the door.

"You're supposed to be in your room," she reminded me under her breath as she opened the door.

Arvil was bent over, still trying to catch his breath and trying to lift his head to make eye contact with Mom.

"Oh my . . . Arvil. What on earth . . . ?" Mom stammered

A solitary drop of sweat acrobatically clung to the tip of his nose, and his glasses had fogged slightly. The thick gray hair on the back of his Esau-ish forearms was matted and moist. As usual, my eyes went straight to his hands—leathery, age-spotted, porterhouse mitts clutching his pants just above his thighs, like a basketball player in a timeout huddle. Massive hands. They never ceased to fill me with a sense of awe—and dread. I had heard the story of how, many years earlier, he retired after being sued for malpractice by a patient of his that woke up during the middle of a wisdom tooth extraction. Arvil had dislocated the poor woman's jaw on accident. Her mouth was so small and his hands were so big that when he reached in to do the extraction it forced her mouth open so wide that her jaw dislocated. Dad says that was before everyone carried malpractice insurance. Apparently, Arvil paid a modest settlement then retired and became a real estate developer like everybody else in town.

"Arvil, what's wrong? Are you okay? What's happened?" Mom asked as she reached over and tried to pull him into the house.

He raised one of his hands as if to say, "Give me a minute."

Mom's questions increased in intensity with each of Arvil's unresponsive pants. Mom thought Mrs. Cooley was dead or something.

"Is Nona okay, Arvil? Is she hurt? Talk to me Arvil!"

Finally, Arvil succeeded in pulling himself together enough to stand up straight and clear his throat. You could practically hear his back creak and his knee joints snap, crackle, and pop as he slowly rose.

"It's your Mother, Linda. I saw her out wandering. She had a book and some kind of picture."

Mom sighed and pushed a strand of auburn hair behind her

ears. She seemed relieved.

"Oh, okay. Where is she—at your house? Is she okay? Is she bothering Nona again?"

Arvil was still doing his best to catch his breath—slowly but surely moving from critical to serious-but-stable condition.

"No, Linda. She's not with Nona. She's lying on her side under one of those wild palo verde trees on the canal bank. I think she just passed out, but her head is bleeding a little bit."

Mom calmly turned to me, looked me dead in the eye, and said, "Call your father." Then she sprinted down the street heading toward the canal.

Hearing the rapid fire of her flip-flops spanking the asphalt of Orchard Way, Curtis, Ben-G, and T. J. paused from their feline hunt to gape as she approached, rhythmically inhaling and exhaling, arms pumping (and by Ben-G's account, nostrils flared wide open like an enraptured tribal dancer in a *National Geographic* article), and then whizzed past them and around the corner—their first exposure to the approaching whistle and passing whoosh of the Doppler effect.

I had no idea she could run so fast.

II

She's untethered from the tubes and monitors now. She's coming home. Back to the master bedroom tucked in the corner of the house. Back to the brass-framed, 1970-something, king-size bed with the eclectic clutter of over- and under-sized pillows. Back to the right side (it's always been her side). Back to the 1980-something peach walls still plastered with her forty-something-year-old matching brass-framed photos of her naked smiling babies, each of us on our bellies, legs kicking and necks lifting, straining under the weight of our oversized giggling heads. Back to the center of our universe—the throne room, playpen, bedtime story spot, hiding place, sick bay, star chamber, refugee camp, sanctuary, and teenage demilitarized zone of our childhood.

4

Runaway

On Grandma Carter's bad days, Mom was "that lady." While Grandma Carter was watching her daily lineup of morning game shows, midday soaps, and afternoon reruns, if she saw that you were up to no good, she'd purse her lips and say, "That lady is not going to like *that*." On her good days, Mom was "Linda dear." On other days, Grandma Carter didn't talk at all. When Grandma was normal she used to say, "Where's your mother, sweetheart?"

Other than Mom, by this time I'm pretty sure Grandma Carter didn't really know who any of the rest of us were anymore. She definitely seemed to have forgotten that Mom was our mom. It's sad to think that after a long, hard life you can end up living six hundred miles, one time zone, and two climates away from home, in a guest room and sharing a bathroom with two girls in a house that's not your own, separated from your husband who can't care for you anymore (and who you desperately loved but only vaguely remember), and stuck with five other people who seem only slightly familiar—one of whom is a strange lady half the time, one of whom you think is a handsome mailman, and four of whom are kids almost seventy years younger than you are and who are—depending on the day—juvenile delinquents (good day) or the pillaging Ute warriors from the stories of your grandfather's childhood in Southern Utah (bad day).

Whether it was a good day or a bad day, Grandma Carter wandered quite a bit—so much so, actually, that she had become a neighborhood institution; she was practically the unofficial mascot of Shady Groves Estates. She wandered in her bath robe, in her nightgown, in her housecoat, in her Sunday best, and in a sweatsuit that Mom bought for her. Once she made it all the way to the front door in her birthday suit. She had forgotten where the shower was. It was a fast Sunday, and consequently the only fast Sunday that I didn't complain about not eating. I fasted the rest of the day to get the seared image of Grandma Carter's pruny, sagging flapjack boobs out of my head.

It didn't work, by the way. That image is still there.

It mortified Mom that Grandma made it out of the house unnoticed so often. Mom usually didn't care what people think about her—she's just that way. But it upset her to think that the neighbors might wonder why she couldn't keep track of her own mother.

Sometimes she cried about it when Dad got home. It was always in their bedroom, with the door closed. All we ever heard was muffled sobbing and Dad's best attempt at a pep talk.

"I just can't take it anymore. I just can't. I can't control her. She won't listen to me. She doesn't even know who I am. Her mind is unraveling, just like that stupid afghan of hers. I can't stand to watch her like this. What am I supposed to do?"

"You're doing your best, and that's all you can do. You're the mother now, and she's the child. You have to be patient, Linda . . ."

Silence would follow, and then Dad would try for a joke.

"At least she's not in diapers . . ."

"Yet," Mom would shoot back.

And then, somehow, she'd laugh. And then she'd cry some more. Sometimes she'd even cry about it to Grandma Carter herself.

One time our neighbor Wendell Miller had been out jogging on the canal bank and found Grandma in her nightgown standing by the canal, staring out into the water in an almost dreamlike state. Wendell had taken her by the elbow and patiently walked her back to the house. When the doorbell rang at 5:30 in the morning, all of us woke up and ran to the door. Mom and Dad got there first. Mom graciously thanked him as we all tried to peer over their shoulders to see what was going on.

Dad walked Wendell all the way down the front walk while Mom hugged Grandma Carter then took a step back and, softly cupping Grandma Carter's cheeks with her hands, stared straight in to the empty black holes of her pupils.

"Mom, please, *please*. You can't do this. You can't just get up and go out without telling anybody where you're going. You're going to get hurt. You've got to come get me if you want to go out. Okay?"

Grandma stood expressionless, watching Dad and Wendell Miller walk down the sidewalk.

"*Okay?*" Mom repeated, the arch of her shoulders revealing how much stress she was holding on to.

Grandma Carter just stood there with her arms at her side. As Dad and Wendell disappeared from sight, she looked up at the chandelier and said, "Why is it so dark in here?"

Mom's lip quivered, and she started to bawl. She put her arms around Grandma Carter and buried her face in her shoulder. They were both wearing the same nightgown—a red and white plaid flannel with tiny green Christmas trees. Mom had bought them for all the girls to wear last Christmas Eve.

Grandma Carter came to stay with us two Novembers earlier. On Halloween that year, she took all of her medicine three times on the same day, even though she was only supposed to take it once a day. Grandpa thought she was so excited to pass out candy to all of the little kids in the neighborhood that she forgot she'd already taken it. She got sick and went to the hospital in an ambulance. They pumped her stomach and x-rayed her to see if she had broken anything when she passed out. Grandpa Carter finally decided he couldn't take care of her anymore.

Grandma and Grandpa and Mom's two brothers—Uncle Ted (older) and Uncle Charlie (younger)—and their families came to our house for Thanksgiving that year. It was a setup. Grandpa couldn't take care of her anymore and no matter how much he loved her and how much he may have wanted to take care of her, the adults concluded that Grandpa wouldn't be able to deal with her alone, or even in person.

She didn't know it, but she wasn't going back to Utah with Grandpa Carter.

They told her after breakfast on the Friday after Thanksgiving.

Dad, Aunt Laura, and Aunt Charlotte (the "nonbloods") took all of the kids on a hike at Papago Park as soon as breakfast was over. I remember thinking that it was strange that Aunt Laura and Aunt Charlotte wanted to go on the hike but Uncle Ted and Uncle Charlie didn't, and that Dad gave Mom a hug good-bye as we left—like he was going away on a business trip or something.

Mom, Grandpa Carter, and Mom's brothers stayed at the house to "do the dishes." As weird as it sounds, there is probably nothing in the whole wide world that Grandma Carter would have wanted to do more than to simply do the dishes with all three of her kids. She had no idea what was coming.

When we got home from Papago Park, the dishes were done and the house was silent. Grandpa was out for a walk, Grandma was in the guest room with the door closed, and Uncle Ted and Uncle Charlie were in the backyard on two lawn chairs that had been pre-positioned like every other pair of suburban lawn chairs on the planet—angled toward one another to induce conversation—except Uncle Ted and Uncle Charlie were both staring blankly into space. Mom was in her bedroom with the door closed too. I watched Dad walk down the hall, pause at the door, and take a deep nasal breath before turning the knob and walking in. It took only a few minutes before I heard the muffled sobs for the first time.

Grandpa didn't eat the rest of the weekend.

None of the kids knew what was going on, but we knew something was wrong, big time. The mood in the house was so somber that we were too afraid to ask what had happened.

Grandma and Grandpa didn't go to church on Sunday. And that afternoon, while Grandma was still in seclusion in the guest room, Mom announced to all the kids that Grandma's joints couldn't take the cold of the Utah winter anymore so she was going to stay with us for a while and that Grandpa would go back to Utah to take care of their house.

Hearing the news that Grandma was staying, all of us kids cheered, and we ran to the guest room and pounded on the door for Grandma to let us in. She finally opened the door. I think our enthusiasm cheered her up a little bit. We all hugged her, and she cried.

She came out of the guest room briefly for Sunday dinner. When she finished eating, she got up, walked over to Uncle Ted and Uncle Charlie, who were still eating, and, without a word, gave them each a silent good-bye kiss on the top of their heads, like she was dropping them off at kindergarten for the first time. Then she retreated back to the guest room.

For probably the first time in her adult life, she didn't offer to help do the dishes.

After dinner, Dad took Uncle Ted and Aunt Laura and their kids to the airport. When he got back, he helped Uncle Charlie load his Suburban for their drive back to Utah. Grandpa rode with them instead of flying back to Utah alone.

Grandma wouldn't let Grandpa in the guest room to say good-bye. Even from downstairs we could hear him pleading with her in his softest voice to open the door.

"Gail, *please*. Open the door. *Gail…*"

"Just go, Charles!"

"Gail, *please*! Don't do this, Gail."

"This is 1960 all over again, Charles! You've been waiting all this time . . ."

"Gail. You're being ridiculous. *Please,* just unlock the door!"

His foreheadrested on the door, and he gazed down at the carpet for any sign of her shadow approaching from under the door. His right hand was on the door knob, wiggling it. His left hand made a fist that punctuated every plea with a knock. Two soft knocks for a period and three or four louder raps for an exclamation point.

"All this time to kick me to the curb. Well you've finally gotten your wish, Charles. You should be proud. You always did persevere!"

"Gail. Not like this. Charlie's got to get on the road. I can't stand out here much longer. Please, Gail. Please open this door!"

Silence.

"Gail?"

"Gail."

"I have to leave, Gail. Good-bye, sweetheart. I love you. You know that I do."

No response.

Grandpa had no other choice but to leave.

We all went out front when Grandpa came back downstairs. Grandpa hugged Mom. It was a long hug. They whispered in each other's ears, and then Grandpa started to cry and then Mom started to cry. It's the only time I ever saw Grandpa Carter cry. They finally let go of each other. Grandpa got into the front passenger's seat. Aunt Charlotte got in back with the kids. Uncle Charlie hugged Mom and said he was sorry he couldn't help more. Mom made him promise and repromise to go by and check on Grandpa every day. Uncle Charlie shook Dad's hand and meekly said, "Thanks, Bob." Then he climbed into the Suburban and slowly pulled away. Grandpa took out his hankie and waved it at us. As they drove off we saw him take off his glasses and use the hankie to wipe his eyes.

After a week or two, Grandma Carter finally accepted the fact that she was stuck in Arizona for good and there was nothing she could really do about it. At first, she was pretty normal. She just forgot things sometimes, like where the guest bathroom was, which drawer the spoons went in, which pills she had to take and when. It wasn't all the time, but she forgot at least one thing every day and had to be reminded. But besides that, she was okay. She even started to talk to Grandpa on the phone every Sunday afternoon. She still made gingersnaps on Saturday afternoons and gravy for Sunday dinner. She still insisted that we read our books out loud to her. She still wore an apron around most of the day, and she still frowned over the quality of the bananas that Mom picked out at the grocery store.

"I guess this means you want me to make banana bread?" She would say to Mom across the kitchen, as she disapprovingly examined the imperfections of a newly purchased cluster of bananas. She was a produce snob and predictably, whenever Mom came home from the grocery store, she'd lament over the low quality or nonexistence of apples, apricots, peaches, plums, and raspberries "in this blasted desert."

When it got to be June and was over a hundred degrees every day, Mom and Dad took a weekend and drove her to Uncle Ted's in Pasadena, where she was supposed to spend the summer. It was Grandma's first summer away from Utah in her entire life and her first summer without Grandpa in fifty years.

Uncle Charlie called in the middle of the night one night, only a couple of weeks after Grandma had arrived at Uncle Ted's. It took four rings before Mom answered the phone, but I was awake from the first ring. The top sheet and all the covers on my bed were peeled all the way back to the floor, and I lay on my back wearing only my boy-kini (that's what Ben-G—a fanatical boxers-only wearer—called regular underwear), arms and legs outstretched like a cadaver on a concrete slab, trying to fully absorb each faint breeze manufactured by the ten-inch standard-issue oscillating fan perched on the dresser in my 87-degree bedroom.

After the first 100-degree day of the year (which sometimes happens in April), Dad would become a tyrant and take exclusive control of the thermostat. He would even tape a small handwritten note on the thermostat: "DO NOT TOUCH."

Every morning, he—and he alone—would make a single daily adjustment to the thermostat in accordance with a formula he concocted. Before breakfast Dad would retrieve the morning papers, retire to the bathroom, and emerge approximately seven minutes later with an announcement of the high temperature forecasted for that day. He would then set the thermostat to 25 degrees lower than the expected high temperature, or 83 degrees, whichever is *higher*. So, for example, if the morning paper said the temperature that day would be 115 degrees, the thermostat would go to 90 and stay there the rest of the day and night, until Dad would repeat his ritual the next morning. But, if the morning paper said there would be some kind of freak cooling period and it would only be 90 degrees, the thermostat would be set to 83. It's what Gregory, who would try to tie every number possible to a Dallas Cowboys player's jersey number, called a "Golden Richards Day" (WR, #83).

Most kids don't even read the newspaper. If they do, it's only for the funnies or, maybe, the Sports section. I think we were the only kids in the universe that anxiously huddled over the morning paper to double-check the weather forecast.

The nights were the most brutal. I begged Mom to at least let us sleep like the pioneers—out on the back porch wrapped in a wet bed sheet—but she never did. During the monsoons in late July it can get unbearably humid too. On days like that, Jericho would say, "It feels like I've got the Mekong Delta in my shorts." A couple of times when it was really bad, Gregory and I slept on the floor in the hall just outside my bedroom, directly under the largest air conditioning vent upstairs.

The night Uncle Charlie called, it had to have been at least 113 or 114 that day—which would have made it a Drew Pearson Day (WR, #88) or a Billy Jo Dupree Day (TE, #89). I usually didn't notice the ring of the phone from my bedroom, especially over the hum of the fan, but in the summertime I slept with the door open to try to get extra ventilation from the vent outside my door.

After answering the phone in her bedroom, Mom must have felt pity for Dad, so she changed phones and talked to Uncle Charlie in the kitchen. And since I couldn't go back to sleep, I went and sat at the top of the stairs.

"What do you mean by *disaster?*"

She listened for about five minutes, sighing, "uh-huh," at regular intervals.

"So where did they finally find her?," she asked matter-of-factly.

More listening.

"Where'd she get *that*?" Her tone became hushed.

Another long pause.

"Well, Dad sent all of her genealogy here, and she insisted on taking it to Ted's, so I knew she had her book with her. That makes a little bit of sense . . . But I have no idea where she'd get the other . . ."

Another pause.

"I don't know whether to laugh or to cry."

She was actually sort of lying, because I could tell that she was already silently crying, trying her best not to sniffle into the phone and give herself away.

"Maybe you're right. Laura is kind of into that disco stuff. I guess . . ."

More listening.

"Oh, man." She sighed again. "You want to know the most ironic thing about all of this? I have *no idea* what to do. I have this instinctual urge to call *Mom* and ask her what she would do in a situation like this, you know? It's just so weird."

More listening.

"So, what does Ted want to do?"

More listening. More sighing. She got up from the kitchen table and began pacing and twirling the extra-long cord of the wall-mounted kitchen phone.

"It's not her fault. Laura's not her daughter. So, really, what can we expect?"

More listening.

"Charlie, honestly . . ."

Pause.

"Honestly? It'll never work. Granted, Charlotte isn't Laura, but she's going to have the same issues that Laura's having—plus, you guys have little kids to take care of."

Listening.

"I know I do, but you and Ted have jobs, and I just don't see how either Laura or Charlotte can handle Mom. Especially with Dad so close by. It's nothing against them. I just don't see it happening."

The call ended a couple of minutes later. Mom stayed in the kitchen for a while, wiping counters and unloading the dishwasher. When the kitchen lights turned off but Mom didn't come back upstairs, I tiptoed down to see what had happened. Through the window I could see her sitting in the dark on one of the patio chairs, listening to the crickets and watching the moonlit silhouette of a queen palm's stringy fronds dance in the breeze.

Grandma was back in Mesa three days later.

5

I Will Survive

As soon as Mom bolted down the street toward the canal to Grandma Carter's rescue, I ran into the kitchen to call Dad.

When I picked up the phone, I heard Lisa on the line talking to her friend Sue Wheeling about what some dork said to some other dork about the way Sue (another dork) looked after PE class.

"That's ridiculous. Your hair doesn't look frizzy after PE—"

"Lisa, get off the phone. I need to use it."

"*I'm* on the phone! Get off!"

"Lisa, get *off* the phone, it's an emergency!"

"Yeah, right."

"I'm serious!"

"Calling the Croshaws isn't—no, wait. Calling *Jenny Gillllllette* isn't an emergency."

Sue Wheeling sniggered in support of Lisa. In my mind I could see Sue's upper lip rolled up, exposing her gums, like a donkey opening up for a carrot.

"Lisa, Arvil Cooley is at the front door. He found Grandma dead or something by the canal. I've got to call Dad. So get off the phone!"

"Shut up, Todd. You are such a liar."

More sniggering from Sue Wheeling.

"I'm serious, Lisa. Get your butt downstairs and ask Mr. Cooley yourself. He's at the front door. Now, HANG UP THE PHONE!"

"Hold on, Sue."

I heard Lisa's bedroom door open upstairs, and she peeked

out. She saw Arvil panting, leaning against the frame of the open front door.

"Oh, my gosh, Sue! He's right. I gotta go!"

Finally.

I called Dad's office. He was almost impossible to get on the phone. He had a new receptionist who had no idea that Dad even had kids, so she thought I was crank-calling.

I wasn't usually one to crank call. Jericho and Ben-G on the other hand loved to crank call—but only if they were at somebody else's house. One time, Brother Croshaw picked up the phone to make a call and instead of hearing a dial tone he heard a phone ringing. Without saying anything, he listened as Jericho proceeded to call Kentucky Fried Chicken and ask the female voice on the other end, "Do you have juicy thighs and large breasts?"

Brother Croshaw took them down to Kentucky Fried Chicken and made them apologize in person to the manager and the poor woman that answered the phone. Jericho later reported that although the lady did have large juicy thighs she had "little chicken nuggets for breasts." According to Jericho, it seemed like they had to overcompensate when apologizing because she obviously did *not* have large breasts. Jericho and Ben-G only learned one thing from this episode: crank calling is bad—if done from your own house.

When I finally assured Dad's receptionist that I was not a crank caller, she compromised by putting me through to Dad's nurse, Shelly Bethune.

"Shelly, it's Todd. I need to talk to my dad. It's an emergency."

Shelly thought she would do Dad a favor by quizzing me on my working definition of "emergency."

"An emergency? Oh, my," she said patronizingly.

"What's wrong? Is somebody hurt, Todd?" she continued, speaking to me as if I was Lassie.

"Just get my dad, please. My mom asked me to call him immediately."

"Well, can I tell him what it's about? He's awfully busy. I'd hate to bother him unnecessarily."

"It's an *emergency*, I swear it. Just get him. Something's wrong with my grandma."

"Oh, dear, what's wrong with your grandma?"

I gritted my teeth. "I don't know. Just get my dad. *Please!*"

"Hold on a minute, dear."

Five minutes later, Dad finally got on the line. Fifteen minutes later, he was home.

At about that same time an ambulance raced down the street and around the corner, following Mom's path to the canal. Twenty minutes after that, it sped back down the street and off to the hospital. Dad rode in the ambulance with Grandma, and Mom drove Dad's car to the hospital.

When Mom stopped at the house to grab Dad's keys, she looked pale and slouchy. She didn't say anything other than "Gregory, you're in charge. I'll call later."

Mrs. Cooley dropped off dinner (some kind of funky Hungarian goulash casserole with zucchini and meatballs that only Maggie was brave enough to eat), and Brother and Sister Croshaw came by for a few minutes to make sure that we were all okay.

Mom would say Sister Croshaw was sweet—which I think was a nice way of saying that she was quiet and plain. It wasn't really Sister Croshaw's fault—anyone looked quiet and plain compared to Brother Croshaw.

Ezekiel Croshaw was only about 5' 7", but he was muscular, like one of those Bulgarian weight lifters that you'd see on *Wide World of Sports*. I heard Mom and Dad refer to him in parental code speak as "The Big E-Z"—it was some little inside joke of theirs. He wore a toupee, talked really fast, had an opinion about everything, did three hundred push-ups a day, and shaved twice a day—once in the morning when he woke up and then again at night before he went to bed. He was fascinated by the end of the world, the assassinations of U.S. presidents, and the State of Israel—which explained why he named his sons Jericho and Ben-Gurion and his dog Megiddo. He believed the Russians would take over the U.S. within his lifetime and would make Daniel Ortega the governor of California and Fidel Castro the governor of Florida.

He owned a bunch of apartments in some sketchy parts of downtown Chandler and South Phoenix, so he carried a gun wherever he went—even to church (Ben-G and Jericho taught me to look for the bulge on the inside of his left calf. If you watched his stride, you could see it). He also paid Ben-G and Jericho fifty cents for every scorpion they caught. Brother Croshaw kept about ten each in little jars on a shelf in his garage, and he always kept one jar in the cup holder of his car. If he had tenants who hadn't paid rent, wouldn't pay rent, and wouldn't vacate the apartment, he'd knock on their door, open the jar, and then fling the scorpions into the apartment as the tenants watched in horror. It worked every time, Jericho said. They were usually out the next day. He was also the teachers quorum adviser and, according to Gregory, he was obsessed with talking about your balls and how your balls are a little factory that you don't want to put into production because once you do, you won't be able to stop production. I didn't get it. I don't think Gregory did either. But, at the time, I couldn't imagine anything more terrifying than sitting in a small windowless room listening to an abnormally short, muscular, hairy man with a gun on his calf and scorpions in his car talk about your balls and how the moon would someday turn into blood.

Sister Croshaw asked if Grandma Carter was okay, and before any of us could say we had no idea, Brother Croshaw was telling a story about when his grandma died. The story went on for about five minutes. It made no sense, but it included something about milking cows, a heart attack, a controversy over temple clothes at the mortuary, and how he was able to cope with his grief by doing push-ups. His grandma was eighty-one when she died, so he did eighty-one push-ups every night before bed in her honor for eighty-one days in a row.

Push-ups were the Croshaw family home remedy—for everything. According to Brother Croshaw, they cured colds, gas, boredom, boners, and, apparently, were also useful tributes when mourning the loss of a loved one. If Ben-G and Jericho got sidetracked when they did their homework, they stopped and did push-ups to get back their focus.

At about 11:00 p.m. Dad came home. We were watching Johnny Carson and eating Cheetos. We should've been in bed. So when we heard the garage door open, we froze, not sure what to do. Should we make a run for our bedrooms? Fake being asleep? Act natural? Before we could reach a consensus, he was in the family room. Gregory was faking sleep, Maggie was running to her room, and I was trying to act natural, if an eleven-year-old fake reading *Time* magazine at 11:00 p.m. on a school night could ever be considered natural.

Dad calmly turned off the TV, cleared the stack of magazines to the side of the coffee table, and sat down on its edge, facing us.

"Grandma Carter fainted while she was out on a walk. She fell and cracked her head open. She had to get four stitches in her head, and she has a mild concussion. X-rays were negative on her hip. Negative means good. She's going to be fine."

As soon as he described her jailbreak as being "out on a walk," I knew he was trying his best to technically tell the truth without blaming any of us—and Mom in particular—for not noticing that she was gone. We didn't have to ask. If anyone asked what happened to Grandma, she had been "out on a walk."

He was talking like a doctor in a waiting room, not like a dad.

"There's one other thing that we need to talk about. As a family."

It was getting serious.

"You might hear from some of your friends that she was found with a couple of things in her possession—things that might seem odd to you."

"Like what?" Lisa was the first to ask the obvious question.

"Well, she had her book of remembrance, and . . ."

Lisa rolled her eyes. "I don't think anyone's going to spread any wild rumors about that. Why did she have it with her, though?"

"Well, we're not sure. But sometimes people with Grandma's condition cling to things that give them comfort or that seem familiar. It's possible that the pictures of her ancestors or some of the other more recent family pictures make her feel secure."

"What else did she have with her?"

"Well, that's where we're a little bit confused. She had . . ."

He hesitated.

"Was it drugs? It was drugs, wasn't it?" Gregory blurted out, unsuccessfully trying to be funny.

Dad frowned at Gregory and gave him a look that needed no explanation.

"No, it wasn't drugs, Gregory. It was . . ." He hesitated again. "She had an album cover with her."

"An *album* cover? Are you kidding? What album? I didn't even know she liked music." Gregory was grinning, testing Dad to see if it was okay to laugh.

"Cream? Led Zeppelin? The Eagles?"

Dad remained serious.

Gregory laughed. When Dad didn't react in the slightest, he added, "Sorry, Dad. Doris Day. Right?"

Dad continued to ignore him.

"It was *Saturday Night Fever*," Dad said matter-of-factly. He was dead serious. Not even a crack of a smile.

We glanced at one another quickly, checking the pulse of the collective mood before daring to respond. He couldn't possibly be serious.

"She was hugging it like a teddy bear when Mom found her."

Gregory's grin spread and widened until his lips parted, exposing his retainer. Then he burst into laughter again.

Gregory was laughing so hard that we all started laughing. But we were biting our bottom lips, doing our best to not get so swept up in it that we couldn't stop if we had to.

Dad gave all of us the obligatory, fatherly, this-is-serious-stuff scowl.

Gregory finally gained control of himself.

Laughing turned to soberness.

Nobody said anything for about thirty seconds. Then Gregory finally blurted—to no one in particular, "*Seriously,* Dad. *What in the hell?*"

Dad didn't even react. He just picked up a *National Geographic* and absentmindedly flipped a few pages. Then, shaking his head, he quietly sighed and said, "It's time for bed."

No one protested. We all marched off to bed like obedient little von Trapps, minus the cuckooing and singing.

III

The sun is just coming up as we turn east down Orchard Way. The jagged silhouette of the bluish gray Four Peaks and the prominent purple-creased forehead of the Superstition's hoodoos are in the process of surrendering to the morning's first burst of sunshine. Water-stained sidewalks soaked from predawn sprinkler cycles, mother's milk to the pubescent green rye just beginning to sprout through the prickly webs of scalped Bermuda, remind us that it is mid-October, the unofficial end of the Sonoran summer.

"It's just up ahead. Third house on the right," Gregory says, leaning forward.

Mark, the quiet and exceedingly courteous ambulance driver with two piercings in his right ear and a nickel-sized neck tattoo of the Chinese character for strength looks in his rearview mirror, makes eye contact with us, and nods respectfully.

I nod back to him.

The ambulance slowly rolls to a stop. Maggie and Lisa are both already there, waiting on the curb. The double rear doors of the ambulance swing open, and Gregory hops out. We hug Lisa and Maggie while Mark gently tugs and pulls the stretcher out onto the driveway. Lisa leads the way to the front door. Mark follows, pushing the stretcher while Maggie walks alongside clutching Mom's hand and murmuring something I can't hear. Gregory and I trail in their wake.

Mark maneuvers the stretcher down the hall, past the framed family poses on mountaintops and beaches, past the prints of Jesus holding the children, past the framed Provo Temple, into her immaculate bedroom. The left side of the crisply made bed is pristine and undisturbed, an unintentional memorial to Dad. Gone for ten years now, a decade, but always present in her life, somehow, even now. The right side, her side, has been turned down, waiting for the crisp sheets to swallow her up.

Mark brings the stretcher to rest at the foot of her bed and unbuckles the safety belt. I bend down and pick her up. I can do this, at least.

She is even more fragile than I expected, no heavier than Lynn, my seven-year-old. I cradle her like I do my daughter when I carry her up the stairs after she falls asleep watching TV.

I place her gently on the bed. Lisa leans in and pulls the covers up, just below her shoulders.

Gregory thanks Mark as he exits, and we unwittingly form a tight semicircle around the bed. We exchange solemn glances and think to ourselves, So this is what it's like to watch your mother die.

6

So Strange

We didn't really see Mom at all for the first two days after they found Grandma. She basically stayed at the hospital the whole time and only came home to shower after we'd already gone to school.

On the day Grandma was supposed to be released, she started asking for Dr. Noah Drake. She wanted Dr. Drake to take out the eight stitches embedded just above her hairline. She informed every nurse, orderly, intern, custodian, and candy striper who came into her room that over her dead body was anyone other than Dr. Noah Drake to touch her scalp. After the nurses told the doctors about the situation, they decided to keep her for observation for an extra couple of days. Despite Mom's efforts, Grandma insisted that only Dr. Drake could touch her.

"Mom, Dr. Drake isn't coming."

"Well, why not? He knows I'm waiting." Grandma grabbed the nurse call button and began impatiently clicking it, like a kid ringing a door bell.

"Don't do that, Mom. It won't do any good."

"Well, why not?"

"Because Dr. Drake doesn't exist, Mom."

"What are you talking about, Linda?" she asked incredulously.

"He's a character on a soap opera, Mom."

"Oh, he is no such thing. He was in here thirty minutes ago asking how my head was. He touched my forehead and looked in my ears."

"Mom, that was Dr. *Wong*. He looks nothing like Noah Drake, and—"

"I thought you said he doesn't exist? If you know that he looks nothing like Dr. Wong, then he must exist or else how would you know that he doesn't look like Dr. Wong?"

"Mom, Dr. Drake exists, but only—"

"So he does exist, then! I told you that he does. And he was just in here half an hour ago!"

"Mom, Dr. Drake is on TV."

"The TV is off, Linda, and it's been off. The only channel that works plays cartoons all day long."

"You're missing the point, Mom. He's not on TV right this second. He's on a TV show—*General Hospital.*"

"Oh, Linda, you're being ridiculous."

Mom sighed in frustration and looked up at the ceiling—a why-me protest and plea for some heavenly help.

"Dr. Drake put my stitches in, and Dr. Drake will take my stitches out."

"Mom, Dr. Drake is Rick Springfield—the *singer*. The one that sings the songs that Lisa plays all afternoon after school. You can't stand it."

"Linda, it's a good thing that we're in a hospital, because I think *you* need to see a doctor."

The nurse answering Grandma's call button came in and asked if anything was wrong. Grandma pointed at Mom and told the nurse to "examine this young lady's head because she must have bumped it."

Mom inhaled long and deep, like a smoker on death row taking his last drag. Withholding any further comment, she walked into the hall and waited for the nurse to come out of Grandma's room. All the nurses—even the veterans who had seen just about everything—thought it was funny. The orderlies and candy stripers began referring to Grandma as "Jessie's Girl."

The next day when Dr. Wong came to examine Grandma and approve her release, he was wearing a sticker—one of those "Hello, My Name Is . . ." name tags, with "DR. DRAKE" unmistakably written in Mom's perfect block print in blue magic marker. Dr.

Wong had protested, but Mom had insisted, and Dr. Wong, despite his better judgment, reluctantly agreed, just this one time.

Mom was exhausted. She had spent the previous forty-eight hours listening to Grandma talk about how *she* was crazy. Grandma just wouldn't let it go—and Mom just wanted the ordeal over with, so she begged Dr. Wong to go along with it.

When Dr. Wong walked into the room, Grandma sat up straight in her bed and smiled eagerly.

"Well, good morning, *Dr. Drake*. So nice to see you," she said more cheerfully than necessary.

Mom rolled her eyes and put down her magazine then stood up to watch while Chinese Dr. Drake examined Grandma's head. He took out a small pair of scissors and carefully removed each of Grandma's stitches. Grandma said nothing but silently stared at Mom the whole time with a huge I-told-you-so smile.

The night before Grandma came home we had a special family home evening. We were on our best behavior. We knew it would be extra serious.

Mom did her best to demonstrate the length of eternity by saying the longest family home evening opening prayer in recorded history. We then sang, "I Am a Child of God" (Dad's pick) with a particularly brutal accompaniment provided by Gregory (He quit piano lessons the previous year. He hated it, and Mom couldn't stand listening to him pound the keys like a chimpanzee for an hour after school every day) and then an acappella rendition of "Bye, Bye, Miss American Pie" (Maggie's pick).

Thankfully, due to the obvious but unspoken topic of this week's family home evening, Dad spared us all by skipping over his standard weekly critique of our behavior in the most recent sacrament meeting, which, with Mom leaning back comfortably in her seat, arms folded in satisfaction, usually went like this:

"You kids have got to learn that *sacra*-ment meeting is a *sacred* time. People come to *sacra*-ment meeting to *worship*. You continue to fail to understand that I can see everything from up on that stand. It's *embarrassing*. And it's not fair to Mom to make her try to be the sacrament meeting police every week. There is to be *absolutely* no _____ [fill in the blank] in sacrament meeting."

Past blank-fillers have included:
- thumb wars
- horse bites
- leaning on your neighbor
- laughing/snickering/giggling
- mocking the special-musical-number soloist—*even if* she [pick one]:
    o can't carry a tune
    o forgets the words
    o drops her violin bow
    o can't get the page of the sheet music turned over
    o vomits (really happened)
    o passes out (really happened)
    o starts to cry (really happened)
- making faces at the speakers
- mimicking the chorister
- singing obnoxiously loud
- singing in a voice like Gomer Pyle, Ronald Reagan, Scooby-Doo, or any other person or character that is not you or your normal voice
- punching
- poking
- pinching
- scratching
- scab/ear/nose picking
- farting
- giggling about farting
- making a scene if you suspect your neighbor is farting
- dry heaving/fake dry heaving if you can smell that your neighbor is, in fact, farting
- burping, either out loud or under your breath

- snorting
- excessively sniffing
- hawking loogies
- asking to go to the bathroom
- asking why you can't go to the bathroom,
- asking to go out in the hall and get a drink of water
- asking why you can't go out in the hall and get a drink of water
- asking to go get a tissue (especially when you have never in your life used a tissue before)
- silently writhing in your seat like a wounded animal after you are denied permission to go to the bathroom/get a drink/get a tissue
- braiding, styling, or otherwise fondling anyone's hair, including your own
- incessantly snapping your head back to get your feathered Farrah bangs in place
- sensuously tickling the back of your neighbor's head, neck, or back
- giving back rubs, back tickles, or back scratches
- writing with your finger on your neighbor's back
- doodling on the program
- chewing, making spitballs out of, or eating the program
- playing tic-tac-toe, hangman, connect four, or any other game
- turning around in your seat
- trying to mouth a conversation to someone on the other side of the chapel
- lying down on the pew/in your neighbor's lap/on the floor
- applying lipstick/lip gloss/Chap Stick
- painting, filing, chewing, or picking fingernails
- administering wet willies
- coloring in hymnbooks
- doing homework

- reading anything other than the scriptures
- making faces or goo-gooing at infants

"It's simple," he continues. "You are to *listen*. You are to pay attention in sacrament meeting, not be paid attention to. Do you understand?"

At some point during the lecture, Gregory would laugh, and then Dad would say, "Keep it up, son. Fools mock but they shall mourn."

So this time, instead of the typical lecture, Dad went right into the family home evening lesson.

There was only one new word discussed in the lesson. It wasn't *celestial, consecration, agency, Atonement, salvation, redemption, exaltation, emigration, persecution, sanctification,* or any other typical family home evening word.

It was *dementia.*

He cleared his throat and, in his serious doctor's voice, began:

"Grandma Carter has lost a significant amount of her intellectual capacity—like her ability to remember certain things or her ability to know where she is and what she's doing at a given time. Because her condition is interfering with her ability to function normally in society, we call it 'dementia.'"

Complete silence.

"Do any of you have any questions?"

"When will she get better?" Maggie asked.

Dad glanced at Mom. It was an "Are you okay?" glance. When she nodded slightly, he turned back to Maggie and said, "That's a good question and I'm glad you asked."

Another "Are you okay?" glance at Mom. Mom was now looking at her hands, twisting her wedding ring.

"Well, let me put it this way. Her condition is not temporary. So, unfortunately, we're pretty sure she is not going to get any better. But we're not sure how much worse her condition will get, or how quickly. There will probably be days when she seems totally normal and like nothing is wrong. But, over time, her condition will probably get progressively worse and become more pronounced." He took a breath. "Good question. Any others?"

"What about Grandpa?" I asked.

"He's going to stay in Utah. He loves Grandma very much, but he's just not able to give Grandma all the care she needs. I hate to say it, but they're both getting old. And it's hard. Excruciatingly hard."

"So why doesn't he just come live here too" I asked.

Mom paused. Tears began to well.

"It breaks his heart to know that she's fading. He wants to be here. But, sometimes what you want and what may be best—best for both of them—aren't the same thing. He understands that."

Brief silence, then Gregory spoke.

"Okay, I don't want to be rude or anything, but basically what you're telling us"—he looked around checking the pulse of the group and then looked at Dad—"is that Grandma is *demented*."

He scanned our family semicircle again, this time with a nervous look on his face—borne not out of his concern for Grandma's condition, but out of fear that he may have earned a trip to his bedroom.

"Right? I mean, really what you're saying is that she's totally nuts."

If somebody had told me before family home evening that Gregory was going to say Grandma was demented and totally nuts, I would have bet all $894 in my First National Bank of Arizona savings account that family home evening would end with Gregory's severe butt kicking instead of the Indian wrestling activity (my pick). Not that there was a history of butt kicking that happened in our house. In fact, quite the contrary—an indefinite forced exile to your bedroom was the preferred generic form of punishment. But Mom seemed to be so exposed emotionally that I could see Dad overreacting to send a message that this was serious, sensitive stuff for which screwing around was not to be tolerated.

I was surprised, though. Dad quietly turned to Mom and raised his eyebrows as if to say, "Would you like to respond?"

No one said a word. Mom paused, staring first at Gregory, and then slowly making eye contact with every other person in the room. Gregory put his hands on his knees and began shifting his weight to his feet, as if to stand up and make a preemptive sprint for his room.

"Yes, Gregory, you're right. Grandma is literally losing her mind," she said calmly.

It was like she was momentarily channeling Mrs. Sidwell, the school nurse, when she gave the puberty lecture for all of the fifth graders—wrinkled brow and double seriousness—and we were the class. Everyone was squirming inside and uncomfortable. But, at the same time, we are all on edge of our seats, hanging on every word.

"She doesn't know where her mind is, and she is losing little pieces of it all the time, and she'll probably never be able to find them again," she explained.

She paused. No one said a word. It was like Mrs. Sidwell had just said the word *menstruation* or *erection,* and it was the first time in your life that you had ever heard those words—adult words, with adult consequences—spoken out loud by an adult, in a serious tone and directed at *you.* Words we had all looked up in the dictionary and giggled about in the abstract but had absolutely no understanding of how they would, sooner or later, forever change our lives.

Part of me wanted to laugh—because it seemed so ridiculous. We would be eating, sleeping, praying that our meals would make us healthy and strong, playing gin rummy, folding laundry, doing dishes, watching TV, and going to church—with a *crazy* person. But the bigger part of me wanted to cry—because it seemed even more ridiculous that this was *Grandma. Our* Grandma. Grandma Carter. The woman who gave birth to our very own mother and raised her, who taught us how to scrape our teeth on the underbelly of a perfectly steamed Artichoke leaf, who covered for us when our "roughhousing" broke the screen door to Grandpa's wood shop and he wanted to know what in the Sam Hell happened here, who slipped us quarters so we could get licorice ropes and cherry Slurpees at 7-11 after Mom had already said no, who turned over a pail and demonstrated for us how to milk a cow ("Now watch here you little Arizona city slickers," she'd say as she laughed), who taught us how to tell the difference between apricots, peaches, and nectarines, whipping a paring knife out of the front pocket of her apron, slicing taste test samples with the speed and dexterity of a world renowned surgeon, who told us with exaggerated grandmotherly animation the stories of her youth and her pioneer grandparents, who still liked to draw a warm bath for us even though we were too old for it, and who would say things that made us cringe, like, "Remember to scrub behind your ears and wash your privates."

"It frustrates us," Mom continued, "because we know a lot of the things that are in her mind. We were there, and they include *us*."

She paused briefly, then continued, sensing Maggie didn't get it.

"It's like her memory is a big purse, full of lots of different things—some things that are super important, like medicine, or her driver's license or her credit cards, and other things that are less important, like lipstick, chewing gum, and tissues. And then there's other things that are in there but you can't remember and so maybe aren't even that important—like an old dry-cleaning ticket, a receipt from a gas station, or a coupon for raisin bran. One by one those things are spilling out of Grandma's purse, and the purse is getting emptier and emptier. In place of those things, she either gets confused or is finding new things that seem important to her."

"So she might think the coupon for raisin bran is her driver's license?" Maggie asked.

"Something like that. And that's frustrating, isn't it? Because *you* know that the raisin bran coupon isn't her driver's license, but she doesn't, and she thinks *you* are the one that's losing *your* mind."

"I don't get it," Maggie said matter-of-factly.

"None of us really does, honey," she said softly. "None of us."

7

Far Out

After Grandma Carter got home from the hospital, everything changed. Mom let her gradually wrest complete, undisputed control of the TV from us kids. *The Jefferson's* was replaced with *Family Feud. Gilligan's Island, Brady Bunch,* and *Big Valley* were replaced by *The Young and the Restless, Edge of Night,* and, of course, *General Hospital.* The only shows that stayed the same were the three that I hate—*Dick Van Dyke, I Love Lucy,* and *Andy Griffith.*

Grandma Carter might not have been totally demented yet, but she wasn't sane either. Every time Dr. Noah Drake came on the screen, she had a conversation with herself, punctuated by fifteen-second pauses.

"Is that Dr. . . . ?"

"No, it can't be."

"He looks so different."

"Did he get in a car accident?"

"I can't believe it. Dr. Drake got a face-lift. Oh, that poor man. They pulled his face too tight. Just look at his eyes! I go to the hospital for three days, and what happens? He gets a face-lift."

"That is not my Dr. Drake."

But even when she wasn't forgetting something or acting like someone we didn't know, she was still different. She didn't seem to look us directly in the eye anymore. She would make eye contact and then focus on something just beyond us, on the wall behind where we stood. She also didn't engage with the grandmotherly generosity we were accustomed to—she didn't care anymore if I got 100 percent on my directed numbers math homework. She didn't care anymore if Gregory hit a game-tying home run. She wasn't interested in Maggie's dolls anymore—even the ones she had given her as birthday presents.

She was sad and soft-spoken. Almost, but not quite, broken—resigned to the fact that even on the very best days, there was nothing to really look forward to anymore.

On her bad days, which became more frequent after she got home from the hospital, all of us avoided her except for Mom. She was a stranger. On her good days, she seemed lost in the past, searching through the sputtering floppy disk trapped inside her skull for those days that meant the most—doing her best to harness and relive the smallest details of the very brightest moments of eighty years, vainly wishing that the grainy out-of-focus snapshots in her brain were full motion video that could be rewound and replayed over and over, and doggedly trying to forget the most painful ones but discovering in the process that the determination to forget only brought them closer to the forefront.

It was almost like when I crashed my royal blue and silver Schwinn Scrambler and cracked the frame. It still looked the same, but it wasn't. It was lopsided and heaved to the right. So, it was put aside, tucked neatly in to a corner of the garage. I would never allow Dad to throw it away or give it to Deseret Industries in one of his unpredictable, impromptu Saturday morning this-garage-is-a-pigsty-let's-clean-this-place-up, I-don't-go-to-work-all-day-so-you-kids-can-trash-this-house, you-kids-need-to-realize-that-the-mortgage-doesn't-get-paid-with-good-times fits of exasperation, but I knew I'd probably never ride it again.

It was there simply as a reminder of good times gone by—the low hum of my knobby tires droning on the asphalt in the silent, crisp, and clear predawn desert mornings of my paperboy days; of pumping faster and more furiously than I ever thought possible, of raising my feet off the pedals as high as I could every few seconds, and of clumsily dropping my panicky feet searching for the familiar plane of the pedals again so I could keep pumping, all to avoid Megiddo's maniacal attempts to bite my Achilles as I rode down the Croshaws' driveway and Ben-G and Jericho laughed and tried to pelt me with oranges to further fluster me. It was a reminder of swerving recklessly through and around Jenny Gillette and the clumps of other girls from my sixth-grade class as they walked home from school, me thinking I was CHiPs Officer Jon Baker on his Kawasaki KZ-1000P, while most of the girls concluded once and for all that I was, without a doubt, a complete weirdo. But Jenny's flirtatious, flabbergasted smile seemed like a dead giveaway that at least *she* secretly appreciated the attention. And that was all that mattered. They were all good times that would likely never return. But the Scrambler sat in the garage next to three beat-up brown vinyl suitcases as a silent and private conjurer of my own best memories.

A couple of weeks after Grandma came home, I was walking through the family room just as Richard Dawson was kissing the five McBride sisters from Paducah, Kentucky. He was slouching in a cream colored leisure suit, waving some blue index cards, and babbling about never having kissed five sisters before. The McBride ding-a-lings twittered and chirped as he methodically smooched them one by one. Grandma unwittingly mimicked each of the McBride girls as they closed their eyes and faithfully puckered the largest pucker they could possibly muster. As I walked through the room, Grandma opened her eyes. Her expectant, raised eyebrows crinkled into a disconcerting but benign semiscowl.

"Young man."

The directive was so uncharacteristically impersonal that I threw an are-you-talking-to-me glance behind me to see if there was somebody else in the room. Nobody was there. She was talking to me.

"Run along and get me my book."

"Oh, hi, Grandma." I was caught off guard. "Sorry, what did you say you want, Grandma?" I tried to add politely.

"Why're you calling me *Grandma?*"

"Where is it?" I asked, ignoring her question .

"Upstairs in that room with the ridiculous pink flowers on the wallpaper."

She was growing more perturbed with every question.

"What book is it?"

"My picture book. Now hurry up if you don't mind."

I knew what book she wanted. She carried it everywhere. I ventured to ask if she was sure she didn't have it with her.

"If I had it, I wouldn't ask you to go get it."

She watched me exit the family room as Richard Dawson asked the third McBride sister to name a common household tool used to clean up messes. I went upstairs and into the guest room, her room now.

Mom had done her best to create a familiar place for Grandma. She had moved an olive green flannel recliner into the corner and paired it with a brass reading lamp. She had placed family pictures from Grandma's house on the walls. They were worn and homey, but they clashed with the floral pastel wallpaper and white-washed furniture. A small basket of yarn, crochet needles, and knitting sticks rested undisturbed in a small wicker basket next to the chair. They had never been touched.

To one side of the recliner on a stout black end table with ball-and-claw feet, there was a picture of Grandma's mother, my great-grandma, seated stoically and completely expressionless, except for an unnaturally wide-eyed stare directly into the pinhole of the camera, exposing her for the novice portrait subject that she surely was, surprised by the pop of the exploding flashbulb. Her dark brown hair was tightly pulled back and folded in a utilitarian bun at the base of her neck. She wore a dark dress that looked too big for her but was nonetheless buttoned tight all the way up to her chin. Her thick, tanned hands rested uncomfortably in the middle of her lap. These were not hands of rest or pleasant parlor conversation; these were hands of planting, picking, plucking, scrubbing, shearing, slicing, sewing, boiling, bathing, mending, canning, chopping, and kneading—of *doing*. These were hands upon which life itself depended.

To the other side of the recliner there was a photograph of a picnic at Mirror Lake in a Uinta summer long since past. On the left, Uncle Ted and Uncle Charlie are flexing like Charles Atlas, and on the right Mom and Grandma are looking out the corners of their eyes at the boys and trying not to giggle. They're all still kids. Grandpa stands in the middle, tall and upright. His barely containable grin spreads wide across his face, drowning the usual prominence of the dimple stamped in the middle of his chin. His full crown of untamed black hair is swept back in wind-molded chaos. A fishing pole held in his right hand is slung back, hobolike over his shoulder as he displays three freshly cleaned rainbow trout on a stick with the other. A model of complete self-satisfaction.

On one nightstand there was a clock radio and a picture encased in sterling silver edges of Mom and Dad's wedding party in front of the Provo Temple, complete with the toothy, relieved smiles of parents who recognized and were grateful that their children had married well. Everyone is framed by the vast gradual incline of a thick spring bluegrass lawn, the autumn gold spire of the temple shooting upward as if out of the bottom layer of a modestly decorated wedding cake, and the fading afternoon light bouncing off Rock Canyon in the distance.

On the other nightstand stood a white-washed wooden lamp with a pink gingham shade that rested in the bull's-eye of an elaborate white lace doily. A small decorative pink wheelbarrow filled with miniature rows of tiny, colorful silk flowers rested next to the lamp. Perched on the edge of the nightstand was an oversized calfskin-covered book with a pregnant bulge. There were so many pages stuffed in the book that its pages fanned upward toward the ceiling at a forty-five-degree angle.

I had seen it a million times, but I never really paid much attention to it. "Book of Remembrance" was imprinted into the worn leather cover in an elegant cursive font along the crown of a stout, flowing tree. The gilding of the imprint had long since flaked away. Stamped in the bottom right hand corner, in no-nonsense block text, was "Gail Esther Pruitt."

I picked it up and almost immediately lost my grip. It was surprisingly heavy.

And then I saw it for the first time. Hidden beneath the bulky heirloom was the *Saturday Night Fever* album cover. I didn't have much time, but after a quick glance, a double-take, and a longer glance, I knew exactly why Gregory had laughed so hard when Dad told us that Grandma had been carrying it around.

There was a guy with the cocky expression of a gunfighter frozen in a flamboyant disco pose on a dance floor made of colorful, illuminated blinking squares. He wore a closely fitted white suit with flared slacks and a black spread-collared shirt. His left butt cheek and left arm were cocked to one side, apparently ready to fire an explosive pelvic thrust. His right arm was extended emphatically skyward like an exclamation point, as if directing the very powers of heaven to take note of the unholy disco carnage he was about to unleash. Inset above him on the album cover was a large photograph of three hairy white men in suffocatingly tight white jumpsuits smiling gaily and benevolently down upon the ultraserious dancer.

I withheld a laugh, murmuring an "oh, my gosh" to myself. Then, since I knew Grandma was probably getting antsy, I made my way out of her room and down the hall with two hands in front of me carrying the book of remembrance like a cafeteria tray. When I came to the first stair, I tucked it under my left arm and grabbed the banister with my right hand for balance. As I began trotting downstairs, I saw something flutter to the side and down a few steps. A piece of paper neatly folded in thirds rested on the carpeted stairs. I bent down to pick it up and noticed that the creases had begun to split.

I could hear the faint familiar jingle of a laundry detergent commercial wafting up from downstairs as I sat down on the stairs and delicately unfolded the paper. The yellowed brittle stationery of the Utah Fuel Company showed a faded black text in a hurried but neat scrawl.

March 14, 1924
Castle Gate, Utah

My Dearest Daisy Petal,
By now you have surely heard news of the great tragedy in mine #2. I can only be grateful for my good fortune. The three explosions were felt even in Helper and Price.

The remains of over 100 men have been recovered now. Women and children mill about the road to the shaft entrance awaiting each change of shift for news of their husbands, sons, and fathers. The young children still do not understand the terrible events of the eighth. They laugh and play games of tag while their mothers wring their hands, endlessly waiting for news that will surely never come. It is all so very sad. As new names of the dead are posted on the board outside the mine portal, the widows wail in their native languages—the Greeks have been especially hard hit.

The company asked those of us with rescue training who were sacked when mine #1 was closed to assist in the recovery effort. The scenes inside the shafts are almost too horrible to describe. The shafts are filled with poisonous carbon monoxide, so we wear heavy gear, goggles, and resuscitators. We look like sea monsters prowling the depths of the ocean. Many of the bodies are charred and mutilated beyond recognition. The skin is burnt so crisp that it peels and flakes at the touch. The bones are so brittle that they snap like twigs. Each body is carefully placed in a burlap sack and stacked on a wagon just outside the mine entrance. Teams of horses carry them into town to the amusement hall, which is now the town morgue—the same amusement hall where we first met two New Year's Eves ago and held hands on the 24th.

The sight of the caskets and bulging sacks on the polished wood dance floor makes all else seem so meaningless and nearly vain. I don't think I will ever bring myself to dance again. To think that I could have easily been one of these poor men lying dead on the dance floor, never to see you again, overwhelms me.

Although I cannot fully understand the reason for His beneficence, and despite the feelings I had only one month ago when I was sacked (solely because I was a single man), I now recognize the provident hand of the living God and I can no longer delay the fulfillment of the ultimate purpose for separating myself from you in the first instance. I am now resolved to use every effort to return to Provo no later than May 1.

Until then and always, I remain yours truly,
—C

Just as I finished the letter and was carefully folding it back together, I heard,

"Young man!"

Oh, crap! I thought. My face warmed with the blush of someone who has just been caught poking his nose into someone else's business.

"Young *man!*"

"Coming, Grandma!" I replied, trying to disguise the startle in my voice.

I had no idea where the letter had come from, so instead of trying to stuff it back in the book, I clutched it in one hand as I hurried down the stairs and hoped I would avoid any what-took-you-so-long questions.

"Man, this thing is heavy," I pronounced, holding out the book.

She ignored my comment, so I cleared my throat and tried to sound nonchalant as I added, "Oh, Grandma, I almost forgot. This piece of paper fell out while I was carrying it."

"What is it?"

"I'm not sure."

It was the truth—but only sort of. Yes, I knew it was a letter from C to someone named My Dearest Daisy Petal (who was probably Grandma), but I wasn't *one hundred* percent sure, and I definitely didn't know what the letter meant. So I wasn't technically lying.

She took the letter and opened it up then squinted at it for several minutes. The McBride sisters had apparently lost their "family feud" with the Willoughbys of Sherman Oaks, California, because a middle-aged Willoughby in his Sunday best was making small talk with Richard Dawson before starting his bonus round. It was not looking good for the Willoughbys

"What is this?" she said, handing it back to me.

I briefly examined it like I had never seen it before.

"It looks like a letter. It's from 1924."

"1924? How long ago is that?"

"Umm, I guess about fifty-five years or so."

"Who's it to?"

"Uh, somebody named . . ." I started in the form of a tentative question.

"Read it to me."

"Are you sure? It looks kinda personal. Plus, I'm not that good at reading cursive out loud," I said lamely.

"Oh, just go on and read it," she said impatiently.

Oh, crap, I thought again.

"March fourteenth, nineteen twenty-four. Castle Gate, Utah. My Dearest Daisy Petal."

I read the whole thing in fits and starts. When I said "Castle Gate, Utah," she furrowed her brow. When I said "Dearest Daisy Petal," her brow unfurrowed and she raised her eyebrows expectantly then stared blankly at the wall. When I got to the part about the dance hall and two New Year's Eves ago, her lips parted and the faintest origins of a smile appeared. She put her head back on the headrest and pulled the afghan up high, nearly to her chin, then closed her eyes and took a slightly deeper than normal breath. By the time I finished the letter, she was asleep.

I folded the letter quietly and put it on the end table next to her book of remembrance.

"Sweet dreams, Daisy Petal," I whispered, only half in jest.

"What *the* . . . Why are you calling Grandma *Daisy Petal,* you weirdo?"

I jumped to my feet in a spasm of fright. Gregory burst out laughing.

"You scared the crap out of me, you idiot."

"Oh. I'm sorry, *Buttercup.* Did I scare you?"

"You're a dork. Why are you sneaking up behind me?"

Gregory smirked. "All I know is I'm walking to the kitchen, minding my own business, when I hear you telling my sleeping grandmother that she's your Daisy Petal, like some kind of weird senior-citizen molester."

"I was reading Grandma a letter, you idiot."

He kept laughing as he walked into the kitchen, opened the refrigerator, drank six large gulps of root beer directly out of the two liter bottle, and then burped, "DE-LI-CI-O-SOOOOOOOOO!!"—holding the *O* until I thought he would pass out for sure.

I have to admit, no one could burp like Gregory.

It was as impressive as it was disgusting.

8

Searchin'

At dinner, Gregory announced that he caught me whispering Daisy Petal in Grandma Carter's ear earlier that day.

Grandma Carter was sitting in her usual spot at the end of the table, next to Mom. She rarely said anything at dinner. She was a silent fixture, not much different than the polished brass chandelier that hung over the kitchen table. For the most part, we pretty much forgot she was present. So it wasn't unusual for someone to mention Grandma in dinner conversation as if she wasn't there.

"Shut up, Gregory. You're totally taking it out of context."

"Oh, sorry. Here's the context: *Family Feud* was on, and Grandma was sound asleep. Then, Todd whispers, 'Daisy Petal' in her ear."

"Shut up, Greg—"

"Stop saying that at the table, Todd. That's twice. Stop it right now."

"You heard your mother, Todd," Dad echoed and scooped up another bite of potatoes. "Tone it down."

"Grandma *is* Daisy Petal, you doofus."

"Boys, seriously. Calm down. Todd, just tell us what happened."

Grandma was obliviously staring at her plate, intently trying to pierce renegade green peas with her fork.

"Grandma asked me to go upstairs to get her book of remembrance. When I was coming down the stairs, a piece of paper fell out of it. When I got downstairs and handed it to her, she opened it up and then asked me to read it."

"What was it?"

"It was a letter from the 1920s. From someone with the initial *C* to someone named Daisy Petal."

Grandma looked up from her plate at me. Everyone stopped chewing and took notice.

"Are you *Daisy Petal,* Mom?" Mom asked gently.

Grandma kept her stare on me for another few seconds and then, ignoring Mom's question, refocused on the peas.

"Go get her book of remembrance," Mom said to me.

I looked at Grandma. She resumed stabbing a solitary, helpless pea with her fork.

"I'm not sure that—"

"It's okay, Todd. Grandma doesn't care."

"Well, I'm not really even sure where it is anymore," I hedged.

"I found it downstairs when I was cleaning up the family room," Mom said matter-of-factly. "I put it back up in her room on the nightstand where it usually is. Go run and get it."

As I scooted my chair back from the table and started to stand up, Grandma looked up at me again.

"You will do no such thing, young man. Sit back down," she said calmly and resolutely.

Grandma looked at Mom. "These are my private affairs."

"Are you Daisy Petal, Mom?"

She didn't answer. She again took aim at a small clique of peas. An uncomfortable silence had settled in the room.

Finally, Grandma looked up at Mom.

"Daisy Petal is what the Dancer calls me . . . If you *must* know."

With an air of disgust, she wiped her mouth with the baby blue paper napkin that had been on her lap, stood up, slowly made her way to the stairs, and then made the deliberate step-by-step, slow-motion ascent to the guest room. We heard her door close. No one said anything. Not even Gregory.

After a couple of minutes, Dad exaggeratedly raised his

eyebrows, an unspoken signal that he was about to attempt to change the subject.

"Okay. Todd and Maggie, you clear. Lisa, you rinse. Gregory, you load."

Amazingly, no one protested.

Mom tried to act unfazed, but we could tell that her feelings were hurt. She quietly helped Maggie clear the table and then began to sweep the floor. Dad followed her around with a dust pan.

The peculiarity of it all—the fact that the entire family was doing the dishes, and even more remarkable that no one was complaining—was palpable.

After a few yeomanlike minutes, Lisa finally broke the silence.

"Who is the *Dancer*?"

"I don't know, sweetie," Mom replied as she ducked the broom into a corner.

"In the letter, C said he didn't think he would ever dance again," I volunteered.

"So, C is the Dancer?" Lisa asked.

"Maybe. Probably," I said on second thought.

Mom said nothing. She acted like she didn't care, but she was definitely listening.

"Why did C say he wouldn't dance again?"

"Because there were dead bodies stacked on the dance floor."

At the mention of dead bodies, Gregory, who had been bent over trying to stuff a handful of forks into the dishwasher's already full silverware basket, stood up and turned around.

"Dead bodies on the dance floor? *What?*"

Mom's purposeful sweeping slowed to a near halt. Dad stopped stalking her with the dustpan and looked my way.

"The letter said that there had been an explosion in a mine and that there were over a hundred dead bodies. They stacked them all in the town dance hall." I felt like I was the Professor explaining a possible way off the island to Gilligan, the Skipper, the Howells, and Mary Ann and Ginger.

Dad became interested.

"Did it say where the mine was? It was the 1920s, you said, right?"

"Yeah, the letter said something about Castle Gate, and I think it also mentioned a specific mine number."

Before they could respond, I continued.

"Oh yeah, I think the letter was from Castle Gate, Utah, too."

"Interesting," Dad said genuinely.

Mom continued to fake like she was sweeping for another minute or two. Then she finally spoke.

"C is Grandpa. *Charles.* He's originally from Price. The Castle Gate mine is only a few miles from Price, by Helper. He used to work in the mines before he married Grandma."

We waited for her to continue.

"They met for the first time when Grandma was visiting her cousins in Helper over the Christmas holidays one year—at a New Year's Eve dance."

"So Grandpa was a *dancer?*" Gregory asked in disbelief.

It seemed absurd. Grandpa didn't seem like the dancing type. A tight end, deep-sea fisherman, forest ranger, or heavy crane operator maybe, but not a dancer.

"I don't know."

"But the letter said he'd probably never dance again because he first met Daisy Petal on the same dance floor where all the dead bodies were stacked," I reported.

Mom offered her own response to Gregory's question.

"I don't know either. I haven't read the letter. I've never known Grandpa to dance, though. There was dancing at our wedding, but he didn't participate at all. In fact, I remember thinking it was so strange—it was at his insistence that we had dancing in the first place. Do you remember that, Bob?"

"Yeah, I do," Dad said. "Strange," he added.

IV

Lisa and Maggie carefully untie the hospice gown and remove it from her. They lift her head, cupping it like a newborn baby's to support her flaccid neck, and slip a fresh white cotton nightgown over her head. They softly lay her head back on the pillow and delicately raise her limp arms through the arm holes. Slightly lifting her hips, they pull the gown down over the rest of her body. She groans and then falls back into a patternless, restless sleep.

With my feet propped up on the foot of her bed, I sit on watch, in the large olive green flannel recliner, the same one Mom put in the guest room so many years previously to give Grandma Carter a sense of home and normalcy. It's still paired with the same brass reading lamp. Mom moved them to her room decades ago, only days after Grandma Carter died. She couldn't bear to let them go. The same black end table with the ball-and-claw feet is here too. On it is a picture of Mom sitting next to Grandma Carter on a chaise lounge. It was summertime. A barbecue. Kids jostled out of focus in the pool in the background. Mom was holding Grandma's hand and smiling effusively. Dad (the photographer) had coaxed a reluctant grin out of Grandma. She hated the sweltering Arizona summers of her exile. It's likely the last photo of Mom and Grandma Carter before Grandma became fully consumed by Alzheimer's.

Her chest heaves and sinks with each palpitated and rhythmless breath. Gregory is napping down the hall in the family room while Lisa and Maggie sit at the kitchen table with notepads and pencils, making notes and speaking in hushed tones of caskets, headstones, and hymns.

9

Boom Boom

"What are you doing? Don't do that."

"Do what?"

"That."

"This?"

"Yeah, *that*. Doofus."

"Why not?"

"Shut up. Here comes a car. Get down."

I tossed my orange into some oleander and wiped my hands on the back of my shorts.

We both crouched behind the spindly arms of an ocotillo and watched the approaching headlights advance.

"Buick," Gregory announced, standing up. "Probably an old fart—not worth the orange."

I stood back up.

"I know this is your first time, but *never* break the orange with your hands. Just step on it once and it'll crack open sideways. That'll soften it up enough."

"Why do you wanna soften it up?"

"Because if we didn't, it would be like throwing baseballs. You'd dent the cars. If you smash it up a bit, it's like throwing a wet sponge. It still scares the crap out of people, but it won't get us killed. The point is to get chased, not killed."

The headlights of another car approached.

"Car. Get down."

We both squatted like big-league catchers behind the ocotillo. The car passed. We stood up.

"If you smash it with your hands, you'll smell like oranges," Gregory said, continuing his tutorial.

"So?"

"So, if a cop thinks you've been oranging, the first thing he'll do is smell your hands."

"How do you know?"

"Trust me, I know."

"You've never been caught by the cops."

"Okay. Keep breaking it with your hands, then."

"They're gonna smell like oranges anyway after I throw it."

"That's why you gotta keep spitting on your hands and rubbing them in the dirt. Why do you think I've been doing that since we got here?"

"I don't know."

"Exactly, Todd. You *don't* know—and you better own up to that fact if you want to go with us to the stake center on Saturday night. It's the last stake dance before the oranges are all picked. Otherwise you'll have to wait until November."

Another car approached. Its brights were on, and it stood taller than a normal car.

"Look at this thing. It's perfect. It's gotta be like a twenty-five-year-old construction worker. "

"How do you know?" I scuffed my shoe in the dirt and squinted at the car.

As it got closer, we could see that it was a slightly jacked pickup truck and that it was loud, possibly mufflerless.

"Shut up and get ready. Here we go," Gregory said, laughing and raising his eyebrows like a crazy man.

A light from the street lamp fronting the house next door reflected a small flash of light off the chrome rims of the truck.

Just as the truck passed, Gregory launched, and then immediately launched again.

Perfect arc and trajectory. He led the truck like a quarterback leading a wide receiver streaking across the middle of the field. He stood in anticipation of contact, momentarily posing, right arm extended in follow-through form.

BOOM!

BOOM!

The effect was bomblike—louder and more sudden than I'd expected. I dropped my orange.

The truck slammed on its brakes, screeching to a halt.

Gregory bounced on the balls of his feet in anticipation of what would happen next. I, on the other hand, had already retreated about fifteen yards farther back and crouched behind a bushy bougainvillea.

The truck stood still, idling for an interminable two, maybe three seconds. Then it suddenly jammed into reverse. The small, white, square lights embedded in the rear taillights instantly illuminated as the truck recklessly raced backward.

"Run!" Gregory commanded.

We scattered like jackrabbits, slaloming our way through a labyrinth of desert landscape—a saguaro, a cholla, a prickly pear, and a palo verde—then hopped a stucco wall into a grassy backyard and bounded through a sandbox full of Tonka toys and an herb garden toward the backyard wall.

The loud humming of the reversing truck was snuffed out by a sudden, skidding stop. A door opened on the truck and then slammed shut.

A man's voice yelled, "Go that way!"

The truck's transmission jammed into drive, peeled out, and then sped off.

We heard someone running through the front yard of the house next door as we vaulted the stuccoed backyard wall into the alley.

Dogs from all over the neighborhood began barking.

We sprinted three perfectly timed strides, like high-hurdlers, across the narrow alley and vaulted another fence into another backyard. We tore through the yard, around a pool, through an open gate and into the front yard. We continued across the street, through another front yard, over another fence and into another backyard, hopped another fence, crossed another alley and another backyard until we were three blocks away, directly across the street from our house. We had completed our suburban steeplechase in less than a minute.

We crossed our street and entered through the side door of our garage. I brought two stools over, and we climbed up and peered out of the galley windows near the top of the garage door. We both spit on our hands and rubbed them on our shorts.

"That guy was perfect. He'll be looking for us the rest of the night," Gregory said proudly.

About fifteen minutes later, a large, lifted, blue Chevy truck with chrome rims and oversized mud tires slowly rumbled down our block, did a U-turn, and slowly rumbled back. The driver peered out his window. A solitary passenger rode in the bed of the truck, leaning against an overturned wheelbarrow as they canvassed the street and yards.

"Too bad we don't have any oranges in here," Gregory said with genuine disappointment in his voice. "That guy's a sitting duck."

We watched the truck troll down to the end of the street and turn left toward the next block up.

"So how'd you like it? Did some hair sprout between your legs?" he asked, stepping off his stool and moving it up against the wall of the garage, next to the lawn mower.

"Pretty cool," I said unenthusiastically, trying to disguise the sheer terror I had just experienced.

"Need to run upstairs and put on a fresh boy-kini?"

"Very funny," I replied, stacking my stool on top of his, while my bony knees knocked.

When we walked inside, Mom was standing at the kitchen sink finishing the dishes.

"Where've you boys been? What have you been doing?"

"Nothing. Just playing dodgeball at the Croshaws'. And then we ran an obstacle course," Gregory added, grinning at me.

10

Do It With Style

Saturday night. Only a tiny sliver of a crescent moon provided a muted yellow glow in the darkness.

I couldn't see Gregory, only the vague bushy outlines of six or seven orange trees and their white-painted trunks.

He called in a loud whisper across the yard to the other four of us—me, Ben-G, Jericho, and Gregory's friend, Jake Nelson. Jake had turned sixteen a few weeks earlier.

"No, not those! *These*. Over here!" Gregory called.

"Over *where*?" someone said.

I found Gregory standing next to the largest tree in the yard.

"What's wrong with these?" I asked, showing him two perfectly round, softball-sized oranges.

"They're navels."

"So."

The other three had finished drifting back toward us, and now we squatted under the orange tree around him, like a young B-team of Sioux warriors taking advice from a slightly deranged medicine man before going out to count coup.

"They're too smooth, and they're too big, and they're too round. Plus, people get mad if you take their navels. These are the last of their navels until next season. Nobody cares about the ornamentals."

"The *what*?" Jake asked.

"The ornamentals. The mock oranges. The fake oranges. The bitter ones."

"What are you talking about?"

Even in the dark, I could see Gregory's look of total exasperation. "Are you guys complete idiots? Half of the orange trees in people's yards around here are fake oranges."

"What?" Jake asked, full of doubt.

"Yeah, they're bitter. You can't eat them. They just look really good hanging from a tree."

"No way. *Serious?*"

"Yeah. Serious," he said sarcastically. "You've lived in Arizona your whole life. How could you not know this?" he continued, exasperated. "They have thick, wrinkly skin and bitter fruit—like an elephant's nuts," he said, laughing.

We all laughed. I was nervous, pacing on the periphery of the group, terrified of the blasts of fear through my extremities that I knew were coming.

"I'm telling you, though, they're softer, smaller, lighter, and easier to grip and throw."

"What are you, the horticulture merit-badge counselor?"

"Listen. If the oranges are softer, you're less likely to inflict any damage. So if you get caught, you're less likely to get your butt kicked. It's the difference between pulling a prank and being a vandal and getting your butt kicked. Think about it."

"You're a psycho."

"If the oranges are lighter and easier to grip, then you ladies can lob your throws from the safety and comfort of the alley behind the stake center. If we use navels, you won't reach the church from the alley." He paused, and I saw the glint of a toothy grin. "And I know none of you guys have the 'nads to step out of the alley and get closer to the church."

"What are you talking about?" Jericho asked, ignoring the insult.

"You weenies are gonna want to stand as far away as possible and make long lobs. That way they won't be able to see you, and you'll have a bigger headstart if we get chased. And remember, the only reason we're doing this is to get chased. It's gonna be awesome."

"You seriously are a psycho," Jake mumbled with a mix of concern and respect.

"Somebody has to be." Gregory laughed.

The five of us picked about thirty oranges, all ornamentals, and threw them in the back of Jake's mom's Suburban. We piled in, Gregory riding shotgun, and then Jake wound through the neighborhood until he found Citrus Blossom Road.

We drove slowly down the alley behind the stake center, lights off, maintaining total silence. On our left, we passed the posterior of house after house, each with its own distinct backyard fence— some bare cinder block, some brick, some stucco, some wooden, a few chain link. On our right was a continuous low-slung wall bordering the back of the stake center.

"Stop right up there by those trash Dumpsters on the left," Gregory said.

We were about forty yards away from the back doors of the stake center, separated by the low-slung wall made of pinkish concrete. On the other side of the wall was a small yard made up of a long row of oleander, a small hedge of juniper shrubs, and a grass border fronting a parking lot that ran the entire length of the stake center. The parking lot was full of beater station wagons, Suburbans, pickups, hand-me-down Hondas and Toyotas, and occasional Mustangs, El Caminos and other high school works-in-progress. On the other side of the parking lot was a wide sidewalk leading to two large double glass doors, providing a direct path to the multistake dance going on inside.

Jake brought the Suburban to a slow, deliberate stop.

"Nobody get out. Put down the back window, Jake," Gregory instructed.

He hopped out, walked briskly to the back of the Suburban, and paused while the back window continued to descend.

"Put it in park!" Gregory whispered loudly.

We jerked our heads around and saw Gregory standing awash in bright red light.

"What?" Jake asked nervously.

"Put it in *park*! Your brake lights are lighting up the whole alley!"

Jake immediately jammed the car into park. With the red light extinguished, we could barely see Gregory.

Gregory pulled down the tailgate and quickly scooped about half of the oranges into the front of his untucked T-shirt, using it as a pouch. He turned around, walked a few steps to the wall, and dropped the oranges against it. Then he came back and did the same thing again. When he was finished, he quietly put the tailgate back up, casually walked back to the front passenger door, and hopped back in.

"Okay, let's go."

I was on the verge of a freak out. I was the youngest of the group and the most vulnerable, the most likely to be caught, the runt. If somebody would have to be sacrificed, I would likely be the one. My hands were clammy and I was about to puke, I was so nervous. But I couldn't embarrass Gregory in front of his buddies. So I kept quiet and acted like I knew what I was doing.

Jake continued stealthily down the alley, exiting right and pulling into a small, unlit cul-de-sac.

We parked next to a large date palm in front of a white stucco house with desert landscaping. The lights were off, and no one appeared to be home.

"Turn off the ignition."

Jake obeyed.

"Okay, let's wait here. We've got about fifteen minutes before the dance is over. When we get there, we're gonna wait until everyone files out into the parking lot—it should get pretty crowded." Gregory looked each of us in the eye. "We'll all throw together. *Nobody runs until we all run,*" he added.

Ten minutes passed in almost total silence. Gregory got out and we all followed his lead.

"Don't lock the doors, Jake," he said authoritatively.

With Gregory in the lead, we jogged around the corner in a tight bunch, like a ragtag, nocturnal cross-country team. We continued down the street, around another corner, and then through the mouth of the alley to the stash of oranges.

We each bent down and huddled around the pile of oranges, as if we were warming ourselves around a flickering campfire.

"Okay, listen, if we get chased, whatever you do, do *not* run down the alley. Hop one of these fences into a backyard and then zigzag your way through backyards for at least two or three blocks."

Everyone nodded.

"We'll meet back at the Suburban. If you get to the Suburban before the rest of us, don't get in. Hide in a yard in the cul-de-sac and only come out when Jake gets there. If the Suburban isn't there, or Jake doesn't show up, everyone meet at the Circle K down on Citrus Heights Road—but stay *off* the road."

At 10:02, the first few kids began to exit the dance.

Just like Gregory had predicted, some of them went to their cars and took off, but most of them stood around by the doors talking and goofing off in the parking lot.

Soon there were fifty or sixty kids milling around the exit. There were a few cars backing up and cruising by the back doors to get one last chance to window shop, while other cars manned by a solitary parent sat idling in line for the kids not old enough to drive yet.

Gregory elbowed me. "Look at the station wagon waiting in line up there," he said grinning slyly. "I think Sister Gillette is thirsty for some orange juice. Leslie must be inside the dance. And look!" he continued excitedly, laughing, "I spy a sprightly young female in the passenger's seat."

"Gregory, seriously, don't. Not them."

"Everybody's fair game, young Skywalker," he said, "Especially, unsuspecting love interests."

He turned his attention to preparation and rolled five oranges out of the stash with his right foot and stepped on each one, creating slight fissures in their sides. Then he delicately picked them up, one by one, like they were dead rodents, and gingerly placed each one on top of the wall.

We all silently copied him, acting like we knew what we were doing.

Gregory spit on his hands, wiped them on the back of his shorts, and then squatted down and rubbed them in the dirt.

He looked down the line at us. "Okay, fellas. Are you ready?"

"Wait! Wait! Are we going for cars or people?" Jake asked nervously.

"Who cares? It's up to you." He looked at us, making sure we were ready.

"Okay—on three."

We all picked up a couple of oranges.

"One. Two. Three. Throw!"

He threw as he said three. Without taking his eye off the mingling crowd, he picked up each orange and, with the efficiency of a Gatlin gun, hurled it as far as he could.

Oranges rained down on the mingling crowd, and we heard faint splats on the concrete.

After the first couple of oranges hit, someone yelled, "What was that?!"

And then there were three loud booms, indicating that three cars had been hit.

Then complete panic broke out as more oranges began to land. Girls standing in the doorway started to scream and run back into the church, kids walking to their cars put their arms over their heads and scurried for cover, and exiting cars that had been leisurely cruising out of the parking lot suddenly gunned their engines.

The barrage was over in about fifteen seconds.

When it was over, Gregory still stood at his post, peering over the fence and laughing.

The rest of us crouched behind the fence, too afraid to laugh or look.

"I told you! *Total chaos!*" Gregory exulted. "Stand up, you guys. Look at this. Quick, you're gonna miss it!"

Jericho and I exchanged glances, but we obeyed and all slowly rose from our crouches.

Just as I brought my eyes over the fence line for a peek, an old Camaro brodied around the corner and roared down the alley toward us, flashing its brights on and off and throwing up a cloud of dust. The sound of gravel ricocheted off of its rear wheel wells.

"Holy crap!" Jake yelled, *"Run!"*

I bolted for the fence across the alley, but my legs got tangled up with someone else and I tripped and landed back against the wall, noticing as I fell the butts of the other four scrambling over the brick wall directly across the alley.

I jumped up and vaulted like a pre-Fosburian high jumper headlong over the opposite wall into the side yard of the stake center.

11

Bad Luck

I crouched in a corner of the black steel trash Dumpster behind the Desert Orchard stake center, feeling like one of those little concrete sombreroed figurines that some of the Snowbirds put in their yards. Although it was nearly pitch black inside the Dumpster, I could feel a mountainous pile of grass on my left and a wall of eight or nine bulging Hefty bags stacked in front of me.

It had been an unseasonably hot, probably record-breaking day for late February—probably ninety-five degrees—and the asphalt of the parking lot and the black steel Dumpster retained most of their heat. At first, the breezeless warmth of the Dumpster felt reassuring, almost cocoonlike, but I soon realized that it acted as a perfect Dutch oven for its putrid contents. I stopped breathing through my nose to block out the smells, but it was no use. The rancid stench of the Dumpster, a stew of week-old dirty diapers, fresh grass clippings, and rotting food was so palpable it almost percolated.

After about twenty minutes, I had begun silently dry heaving. I was getting desperate to stand up and stretch out, and even more desperate to open the lid of the Dumpster to take a deep breath of fresh air.

After barreling over the wall into the side yard of the stake center, I had furiously slithered on my stomach between the row of oleander and juniper bushes to the farthest corner of the parking lot where the Dumpster sat. The chaos near the back doors of the stake center had calmed by that point, and I could hear dogs barking and the occupants of the Camaro calling to each other and yelling random threats toward the houses behind the alley.

Upon reaching the end of the hedge of oleander and juniper, I had instinctively jumped up, opened the lid of the Dumpster, catapulted myself in, and lowered the lid.

The grass clippings were starting to stick to my sweaty arms and legs, and something had begun oozing out of one of the Hefty bags onto my right elbow. I had no idea what it was, but to calm my nerves and to stave off accelerated dry heaving, I imagined it was nothing more than melting Jell-O salad that had been tossed out after homemaking meeting.

Cars were still exiting the parking lot, stragglers from the dance. And I could make out the sounds of faint flirtatious laughter coming from the direction of the exit doors.

My pulse spiked as I heard a car drive up and park in one of the spots adjacent to the Dumpster. At least four guys piled out and shuffled to the front of the car. A couple of them leaned against the side of the Dumpster.

"I'm telling you, for that many oranges in that little of time, there must have been at least six of them."

"Yeah, 'cause when we drove down the alley I saw three jump a fence into a backyard, and at least one other guy jumped a fence into that side yard right over there."

"So did I."

"He's probably hiding in the bushes somewhere around here, or I guess he could've gotten a ride with someone leaving the dance."

"I bet he's still hiding. These guys weren't wearing church clothes. There's no way they'd come over here and risk trying to bum a ride off somebody."

"I wish we could find one of them. I could whip out my baseball bat and scare the crap out of him."

"Is your bat in the car?"

"Yeah, it's in the trunk with my glove and stuff."

"Get it out."

"Why?"

"Just get it out. I wanna see it."

I heard the trunk pop and then the swoosh of a swing.

Please don't look in the Dumpster, please don't look in the Dumpster, I silently pleaded.

I could feel myself starting to come unhinged. I couldn't remember if I had spit on my hands or rubbed them in dirt.

I quietly let some spit dribble out of my mouth onto my hands. Then I grabbed two handfuls of grass clippings and squeezed them as tightly as I could and scrubbed my hands with them like they were soap.

My ears perked up as I realized that the conversation of the searchers had briefly turned to the dance and their failed conquests.

The guy with the bat had begun tapping its barrel on the corner of the Dumpster, making a torturous pinging sound.

I began furiously making lifelong promises to God if He could get me out of the Dumpster without getting torn a new one, and simultaneously resolving to never tap on the glass of an aquarium again.

"Wait, so what happened with what's-her-name?"

"She didn't want to slow dance."

"What? She said that?"

"No, but I could just tell."

"What? How?"

"I don't know. I could just tell."

"You're a wuss, man. A serious wuss. Did you leave your gonads at the door?"

"Whatever."

"She's pretty fine, though, I have to admit."

"Yeah, but she's pretty much a wench."

They all laughed.

"So what are we gonna do?"

"Let's drive down the alley again and see if we can find 'em."

"I'm telling you, one of them is holed up around here somewhere."

"Screw that. I don't want to go searching through bushes. Let's see if we can see anything down the alley."

The pinging of the bat stopped.

"If we find you, you're *DEAD MEAT!*" one of them yelled.

They began climbing into the car.

Two doors slammed, then someone asked, "Are you guys done with these?"

"I'm done."

"Yeah, I'm done too"

"Well throw them away, then. Geez."

My heart stopped.

"Don't be so uptight"

"Screw you. I don't leave trash in your car. Oh yeah, I forgot, you don't have a car."

"Mellow out."

I heard the car door open and someone get out.

I buried my head between my knees, held my breath, and closed my eyes, squinting as hard as I could as if the tighter my eyes were shut the less visible I would be.

The lid of the Dumpster lifted and two Thirst Busters half full of warm Coke fell on my back.

The metal lid banged shut.

Through my ringing ears, I heard another door slam shut, the ignition turn over and hiccup, and then the low gurgle of the idling engine. The Camaro reversed, shifted into drive, and then slowly accelerated away from the Dumpster.

12

You Got What It Takes

My guess is that I had been completely motionless for a total of forty-five minutes.

The prickly sensation of my legs falling asleep had passed about twenty minutes earlier, and both legs had gone completely dead-man numb. I couldn't feel anything below my waist. For all I knew I had crapped my pants.

My allergy to Bermuda grass had kicked into high gear, and I could feel the storm clouds of an approaching asthma attack beginning to gather in my lungs and throat. Somehow, I'd miraculously been able to stave off sneezing, but my nose was running, practically bubbling like a mountain spring, and my eyes were watering and swollen. I'm sure I looked just like Maggie did when she was two-years old, standing in her crib staring desperately at her bedroom door, exhausted and all cried out, longing for someone, anyone, to open the door and pull her out of her crib.

I was really screwed, I thought to myself. I couldn't run even if I wanted to. I was a dead man, I concluded. A hairless eleven-year-old kid from the suburbs dead in a Dumpster, I obsessively catastrophized to myself. *I'll never hit a legitimate over-the-fence home run, reach the summit of Red Mountain, ride a bull for seven seconds, glide down the glassy face of a breaking wave, see a cheetah take down a gazelle, or feel Jenny Gillette's perfectly pouty lips stretch thin into a broad smile while we kiss.*

After my mind temporarily stopped racing. I resolved to count to one hundred, and then I was going to try to stand up and get out of the Dumpster, no matter what.

Just as I hit sixty-three, I heard a car in the distance. It came closer and closer until it was parked next to the Dumpster.

My heart sank and a new surge of adrenaline coursed through my veins. *They're back. Now I'm really dead,* I thought.

I pulled the collar of my T-shirt up over my nose and pinched my nostrils together, wiping the discharge on the inside collar of my shirt and burying my head between my knees again.

The car stood idling. Doors opened, and a few people got out and then ran off.

The car backed away, then slowly retreated and sped off toward the exit.

It was dead silent for a full three minutes, and then I heard running footsteps approach and stop. Low voices whispered softly and unintelligibly. Another set of footsteps approached. More whispering, this time louder, but still unintelligible. The whispering became more urgent, almost heated.

"Screw you guys, then. Go ahead and go. I'm not leaving, though. I'll walk."

It was Gregory.

I started banging on the side of the Dumpster.

"Gregory! Gregory! Gregory!" Each iteration was increasingly desperate. "Gregory!"

The lid of the Dumpster slowly opened.

I looked up, but the orange glow of the parking lot's street lamps momentarily blinded me. I squinted and tilted my head to the side. There was Gregory peering down, eyes wide open, a proud, incredulous grin on his face.

"Here he is! Holy crap! Look at him!"

The others ran up to ogle. None of them laughed. They stood in disbelief.

Jericho simply declared, "Dude!"

"Awesome!" Gregory smiled as he reached down in the Dumpster. I grabbed his hand and pulled myself up. When I was fully upright, my shoulders reached the Dumpster's edge.

"You guys've gotta help me out of here."

They pulled me up and over the edge of the Dumpster. I came down on my feet and leaned up against the side. The blood starting rushing down to my feet, and I could feel the pins and needles of returning circulation.

Headlights turned into the parking lot. I quickly crouched.

"It's just Jake. Don't worry," Gregory said.

Jake passed then made a wide 180-degree turn and pulled up right next to us.

"You found him?" he asked incredulously.

"He was hiding in the Dumpster!" Gregory jubilantly proclaimed.

Gregory climbed in shotgun, and I climbed onto the front bench seat next to him. He wasn't expecting it, but he slid over toward Jake without saying anything.

Jake put it into drive, and we passed by the carcasses of smashed oranges scattered around the parking lot and the sidewalk leading up to the double doors of the stake center.

As Jake turned on to Orchard Road, Gregory elbowed me lightly in the ribs, "Unbelievable, bro. Absolutely unbelievable." He laughed admiringly.

"I think I'm done with this," I announced softly.

"You can't hang it up now. Sitting in a Dumpster for an hour? Are you kidding? There aren't many orangers with the balls or the ingenuity to pull that off. You'll be a legend!"

"I'm done. From where the sun now stands, I will orange no more forever."

"Nicely done, Chief Joseph." Gregory laughed.

I rolled down the window, put my head back on the headrest, closed my eyes, and let the dark current of crisp desert air rush across my face.

V

It's just the five of us—Mom and her four kids. No spouses, no grandkids—they will join us later, when it's time. The four of us haven't been alone together in this house since Gregory left on his mission to Hong Kong.

Now, we're left to ourselves. To reflect. To wonder and wish. And hope.

I sit and wander back through the angst of my high school years as I watch her nearly lifeless shrunken shell grow more exhausted with each passing hour.

Years race by in my thoughts. Why was I an immature, purposeful, premeditated jerk in high school nearly every time the opportunity to be one presented itself? Why did I rebuff nearly every effort she made to know my feelings and dreams and fears? Why did I challenge every opinion? Why did I pick on her by rolling my eyes at nearly every expression of love, every attempted teaching moment, every intimation of things spiritual that she expressed? She was just doing her job. The same job that I'm trying to do with my own teenagers. Was I trying to deny her somehow? Was it some kind of power trip—to make sure that she didn't take me for granted? Was it to punish her somehow because I was embarrassed that she was unapologetically my biggest fan?

I don't have any answers. The only thing I know is that she ignored it all. By the end of my mission to Stockholm, she was the only one who was still writing, my only true friend—she never missed a week. Even Dad missed a week now and again, but she never did. But even then, even after she proved her steadiness and absolute maternal reliability, somehow as soon as I got home, I took her for granted all over again. When I was home, I wanted to be out. There were friends to reacquaint with and girls to chase. She was always there, she always would be there, I thought. I knew that someday I would make time for her, someday I would come back and bare my soul, apologize for the idiocy of being twenty-one and knowing everything without, in reality, knowing anything, tell her thanks, tell her the truth—that I owed everything to her.

Had I ditched her by returning to Europe for grad school? Had I abandoned her by purposely not looking for a job in Arizona? Had I completely failed to learn from her example, to do what she had done for Grandma Carter—to swallow hard, grit my teeth, and sacrifice for the one who had made my life possible? Of course I had.

Where will she be tomorrow or the next day—or whenever it is that she is no longer here? Will she really be reunited with Dad? Will it be immediate? Will it be delayed? Will it even happen at all? Or is the idea of their reunion nothing more than some midlife elixir for those of us who have to rely on things hoped for rather than actual knowledge. If she could speak, I know what she would say. She would say, "Of course, Todd. Of course I'll be with your father again. Of course we'll be together. There's no question."

And she will know soon.

13

I Love You Dancer

It was only a couple of hours later—the middle of the night, 12:41 a.m.—or in Gregory time, it was Roger Staubach (QB, #12):Charlie Waters (SS, #41).

My door was wide open. My fan was oscillating down the backstretch of its perpetual seventeen-second loop around the perimeter of my saunalike bedroom.

Even though it was only February, because it had been so freakishly hot Dad had made sure to set the thermostat at 83. And even though it was a Golden Richards Day, it had been exceptionally humid, too. Thankfully, the air conditioner periodically provided some relief every fifteen minutes or so, but it was still uncomfortably hot.

I had been sleeping fitfully, still itchy and wheezy from my Dumpster experience, waking up every time the air conditioner clicked and began spewing 83-degree air, interrupting a dream that I was eating a steaming plate of breakfast heaped on Mom's fine wedding china. I was standing, fork in hand, on the playground at William Ellery Channing Elementary School under the monkey bars watching Jenny Gillette with her lemonade-stand smile and fluttering purple sundress on the middle swing across the playground. She would make one solitarily pump to the perfect height—that point where for a split second you feel just barely outside the grasp of the apogee of the swing's orbit, the instantaneous prelude to the stomach-dropping yank back toward the ground—and then back down again. She straightened and extended her suntanned legs and bare feet in perfect harmony with every ascent and gracefully tucked them back under the rubber strap of a seat with every descent. Her bangs fluttered, and her long brown hair ebbed back and forth in hypnotic unison with every rise and fall of the swing, like the rush and corresponding retreat of sea foam at high tide. Just as I poked my fork into the puffy, yolky pouch of a perfectly cooked over-easy egg and watched the thick protein gold ooze to the rim of my plate, a snow white gorilla dropped from a nearby tree, stormed the playground, forcibly removed the plate from my hand, and unceremoniously dumped all of it—eggs, sausage links, hash browns, and wheat toast with raspberry jam—into the sandbox. Jenny tilted her head back, closed her eyes, and giggled ecstatically.

I was just beginning to notice how the yellow yolkiness was coagulating into small clumps of darkened sand around my bare feet when the startling hiccup of the air conditioner and the approach of what sounded like someone rhythmically cracking his knuckles woke me up.

Half asleep and still groggy, my instincts convinced me that the white gorilla was coming down the hall, cracking his knuckles in preparation to beat my skull on a rock. I was sure that any second my brains would be commingled with my now sandy breakfast.

Although I was firmly stuck in the haziness of dream hangover, my stronger natural instincts of self-preservation somehow managed to take over. Bracing myself to be mauled by the knuckle-cracking ape that was methodically approaching my bedroom, I sat up and raised my hands in front of me, stammering a panicky, "No! No! *Noooo!*"

"Young man," a voice whispered.

"Holy crap! Holy crap! Don't kill me!" I begged, half asleep.

"Young man," the voice said firmly.

I couldn't see a face. The glow of the night-light in the hallway outside my door provided a backlit silhouette of a slightly hunched figure with a lopsided head wearing a white robe.

"Young man."

Coming to, I recognized Grandma Carter's voice. Her pillow had matted her hair to one side. She looked deformed. But it was just a severe case of bed-head.

"Grandma, what are you doing?" I sputtered.

She came closer to my bed. Her hips and knees popped and cracked with every step—the sound of the bloodthirsty, knuckle-cracking gorilla.

"Young man."

"Grandma, what is it? Do you want me to get my mom?"

She didn't answer. She just stood there.

"The Dancer doesn't dance anymore, young man."

"Um . . ." I said it politely, not knowing the right thing to say when a demented sleepwalker wanders into your bedroom in the middle of the night.

"Oh. Really?" I continued, trying to collect myself.

She didn't respond. The silence was beyond awkward.

"Um, why doesn't the Dancer dance anymore, Grandma?"

She sat down on the edge of my bed, next to my feet, holding something in her arms, close to her chest. The sheets were kicked back to the foot of the bed. I was sitting bolt upright.

She fixed me in an intense stare and put a hand on my left ankle. I almost screamed like a little girl.

"Because the Dancer is angry."

I had no idea what to say. My skin was starting to crawl, like I was about to break out in hives. The dream haze was gone. I was awake, more awake than I'd ever been in my life. I wanted to scream at the top of my lungs, "MOM, DAD, GREGORY, LISA, JOHN BOY, JIM BOB, SOMEBODY, ANYBODY, *PLEASE*!!! GRANDMA IS ABOUT TO MURDER ME!"

I swallowed hard and said instead, "Why is the Dancer angry, Grandma? Are you sure you don't want me to go get my mom?"

Please say yes, I thought. *Please say yes. Oh, Lord, in the name of all that is good and holy, please let her say yes*, I prayed.

She just stared and then looked down at her lap. I couldn't tell if she was asleep, completely normal, or completely demented. There was nothing I could think to do except keep asking questions.

"That lady will only make me go back to that room."

I said nothing.

"The Dancer is angry because those men, those boys. They're all dead. And he can't dance anymore. He won't dance anymore."

My stomach began to slosh and churn like a cement mixer.

"You mean the guys in the mine?"

"Just look at him, young man."

She gently lowered what she had been holding against her chest down to her lap. It was the album cover.

My room was pretty dark, but John Travolta's leisure suit and the white jumpsuits of the three guys smiling down on him from above practically glowed in the dark.

"Um hmm," I mumbled.

I was speechless. It felt like my bowels were beginning to part like the Red Sea. Maybe crapping in my bed was the only way to save myself, I thought desperately.

"Look at him."

She put the album cover in my face, practically against my nose.

"He's angry, young man."

"Yeah, he is, isn't he?"

"He's beautiful."

"Yes, Grandma."

I involuntarily passed gas. Grandma Carter was unfazed. I was in serious danger of dumping a load in my shorts. I would never hear the end of it from Gregory. Wetting the bed could be written off as just a wet dream—or, as Dad would say, with awkward medical precision, a "nocturnal emission." I could endure a few days of ribbing from Gregory about that, but a scoop of Rocky Road in my bed, in front of my own grandmother? That would live on in family lore *forever*. I could just see Uncle Gregory telling my kids every Thanksgiving about "that time when Grandma Carter literally scared the crap out of your dad."

The fan's manufactured breeze oscillated past Grandma, causing her matted gray cockatoo plumage of bed-head to sway from side to side, injecting our conversation with an extra dose of creepy bizarreness.

"He's beautiful *and* angry."

"Uh huh."

She pulled back the album cover and once again placed it face up, in her lap. She stared at it for a quiet minute. I glanced at the clock. The red digital numbers indicated it was now Roger Staubach (QB, #12):Robert Newhouse (FB, #44)

"Young man."

She looked me directly in the eye and paused.

"He's my sweetheart. And I love him."

I was out of questions. What did you say to a crazy old lady who you thought was a homicidal albino primate, who appeared in your darkened bedroom in the middle of the night and confided that John Travolta was her beautiful, angry sweetheart?

"Yeah, okay," I managed to stammer.

She slowly stood up, her eyes still intently fixed on mine. Her joints popped and cracked, like tiny air pockets in a piece of dry firewood being consumed by a campfire's flame.

"That lady doesn't like me to come out of my room when she's not awake, so don't tell her about our chat."

"Uh, sure, Grandma."

She carefully pivoted toward my open doorway and walked, snapping and cracking, toward her room.

I unclenched my butt cheeks and let loose the fizzy burn of pent-up gas, then, in exhausted relief, did the Nestea plunge back onto my pillow.

14

Midnight Girl

I decided not to say anything to Mom about Grandma Carter's midnight visit. Mom was worried and depressed about Grandma as it was. There was no point in telling her about Grandma's pledge of undying love for John Travolta. It would only have upset her even more, and she would have never slept again.

The next day, after Gregory and Lisa both complained about how hot their rooms were, I suggested that it was *way* cooler at night if they left their doors wide open, hoping that Grandma's nighttime foraging would lead to their rooms instead of mine.

I went to bed each night with my door wide open as well, so as not to arouse the suspicion of Gregory and Lisa. But I lay awake until the lights in Gregory's and Lisa's rooms went dark—and then closed my door.

It didn't work. Four days later, she was back.

I had been asleep. I was a spy, and me and Scooby Doo were being chased through East Berlin by a German Shepherd named Dieter and the big red Kool-Aid guy. The turn of my bedroom's door knob and the squeak of a hinge woke me.

I sat up, startled. The back of my head and back were covered in sweat. Grandma's silhouetted figure stood in the doorway. I glanced at the clock on my nightstand. Danny White (QB/P, #11):Randy White (DT, #54).

"Young man."

"Young man."

"Yeah, Grandma? What is it?"

She was holding the album cover and the book of remembrance

in both hands in front of her, like she was carrying a casserole
dish full of scalloped potatoes from the oven to the dining room
table.

"Take this." She set the book of remembrance in my lap but
kept the album cover. She retreated toward the doorway, closed
the door, and then turned on the light.

She appeared to be completely in control of herself. The
slightly deranged and far-flung look in her eyes, which was
becoming more and more common, was not present.

She was not wandering aimlessly tonight. There was purpose.

She stood in front of me for a moment and then sat on the
edge of the bed. Then she reached for the book in my lap and
began turning pages, looking for something.

About one-third of the way through, she found what she was
looking for. Another crisp, yellowed, perfectly tri-folded piece of paper.

"Here." She handed it to me. "Read this. I can't find my
reading glasses."

I didn't know she could still read. Actually, I'd just assumed
she couldn't.

I carefully unfolded the paper. Tucked behind the creases was
a piece of tissue paper. Inside the tissue paper was the perfectly
flattened head of a crispy white daisy and a small black-and-white
photograph about four times larger than a postage stamp.

I handed it to Grandma. As she placed them in the palm of
her hand and admired them, I began to silently scan the paper—
another letter.

"Out loud, young man."

"Oh, sorry."

I sat up and crossed my legs, Indian-style. The covers were
rumpled at the end of the bed. It was just me, my Mervyn's-
brand, white cotton loincloth, and Grandma Carter. A poster of
Paul Westphal tossing a basketball high in the air while he walked
off a grungy urban playground hung on the wall above our heads.
"Goin' Home," the caption said.

I cleared my throat and began to read.

April 1, 1923
Castle Gate, Utah

Dear Gail,

Can you believe it? It has been exactly one month since I left Provo, and three full months since we first met. I never imagined so much could happen in such a short period of time. I would have never imagined that Mary's simple introduction and insistence that we share a dance could have set me on my current course.

I know you do not agree with my decision to leave the BY. It was difficult to leave. But things must be done. I received a letter from Dr. Harris last week reminding me that he viewed my decision to return to the mines as a "grave mistake for a young man of your intellect." Mother was also displeased with my decision and did not speak to me for several days after my return. She would not even set a place for me at the dinner table! Fortunately, her disappointment did not last long. My charm must be too great to resist! In truth, I think she is secretly glad to have me back.

Father is clearly pleased to have me back in his company in the dark bowels of the mine, although he would never admit it. I know that he thinks university study is a "fool's game."

The work is monotonous, difficult, and dirty, but the pay is better than I can find in Provo or elsewhere in Helper or Price. The shift foreman has taken a liking to me and requested that I be trained in mine rescue and first aid, which will entitle me to an increase in wages.

I do not doubt that being an "educated man" is something to strive for, but presently it stands as an

*obstacle to more pressing ambitions. What matters
most now is for me to earn and save an honest income.*

*As I do not know when I might have occasion
to return to Provo, I confess that your last letter's
mention of a possible July visit to Helper made my
heart leap in anticipation. I do hope you will be
able to visit your aunt and uncle for the 24th. I have
circled the date on Mother's calendar. Each dance
is (and shall remain) reserved for Ms. Gail Esther
Pruitt of Provo, Utah County.*

> *Yours truly,*
> *—C*

*P.S. The Company requires a photograph for
identification purposes. I had an extra print and
thought you might like it.*

*P.P.S. I saw this solitary daisy springing from
a crack in the sidewalk just outside the post office.
Such a beautifully defiant and lonely little blossom! It
reminded me of someone I know in Provo!*

I looked up at Grandma. She blinked and faintly smiled, savoring the moment.

"Do you want me to put the flower back inside the letter, Grandma?"

She silently handed it to me, but she kept the photo, cupping it in her hands like a little girl examining a ladybug she'd just caught.

I carefully folded the tissue paper around the daisy and gently placed it in the middle section of the folded letter, allowing the bent pages to involuntarily fold back into place.

"Where do you want me to put it, Grandma? I asked, flipping through the pages of the book of remembrance."

"Anywhere is fine."

I flipped a few pages and found a spot in the middle of the book where I could snugly secure the letter, then closed the book.

She stared studiously at the photo for a few moments and then handed it back to me.

It was Grandpa. Young. Wiry and sturdy. His jaw was clenched, and his cleft chin jutted toward the camera. His coal black hair, wild and furious, was pushed back from his forehead, unparted. He held back a grin that was beginning to take shape on his lips. His eyes were confident, friendly, determined. This was a man. A man who knew his future and was confident that he would take hold of it, even grab it by the throat—just as soon as he could figure out how.

I found the letter again and unfolded it, then inserted the photo back between the tissue paper and the daisy.

Grandma was blankly staring at Paul Westphal, lost in quiet reflection.

"So, Grandma, who is C? I mean, it's Grandpa, right?"

"C is the Dancer," she said matter-of-factly.

Her answer was quick, her tone authoritative, like a puncher's jab. I realized that another late night episode of the *Twilight Zone* was likely beginning.

"But, I thought you said the Dancer was . . . him? " I said, resting my index finger on John Travolta's poofy Brillo Pad hairdo.

"He is."

"So, *he* . . ." I said, tapping my index finger on John Travolta's disco dancing game face for emphasis, "is *C?*"

She sighed impatiently and resolutely. "Well, of course."

She stood up, retrieved her overweight book of remembrance from my lap, and shuffled out of the room, switching off the light and closing the door as she left.

And then it hit me. Grandpa—with his young, twenty-something pose, confident smile, dimpled chin, black helmet of hair, dark eyes—really did look like John Travolta. A lot.

Suddenly, I wasn't so sure anymore that Grandma was, as Gregory often described her to friends visiting the house for the first time, "totally demented."

"Don't be scared when you come in, it's just my grandma in

there. She's totally demented—seriously; but she's harmless," he would explain apologetically.

Maybe she was just confused and completely frustrated, like a blind person locked in an unfamiliar room. How could she even hope to understand the present, much less think about the future, if she was losing grasp of the past—of those fundamental, basic defining features of life, like my name is Todd. I live in Mesa, Arizona. My Dad is Bob. My Mom is Linda. I have a brother and two sisters. I'm Mormon. I'm about to turn twelve years old, become a Scout, and a deacon, and go to junior high. I love biographies of Indian chiefs and every sport I've ever heard of and ice-cold water that makes your teeth hurt and your brain freeze and chicken enchiladas with red sauce and the frozen toy soldier poses of ancient saguaros and the whitewashed sunscreen on the trunks of citrus trees and the chalky yellow scar across the forehead of Usery Mountain.

Grandma had a vague sense, an almost instinctual, gravitational pull, to some of those answers. I was sure of it. But, I also was convinced that she didn't really know the answers and certainly couldn't express them. I was beginning to realize that she found comfort from us, from me, even if I couldn't provide any of the clarity that she seemed to be longing for. With no future, she seemed to be focusing all of her energy on a solitary journey to reclaim her past, and I was her secretary designate.

But who really knew? Maybe she understood it all perfectly and had rationally concluded that she had no real future, nothing to set her calendar to—so why care if peaches were ripe, if dishes were done, or if dinner table conversations about our latest comings and goings were stimulating? Maybe she had given up and checked out. None of us could blame her. Maybe she had concluded that she was like a death-row inmate who had exhausted all of her appeals. It was only a matter of time, only a matter of running out the clock.

So, despite Dad's thorough medical explanation during family home evening and Gregory's hyperbolic ramblings about insanity, craziness, and lunacy, that moment—that precise instant in time—was when I finally understood that although Grandma, *my* grandma, my only living grandma, was losing her mind, she was, more importantly, just desperately alone and hopelessly heartsick. She had been left to aimlessly and tediously pan for the priceless golden nuggets of memories that were buried in the bed of a swollen river that continued to rush past.

And so was Mom—because there was absolutely nothing of substance that she could do to help. Sure, she could give Grandma the necessities of life. She could give her clean sheets, hot meals, and cocktails of pills and tablets. She could help her out of bed, help her up off the toilet, and tuck her into bed. She could make small talk with her. But she couldn't give her what seemed most important—a link to the past, a connection to memory. She could only watch Grandma slowly fade away like the waning intensity of the sunsets that appeared daily right outside her bedroom window.

VI

She labors all afternoon until her breath begins to flicker and fade, only to be interrupted by intermittent gasps and desperate gulps for air. The words that have failed me as I sit by her bedside seem to solidify in my throat in a hard lump. I go and find the others. They are sitting by the pool on chaise lounges speaking in reverent tones about the logistics of death.

A brilliant sunset illuminating the wispy streams of cumulus clouds begins to appear and slowly develop, like an instant Polaroid.

They hear the French doors open, become quiet, and watch me approach them poolside.

I stand silently for a moment, trying to maintain my composure. They stare patiently, waiting for me to say something.

I swallow hard.

"I think this is it," I say.

15

Summer Fever

Except for Grandma's random midnight visits, every day that summer was pretty much the same.

Woke up at eight or so.

Watched *The Jefferson's* at eight-thirty—assuming we could get control of the remote.

Ate breakfast while Mom bugged me about memorizing the Articles of Faith.

Rode my bike with Gregory and T. J. across town to Arroyo Vista Junior High School for summer basketball camp where we were supposed to be taught the finer points of basketball by Coach Rory Rawlings, the pumpkin-headed, pork-bellied, pin-wheeled typing teacher/freshman basketball coach. He had a tendency of pulling the waistband of his blue (Mondays, Wednesdays, and Fridays) or red (Tuesdays and Thursdays) polyester coaching shorts into the vicinity of the flabby overhang of his male boobage every time he stood up. He liked to yell out shrill commands as he reclined over the top three rows of the bleachers, usually addressing us as, "ninnies," "knuckleheads," or "Princess Uglies" and, when especially irate, muttering, "friggin' Special Olympians," under his breath to himself.

Each camp session ended with a free-for-all, hack-a-thon of a scrimmage that usually concluded with someone yelling that someone else sucked, which was followed by the predictable, "No, you suck!" refrain. And then just as the to-and-fros were devolving into detailed suggestions of how and what ought to be sucked, Coach Rawlings would rise from his piney, makeshift La-Z-Boy.

"All right, all right . . . that's enough! Get the hell out of here,
you ninnies!"

After riding home three miles toward the teasing, liquefied
waviness of mirage that hovered over the 160-degree broiled
asphalt road, we dumped our bikes in the driveway, ran through
the back gate, quickly peeled off our shirts shoes and socks, and
jumped into the pool in our basketball shorts. Then we ate lunch
while Mom bugged me some more about memorizing the Articles
of Faith.

After lunch we always went back out for more swimming
until *Gilligan's Island* came on. Next was the *Brady Bunch*.
Then *Big Valley*. *Big Valley* lasted for an hour. It was about the
Barkley's—some ranchers in Stockton, California. Jared was the
oldest—the smart mama's boy. Nick was the middle brother with
a bad temper. And Heath was the youngest brother. Lisa thought
Heath was a fox. Heath was also the Six Million Dollar Man.
Audra was the sister who was supposed to be beautiful but really
looked like an albino. Mrs. Barkley scared me. She always wore a
black hat and a black leather coat when she rode her horse. They
never tell you what happened to Mr. Barkley. I bet Mrs. Barkley
had him killed so she could have the ranch.

The rest of the day was usually more swimming. Jericho,
Ben-G, T. J., and sometimes Curtis, usually came over. We played
Marco Polo (in the shallow end only) and the Match Game (take
a wooden match in your hand, dive head first into the deep
end, and place the match on the bottom. The wooden match
ultimately floats to the surface and whoever snatches it first gets
a point and then gets to take it down to the bottom. First one
to fifteen wins). I was the undisputed champion of the world of
Match Game. No one ever beat me, not even Gregory.

The best part of swimming was hopping out real fast and
laying down on the hot deck after you'd been in for a while. It
burned your bare stomach at first, but then your whole body
started to tingle. You could feel the skin on your back get tight
and warm, like the Sunday dinner rolls you can see rising and

browning through the glass oven door. I sometimes worried that my back was going to get bigger and bigger until the skin eventually split—like unevenly roasted marshmallows, getting crunchier and crunchier on one side until oozy goo dripped out of the crack.

The very best was lying on your stomach, resting your chin on the back of your hands, and looking close up at the cool deck. It looked like a mini Grand Canyon. Lots of canyons and side-canyons. You could watch the water dripping off your nose fill up one canyon and spill over to the next one, washing away little pieces of dirt and grass that had collected on the deck. The little brown ants that made a trail from the garden along the ridge of the deck ran away from the flood like the Teton Dam just broke.

My Great Grandma Willey, Dad's "Grammuh," used to live in Sugar City, Idaho, and her house washed away a few years ago when the dam broke. She called it the damn dam. She used to make us ginger snaps whenever we visited. She eventually had a stroke and started swearing. After the dam broke Great Grandma Willey ate pickled beets and canned apricots for two weeks straight. Some stake in Kaysville, Utah, donated three trucks full of food from the bishop's storehouse to help the people in her stake out. For about a year afterward, Dad talked nonstop about how great the bishop's storehouse is. Gregory still teases Dad about it.

"Dad I'm feeling a bit irregular and wondered if you could get me some prunes from the bishop's storehouse—there's no more ex-lax in the medicine cabinet."

"Fools mock, but they shall mourn, Gregory. Remember that. If you want I can prescribe you a little something to keep you on the john until Christmas, smart-guy."

Every Sunday of the summer Dad made an announcement in sacrament meeting about the ward's annual bishop's storehouse project that would happen in August. He even made sure he personally made the announcement, even when it wasn't his turn to conduct the meeting. By the first week of July, everyone in sacrament meeting rolled their eyes when the counselor who was conducting said, "And now the bishop would like a minute for some special ward business." They all knew he was going to blab on about the bishop's storehouse.

It was Dad's fifth summer as bishop. Mom knew what was coming. She bowed her head and wouldn't even look at the pulpit when he started with the announcement. She acted like she was shushing one of us or like she was looking for something in her bag, but she was really just too embarrassed to look at Dad or to make eye contact with anyone else.

"Brothers and sisters, we've got a very special opportunity on Saturday the twenty-fifth to participate in the 49th Ward annual summer bishop's storehouse project—a service project that will provide others with the very bread of life. It will provide spiritual sustenance for you and may literally serve as manna did to the children of Israel for the nameless and faceless Saints that you will be providing for. Many of you may recall last year's ward service project of weeding the grapefruit orchard at the Church's regional farm in Queen Creek. We had about forty or fifty members of the ward come out to weed. What a tremendous experience that was for all those who participated, and what an equally tremendous experience it will be for all those who participate this year. Brothers and sisters, as you know, the orchard that we weed will allow the grapefruit to flourish, and that grapefruit will ultimately be sent to the bishop's storehouse, where it will be distributed to those of us who are less fortunate or who have fallen on hard times. Brothers and sisters, I promise you five things. You will be tired! You will be hot! You will be sweaty! You will be dirty! But, oh, brothers and sisters, what a great and marvelous opportunity! For, brothers and sisters, you will feel the Spirit of the Lord and know that you are helping those who for some reason or another at this time in their lives cannot help themselves! Brothers and sisters, let me tell you something. When the Teton Dam broke near Rexburg, Idaho, four years ago my own family was blessed by the divinely inspired bishop's storehouse program. My Grammuh Willey was left homeless. She was one of the hundreds who lost their homes. She was left without shelter. Without food. That's when the good Saints of Kaysville, Utah, sent truckloads of food to the flood-stricken Saints of Sugar City. Let me ask you something—on that appointed Saturday afternoon, did Brother John Doe of the Kaysville Umpteenth Ward of the Kaysville Umpteenth Stake know that the apricots he picked would help feed an anemic widow hundreds of miles away? No, he did not. Did Sister Jane Doe know that pears she canned would feed that same anemic widow hundreds of miles away? No, she did not. But their dedicated service *literally* saved lives. Brothers and sisters, I hope you will join me on the twenty-fifth of August at 5:00 a.m. in Queen Creek."

After that the whole congregation would breathe a sigh of relief.

After church Mom always told Dad he sounded like Elmer Gantry.

In any event, the fun always ended at 4:00. Even on summer days, Jericho and Ben-G had to be home by 4:00 every afternoon to do their chores before Brother Croshaw got home. If they weren't finished with their chores before then, Brother Croshaw would wake them up at 4:30 the next morning to finish them just to teach them a lesson. T. J. usually left at the same time they did. He always said, "Yeah, I gotta go too," even though he didn't really have to.

After they all left and I walked into the kitchen to get a snack, Mom usually started bugging me *again* about memorizing the Articles of Faith.

"Todd, let's review those Articles of Faith."

"Yeah right, I'll go get back in the pool if you want."

"Todd, I'm serious. You need to focus on the Articles of Faith so you can pass them off."

"I've never heard the prophet say that I have to pass them off."

"Okay, Todd. But just wait, you'll see what I mean."

"Oh, brother, Mom."

She put down the paper and stood up to put the milk back in the fridge.

"C'mon, Todd, what is the seventh Article of Faith?"

"Mom, this sucks. Please give me a break."

"Todd! I won't stand for that! You know how your father and I feel about *that* word in *this* house. Don't say it again. Especially when you're talking about the Articles of Faith."

She was serious.

"Big deal. Joseph Smith wrote them in about ten minutes for a newspaper or something."

"Todd, I'm serious. You're really skating on thin ice."

"Good. There's no ice in Arizona. Why do I have to memorize all of these stupid things anyway? We believe. We believe. We believe. I don't even think I'm part of the *we*. Maybe I'll stand up in sacrament meeting and say, "My mom believes," or "My dad believes.""

"Todd, you're being ridiculous. Do you want to graduate from Primary?"

"Yeah. Just so I won't have to memorize anymore Articles of Faith or sing any more stupid songs."

"Do you want to be a deacon?"

"Yeah, I guess."

"Do you want to be in Scouts?"

"Yeah."

"Then you have to memorize all thirteen Articles of Faith, pass them off to Sister Smiley, and then say one in sacrament meeting. That's the deal."

"Well, Sister Smiley—"

"Don't say it, Todd!"

"Mom, I'm telling you she's a weirdo."

"Todd, I'm not going to sit here and listen to this anymore. I just won't. Now please, for heaven's sake, just tell me the first Article of Faith. I know you know it." A hint of a smile curved her lips. "I'll even give you a hint. It starts with 'We believe.'"

"Thanks a lot."

Deep breath.

"We believe . . ."

Pause.

"Ingodtheeternalfatherandinhissonjesuschristandintheholyghost."

Exhale.

"Good, but say it about ten times slower."

"Weeeee beeeelieeeeevvve iiiiinnnn—"

"Todd, will you please just cooperate with me? You could have been done ten minutes ago if you had just said it in your normal voice."

"We believe in the God the Eternal Father, and in his Son, Jesus Christ, and in the Holy Ghost. Amen. Hallelujah."

"Very good! But I don't think there's an amen or a hallelujah in there." She smiled and then put a hot dog in the microwave for me.

16

We Are Family

One day that summer Mom matter-of-factly announced that Grandpa Carter was sick too.

He had a heart attack that afternoon at 1:15. Mom was on the phone all afternoon with Uncle Ted and Uncle Charlie.

Dad came home from work so Mom could get ready to go up to Utah the next morning to help take care of Grandpa. Dad said that even though the heart attack was mild, it was more serious than normal because of Grandpa's lungs.

Grandpa Carter wheezed and coughed a lot. Even when he was just sitting in a chair watching the news, he breathed like he was getting ready to do something really scary—very slowly but with deep breaths. It was like he was concentrating on every breath. It reminded me of how you breathe when you go to the doctor and he puts the freezing cold stethoscope all over your back and chest. I would get nervous and concentrate about my breaths.

"Okay, Todd, deep breath."

Inhale. Pause. Exhale.

"Good. Again."

Inhale. Pause. Exhale.

"Good, and again."

Inhale. Pause. Exhale.

"Good job, one more."

Inhale. Pause. Exhale.

"All right, sounds fine."

Every time I saw Grandpa, I told him a new joke. He loved jokes even though whenever he laughed it made him cough for about three minutes. He always said it was worth it after he finished coughing, to let me know that he liked my jokes. His favorite was the one about the streaker in the church. I told it to him a couple of summers earlier when we were in Provo.

"Hey, Grandpa, did you hear about the streaker in the church?"

"No, I don't believe I did hear about a streaker in the church." He called into Grandma.

"Gail, did you know there was a streaker in the church?"

He was just playing along.

Then you could faintly hear Grandma calling back.

"Charles, you'll have to come in. I can't hear a word you're saying!"

"Sorry, Todd, what about that streaker in the church?"

"They caught him by the organ."

He had one burst of laughter and then he started to heave and cough. For that one burst of laughter he sounded just like Gregory did when he laughed. Like he was young.

He coughed and slapped his knee at the same time. He didn't stop coughing for about five minutes. Grandma even came out from the kitchen to see if he was okay. She was wearing an apron with flowers on it and had a paring knife in her hand. He just kept coughing and waved his hand at her to go back to the kitchen

"Boy, oh, boy, that was a good one. It was worth it. Definitely worth it."

After dinner we sat out on the porch swing and watched the reflection of the sun setting on the snow caps of Mt. Timpanogos. Grandpa always did that after dinner. He gently swung back and forth, back and forth, perfectly timed with a deep asthmatic breath between each swing. Rock, squeak, wheeze. Rock, squeak, wheeze. Rock, squeak, wheeze.

"They caught him by the organ, did they?" he asked me.

"Yup, that's what they say."

"That sure was a good one, wasn't it."

"Yeah, pretty good, I guess."

I gave Mom a joke to take to Grandpa in the hospital. I wrote it down so she wouldn't forget.

Dear Grandpa:
Question: What are pigskins used for most? (turn the page over for the answer)
Answer: To hold pigs together. (Did you think footballs?)
—Todd

I knew it was a dumb joke, I could've given her a funnier one, but I didn't want Grandpa to laugh and cough. After he read it, he probably just cracked a smile and nodded his head. That's what he did sometimes.

Whenever Mom was gone we got to eat out for dinner and have cold cereal for breakfast. Mom wouldn't let us have Trix, Froot Loops, Lucky Charms, or Frosted Flakes. She said they had too much sugar and weren't healthy. If we wanted cold cereal it had to be Cheerios, Raisin Bran, Shredded Wheat, or All-Bran.

Whenever Mom went out of town the first thing Dad did on the way home from the airport was stop at Circle K and buy extra milk and whatever cereal we wanted.

For dinner we got to choose where we wanted to go. Dad always hated eating out, but he never learned how to cook so he had no choice when Mom was gone.

The only time Dad ever cooked was on campouts. He usually just packed Cup-a-Soup. All you had to do was boil water and wait five minutes. Once, on a campout we had freeze-dried beef stew. It was disgusting. He knew it.

"Well, boys, if that doesn't put hair on your chest I don't know what will. Next time we'll stick to the basics. Cup-a-Soup, beef jerky, and black licorice."

The first night that Mom was gone, the girls always got to pick—because they're ladies, Dad would say. They always chose

Kentucky Fried Chicken, but I think Dad hated it. He would only get mashed potatoes and gravy. Grandma would suck every last piece of cartilage off the bones like she was a scavaging hyena. It was always a little disgusting to watch her silently bite, nibble, slurp, and suck a drumstick down to pure bone.

On the boys' night we always chose Mexican food. Dad liked Mexican food too. He always got a chicken chimichanga. I always got shredded beef tacos. Gregory would get tostadas. The girls always ate too much chips and hot sauce before the food arrived and then would whine the whole time that their mouths burned. Grandma had no idea what to get, so Dad would just get her a cheese crisp, rice, and refried beans. She always complained about the beans.

"I've never eaten a cow pie, and I'm not about to start now," she would protest. "These are not *beans*."

Mom had planned to leave for Utah right after we went to school that next morning. Her bags were next to the kitchen table.

"Hurry up and pass the bacon, piglet."

Maggie was taking forever.

Dad wrinkled his forehead and gave me a look.

"Todd. Nice and easy—"

"I know, I know," I said rolling my eyes. "But—see—look at her! She's taking forever, and she's fondling every piece of bacon. Look! I'm telling you she's a molester. Pass it over, Maggie."

"Excuse me, Todd?"

"Please, please, please, *please* pass the bacon."

"Don't pass it to him, Maggie. We don't understand heathens."

"Please pass the bacon, sir. By the way, sir, what is a heathen, sir? Do tell."

I said it with an English accent. He almost laughed. You could tell.

"A heathen is someone with no manners."

He was trying to look too strict. I think he was trying to show off for Mom—trying to show her that he would be able to handle us for four days all alone.

"*Please* pass the bacon."

He passed it. "Much better."

Mom had her purse on the counter and was counting some money. Without looking up, she said, "Todd, when I get back I expect you to have memorized the second and third Articles of Faith. The fourth would be nice too."

"C'mon, Mom."

I was whining on purpose.

"Todd, we have already had this discussion."

"I knoooooooww."

The first night we had Kentucky Fried Chicken. As we drove there, Dad turned off the radio and cleared his throat. We knew what was coming. Whenever we all drove somewhere together, Dad turned off the radio and tried to quiz us on something.

"Maggie . . ."

"Yes, Daddy?"

"What iiiis . . ."

He always waits on purpose, acting like he's trying to think up a really hard question.

"What is, hmmm, let me think. What is three plus two?"

"Oh, that is so easy, Daddy!"

"Lisa, I wasn't asking you, honey."

"But, Daddy, it's so simple!"

"Five!"

"Nice job, Maggie."

"You're a dope if you don't get that one."

"Be quiet, Todd."

"Yeah, Todd, shut up."

"You shut up, Lisa." Then I mouthed, "kiss my butt" at her.

"Daddy! Todd said, 'kiss my butt!'"

Gregory laughed.

I looked at the rearview mirror from the backseat. Dad's eyes were staring back at me.

"Did not."

"Daddy, Todd said to kiss his butt!" Lisa insisted.

Gregory laughed again.

"I swear, Dad, I didn't say anything."

"All right, Todd."

I mouthed "butt" again when he looked at the road.

"Daddy, he's still doing it!"

"Okay, okay, you two. Todd, tell us the second Article of Faith."

"Oh, brother, Dad."

"Come on. I'm serious. Don't you know it?"

"I know it."

"You're a dope if you don't get this one."

"I didn't ask you, Lisa."

"Come on, Todd. Tell us. Enlighten us," Dad coaxed.

"We believe that Kentucky Fried Chicken stinks."

Everybody laughed except for Dad. Grandma sat stonefaced in the front passenger's seat.

"Come on, Todd. You're stalling. You really must not know it."

"I know it."

"Then spit it out. Prove it."

"We believe that men will be punished for their own sins and not for Adam's transgression—and that Kentucky Fried Chicken stinks."

"Good job, Todd. That's exactly right."

Confused, Grandma wrinkled her brow and turned to look at Dad, but said nothing.

I knew he didn't like Kentucky Fried Chicken.

VII

"We're here, Mom. We're going to give you a blessing," I say softly, finding words.

"Okay, Mom?" Greg softly asks, knowing there will be no response.

Somehow she manages to open one eye, then the second. She blinks glacially, practically coaxing her eyelids to open again.

Lisa and Maggie stand in the doorway with sore, puffy eyes and silently weep.

I have run out of words once again. Don't close your eyes, Mom, *I think.* Leave them open. Never close those eyes.

Gregory looks at me and nods.

He delicately places his hands on her head. I step closer to the bed and follow his lead. There will be no oil, no healing.

We take deep, reluctant breaths. Our fingertips touch each others' as they rest on her tangled mess of week-ago washed, pillow-matted hair.

"Linda." His voice cracks and he pauses. "Carter. Whitman," he continues deliberately, cautiously.

Her body twitches, and the sheets rustle slightly as Gregory pronounces her name. She somehow manages to lift her right hand. It moves slowly out over the bed and then back and up toward her body, like a pivoting crane, and comes to rest gently, almost reverently, on top of our hands—on top of her own head—as if to say, "Go ahead, son. Don't be afraid. You can say it."

17

The Hustle

Mom was back the next day. Grandpa was out of the hospital, but he had to take it easy. He couldn't work in his yard anymore. Grandpa's heart attack was mild, Mom said. He was going to be "just fine," Dad said. But Dad also said that even if another heart attack didn't kill Grandpa, paying someone to mow his lawn and prune his bushes would.

"Add *that* would be a mighty painful death," Dad said, trying to make light of the mention of death.

Mom didn't laugh. She acted like she didn't even hear it. Dad looked at us and raised his eyebrows. That's sign language for "oops—guess I shouldn't have said that."

He was only trying to cheer her up. She was still sensitive. You could tell just by looking at her. She hadn't really talked since she'd been home. She didn't joke around or let us whine. I hadn't even tried to whine because I knew she wasn't in the mood.

"Todd, I need you to take out the trash."

"Todd, I need you to do your homework."

"Todd, I need you to help Lisa finish the dishes."

"Todd, I need you to quit bothering Gregory."

When she said, "I *need* you to do something," I knew that meant to just do it and don't mess around.

She hadn't even smiled in a couple of days. She looked determined, or irritated. I couldn't tell which. So I decided to recite the fourth Article of Faith to cheer her up.

The fourth Article of Faith was the easiest one of all for me. It's the fourth one, and you just had to remember four things.

I said it on one of those rare occasions when Grandma Carter didn't protest our takeover of the remote, while I was watching *Gilligan's Island*. Grandma was sitting next to me staring blankly at the Professor explaining something to Thurston Howell the Third.

I had the green and red afghan wrapped around me as I watched. After you've been in the pool all day and you come into the house in your wet swimsuit, the air conditioning hits you and you can get really cold—even at 83 degrees. That's why I always watched *Gilligan's Island* with the afghan around me. It was the episode where the Professor hears on the radio that astronauts are going to be flying over the island, so they put a bunch of palm tree logs out to spell SOS. Just when the astronauts are flying over, they light the logs on fire. But Gilligan catches on fire like an idiot and knocks all the logs around so it really just spells, "SOL." The astronaut's name is Sol too, so they just think it's someone saying, hi to Sol. Gregory said "SOL" means something else, but he wouldn't tell me what. He said that whoever wrote the script for that episode was making a secret joke that only "sophisticated people with an appreciation for fine humor" could understand.

"If you have to ask, then I can't tell you," he said when I asked.

I bet Gregory that they'd never get off the island. I was convinced that if they ever wanted to have a chance at it, the first thing they would have to do was kill Gilligan.

If you sat on the couch after you'd been in the pool, you had to make sure that your towel was tucked under your bum. Mom would get mad if you got the couch wet. Although sometimes it was cool to get the cushion wet—there would be a perfect wet shape of two butt cheeks on the couch.

"Hey, Mom," I said to get her attention.

I was still staring at the television. The Skipper was chasing Gilligan around trying to hit him over the head with his skipper's hat. Skipper should kick him in the nuts just once, I thought. That would make Gilligan shape up.

"We believe the first four principles and ordinances of the gospel are first," I stuck out my index finger like a salesman, "faith in the Lord Jesus Christ, second repentance." I jumped up on my feet and stuck out two fingers. "Third baptism by immersion for the remission of sins." Three fingers. "Fourth," four fingers and in the voice of a preacher, "the laying on of hands for the gift of the Holy Ghost."

Mom looked genuinely surprised. She loved it when you went out of your way to start a conversation with her. Especially about church stuff.

"Todd, that is just peeerrrfect!"

She sounded like a content little kitten when she said it. It was the first time I had seen her smile since she got back from Utah.

Gregory walked in right at the end, looked at both of us, and rolled his eyes.

"What a dork," he said and then walked out of the room.

Mom was beaming, though. I had completely caught her off guard. Mom remembered things like that. She thought you were an angel if you said something out of the blue about the Church.

Right after that, though, Mom turned the tables on me. Just as Nick Barkley was beating the crap out of some poker-playing city slicker at the start of *Big Valley*, Mom came in and announced that if I didn't memorize the fifth Article of Faith by dinnertime, I couldn't go outside the next day.

"That means no swimming too, Todd."

"That's not fair, Mom," I protested, reeling from the sneak attack. "That's cruel and unusual punishment. Did you forget we live in the Sonoran Desert?"

"That's all the more reason to learn it by dinner."

The fifth Article of Faith is a boring one. After the first four they really go downhill, I thought. The first one has all three Guys. The second one has Adam. The third one has Jesus, and the fourth one has four things. The fifth one is boring.

I decided to appeal.

After making sure Mom was otherwise occupied, I hurried to the phone.

"Dr. Whitman's office. How may I help you?"

"Hi, this is Todd Whitman, Dr. Whitman's son. I need to talk to him."

She patched me through to Shelly Bethune.

"Shelly Bethune speaking."

"Hi, Shelly, it's Todd Whitman. Can I talk to my dad, please?"

After my frantic call when Grandma fell on the canal bank, there was no more gatekeeping by Shelly. Dad had told her to always patch us through if we called. Dad didn't mind if you called him at work, as long as you didn't do it too often.

"Sure, Todd."

A few minutes later, Dad came on the line.

"Hey, Todd, what's up?"

"Dad, Mom says I have to learn the fifth Article of Faith by dinner or else I have to stay inside all day tomorrow."

He didn't say anything.

"Dad, can you hear me?"

"Yeah, I heard you. So what's the problem?" he asked unsympathetically.

"The problem is that it stinks—"

"Hold on, hold on. Do you have all of the Articles of Faith right there?"

"Yeah."

"How many words are in the fifth?"

"What?"

"Count the number of words."

"Just a second."

I put down the receiver and counted as fast as I could.

"Thirty-five."

"That's it?"

"Yeah."

"You already know "We believe," so it's really only thirty-three."

I didn't say anything.

"Todd, what time is it right now?"

"I don't know."

"Well, I can tell you. It's 2:30. That gives you three and a half hours to memorize thirty-three words. That's about ten words *an hour*. If you really concentrated, you could memorize the rest of the thirteen Articles of Faith in that amount of time. So, thirty-three words is nothing. Piece of cake. I'll see you at dinner."

"Ooookaaay. Bye." I said it in the whiniest voice I could muster.

We had goulash for dinner. No one was excused when they were finished. Mom said that we all had to wait until I said the fifth Article of Faith.

"Go ahead, Todd. We're waiting."

"Geez, Mom, are you serious? I have important stuff to do, and I already graduated from Primary. Can't I be excused?" Gregory said.

"Yes, I am serious. And whether you may be excused right now or not depends entirely on Todd. So, go ahead, Todd. Show us if you will be playing outside tomorrow and whether Gregory will get a chance to start working on his 'important stuff,'" Mom said, skeptically glancing at Gregory.

"What's the big deal?" I shrugged. "We believe that a man must be called of God by prophecy, and by the laying on of hands by those who are in authority to preach the gospel and administer in the ordinances thereof and that Gregory doesn't really have anything important to do—he's just trying to get out of doing the dishes," I said, smirking.

"That's total BS," Gregory interjected.

"You know, that's actually a good idea," Dad said. "You haven't done them in a while, Gregory. I'll rinse, you load."

"I correct my earlier statement. *This* is total BS," Gregory protested.

"Wha, wha, wha, whaaaaaaa," Maggie chimed in, like a game show sound effect.

It was the first time Mom laughed since she'd been home.

18

What You Gonna Do About It

We had another new Primary teacher the next Sunday. Her name was Sister Mason. She cried. It had been four teachers in a row that we made cry. It only took us seventeen minutes this time. We were all convinced it was a new record. T. J. had a stopwatch on his watch, and he kept track of everything. He timed himself doing everything and wrote the times down on a special notepad, like he was a scientist or a newspaper reporter.

He knew how long it took for him to brush his teeth (33.33 seconds), to take a whiz (3.48 seconds was his shortest ever, and 49.01 seconds was his personal best), to walk to the bus stop at a normal pace (1 minute, 42.41 seconds), to say the Pledge of Allegiance (11.12 seconds), to eat a bowl of corn flakes (3 minutes, 10.39 seconds), to say the sacrament prayer on the water (17.98 seconds), and the time it took for all of the deacons to leave the sacrament table and sit with their families after passing the sacrament (23.01 seconds).

I thought there should be a *Guinness Book of World Records* for the Church.

Sister Hammond would definitely have won for longest prayer (4 minutes, 33.29 seconds). She even blessed flowers.

"We thank Thee, our kind and loving Father, for the lovely petunias, whose budding blossoms testify to the birth and Resurrection of thy dear, beloved Son. We ask Thee to remind us, dear Father, that even Solomon in all of his glory was not arrayed as one of these . . ."

She would go on forever.

Jeffrey Peterson would have won for most times saying the sacrament prayer in one sacrament meeting. He had to say it four times once. He said, "excuse me" twice and "dangit" once. Then he finally said it right. All of the deacons were laughing. Everyone in the congregation could see them bowing their heads in embarrassment and their shoulders heaving up and down trying to stifle the laughter. Dad said it was a fiasco.

Jimmy Morton would have won for heaviest sleeper during church. Once his older brother Johnny colored his face with a green magic marker during sacrament meeting. He had a green beard and mustache, and even green eyelashes. Then Johnny and his other older brother Glen played Tic-tac-toe on his forehead. Glen got three *X*'s diagonally. The green stayed on his face for about four days. He had some scabs, too, because his mom scrubbed his face so hard to get the ink off.

Sister Bybee would have won for most crying. We all called her Sister Bawl-Bybee. She moaned and wept *every single* fast and testimony meeting. Each month she made it to the pulpit without incident, adjusted the microphone, calmly smiled, and then stood there in silence for about thirty seconds trying to keep the inevitable at bay. She looked like she was using all of her concentration to hold back a seizure. Then she would raise her hand as if to say, "Just a minute, I'm in control," and would eke out, "My heart is so full . . ." Then she would start babbling and sniffling about her dog, rock music, or pretty much anything else.

Seriously. She cried about *everything*.

One time she even tried to *sing* her testimony. It was that song, "O That I Were an Angel."

"Brothers and sisters, my heart is so full today that I can't even speak. I think that I would rather sing praises to the Lord."

Then she cleared her throat, took one deep breath through her nose that made juicy sniffling, noise and . . .

"Ooohooooooooooh that I were an Annnn . . ."

Her voice cracked, and then she started bawling so badly that nobody could understand her. She was slobbering and singing at the same time. It was gross. Dad stood up from behind and handed her the strategically placed box of tissues as a subtle nudge that it was time to sit down. Dad called her the book of Lamentations. I didn't really get it. Mom thought it was funny.

And Sister Doyle would definitely have won for shortest time as a Targeteer teacher. She worked at a grocery store, and that Sunday she brought her scriptures, lesson manual, and a picture of Ammon in a Michelob Light box. Trevor was the first one to notice the box.

"Sister Doyle, do you drink beer?"

"What?"

Confused, she looked down at the box. She smiled and opened her mouth as if to explain, but Trevor interrupted before she could start, and singsonged:

"Sis-ter Doy-le drinks Mi-che-lob! Sis-ter Doy-le drinks Mi-che-lob!"

After that Trevor started singing the Michelob Light commercial that's on during all of the football games—the one where people bet each other for a Michelob Light and practically kill each other to win.

"Miiii-che-lob Light for the winner! Miiii-che-lob Light for the winner! Sister Doyle, you're a *beer* drinker!"

"No, listen boys, I just picked it up on my way out of Smitty's."

"Recognizing your problem is the first step, Sister Mason!" Trevor said gleefully.

"Yeah, Brother Doyle does have a beer belly, doesn't he!" one of the other kids piped in.

Everybody laughed. Even the girls—except for Jenny. They bowed their heads like they were embarrassed, but they were snickering too. Jenny sat up straight and defiantly scowled at all of us.

Sister Doyle tried to laugh about it, but we had her. No one listened to her lesson after that, except for the part where Ammon chopped off the arms of the Lamanites.

We all started yelling and karate-chopping each other's arms. And Trevor kept singing, "Michelob Light for the winner!"

"Miiii-che-lob Light for the winner! Miiii-che-lob Light for the winner!"

"Please, boys, please! Do you want me to go find your mothers in Relief Society?"

That quieted us down for a few more minutes, so she started telling us how King Lamoni asked to see Ammon.

Then Trevor finished her off. Sister Doyle asked for someone to read Alma 18:15, and Trevor raised his hand like he was being polite and serious. He started to read.

"And it came to pass that Ammon said unto him again: What desirest thou of me? But King Lamoni answered him not. And then Ammon said, King do you have any Michelob Light? And it came to pass that the King said, Yes, I always have Michelob Light for the winner! Miiii-che-lob Light for the winner!"

Now he was singing it *and* dancing a jig. Some of the other boys joined in as well. I held back on account of the death-stare Jenny was still giving all of us.

"Miiii-che-lob Light for the winner! Miiii-che-lob Light for the winner!"

"You kids! Stop!"

That's when she started to cry. And then she ran out of the room.

Trevor shrugged his shoulders, said oops, and sat down.

I glanced at Jenny for a moment, hoping she'd see I hadn't been the instigator or an active participant, but she only glared and gave me a motherly I'm-so-ashamed-you-should-know-better shake of the head. I was cut, deep. Then she stood up, scowled at Trevor, and said, "You are *such* a jerk." Then she left the room.

19

Darlin' (I Think About You)

A couple of weeks after Mom came home from taking care of Grandpa, Grandma paid me another middle-of-the-night visit. This time she was sitting on the edge of my bed, lights on, flipping through pictures in her book of remembrance.

When I woke up and saw her there, it looked like she had been sitting there for hours, engrossed in the photos and stories glued onto the pages of her book. I surprised myself with how calm and collected I felt.

The album cover sat on my bed, next to her. When she noticed that I was awake, she stated matter-of-factly, "The Dancer is *not* dead."

"I know. Who told you he was dead?"

"He's alive."

"Yeah, Grandma. He is."

"Peter, James, and John will take care of him."

Here we go again, I thought, but kept my mouth shut. She kept hers shut too, but continued slowly flipping pages in the book.

Finally I mustered, "You mean, like the Apostles?"

"Well, of course. I don't know any other Peters, Jameses, or Johns. Do *you?*"

"No. Mom has a Peter, Paul, and Mary record, though." I was trying to make a joke, but I knew it was pointless. Grandma's sense of humor was lost too.

She looked at me like I was the one who was crazy. There was an awkward pause. She continued to flip the pages of her book.

"How do you know, Grandma?"

"How do I know what?"

"That Peter, James, and John will take care of him."

"They have been for some time."

"How do you know?"

She picked up the album cover and handed it to me without lifting her head up from the book.

"Well, just look at them. It's *obvious*."

"At who?"

"Them."

She was pointing at the three smiling, shaggy men in white jumpsuits on the album cover. The Bee Gees.

"What do they have to do with anything?"

"Young man, do you mean to tell me that you have never seen Peter, James, and John?" she asked, pointing at each one of the Bee Gees in succession.

"Uh, no. I've never seen them before, Grandma. How do *you* know they're Peter, James, and John, Grandma?"

"Well, how do I know anything? How do I know that the sky is blue? How do I know that I'm hungry?"

"Uh, well . . ."

"Because I can see it. And because I can feel it."

I didn't press it any further. There was no point. Grandma didn't even really know who *I* was—other than some half-naked kid she found some vague sense of security in talking to during the middle of the night. It was odd. It made no difference that I called her Grandma. As far as I could tell, she didn't even know what "Grandma" meant. For all I knew she just thought it was her name. She was at a point in her life where she probably knew less than she had ever known in her life. At least as a toddler, she had known who her mother was. She had known her by sight, by scent, even by taste. It was unmistakably imprinted upon her. Now, she knew almost nothing. She woke up and stumbled, mumbled, and grumbled her way through the foggy mists of memory and a daily routine of TV shows, three solid meals, and the chaos of a young, rambunctious family who she viewed alternately as prison guards and fellow inmates.

She didn't even know Grandpa anymore. When Mom would put the phone to her ear on our Sunday night calls to Grandpa, she would listen and stare blankly.

"Here you go, Mom. It's Dad."

The room would go quiet. We could hear the faint garble of Grandpa coming through the earpiece—a heartbreaking monologue of random sentences about mundane tasks, fruit, and the weather.

"Gail, dear. Are you there?"

"Gail?"

"Are you there?

"I picked a dozen peaches yesterday. They're perfectly ripe, even "succulent"—as you might say."

"It's been a little cool the last few days, but pleasant."

"Are you roasting down there?"

"Make sure Linda keeps those ceiling fans on full tilt."

"Charlie says hello. His kids are getting big. You won't recognize them when you see them."

"We all miss you."

"Give Linda and the kids a kiss for me."

"Okay?"

"I love you, sweetheart. Good night."

"I'll talk to you next week."

And with that, Mom would take the phone and say, "Okay Dad. Be careful. Talk to you soon. Love you. Bye-bye."

I just assumed—and I was pretty sure everyone else assumed—that Grandma knew nothing and felt nothing that was genuine, clear, or unconfused. We only spoke about her in hushed tones punctuated with deep sighs. Everything she said or did was somehow suspect, or not to be taken seriously.

But I was wrong.

There were two things that she knew absolutely and without

a doubt: the Dancer was alive, and Peter, James, and John were taking care of him.

20

Tragedy

Dad bought Mom a new Suburban two Tuesdays ago. The station wagon was getting too old. Dad wanted to get it fixed again, but Mom said she was putting her foot down.

For family home evening we went to test-drive cars—although we knew we were either going to end up with a van or a Suburban. Usually, family home evening was a disaster. We teased and mimicked the girls as they tried to lead a song or teach a lesson and fake dry heaved when we tasted the brownies they baked. If family home evening lasted more than fifteen minutes, at least one of the girls would be sure to be bawling and storming off to her room. But this family home evening activity was better than even the occasional "football home evening" when Dad completely scrapped everything but the prayer and we got to watch Monday Night Football. In fact, it was the only family home evening I remember where we didn't make the girls cry. We didn't want to ruin it. We drove to Dairy Queen in the van during the test drive. I got a chocolate-dip with sprinkles, everybody else got Dilly Bars.

I liked the Suburban best because it looked cool. The middle seat even folded down. You could sleep on it when it was folded down. And since Mom didn't like the van, the Suburban was what we went with. The van was white, and she thought it looked like a big ambulance or one of those vans that you see carrying Mexicans to and from the orange groves.

The Suburban made its debut at the fathers and sons outing that weekend. It was at a place called Sunflower, which is about halfway to Payson.

We ate hobo dinners, which are pretty tasty. You take half-cooked carrots, potatoes, and steak, and some onion, and wrap it all in aluminum foil. Then you put it in the coals of the fire for about forty minutes or so, and it's done. Gregory said Brother Hansen put some frozen burritos under the hood of his truck once on his way to a camporee. As soon as he got to the campsite, he opened the hood and started to eat. It was perfectly cooked. So Gregory always bugged Dad to let him put the hobo dinners in the engine. Dad always said no. Gregory said Dad didn't understand combustion.

"Dad, I'm telling you if you just put the hobo dinners under the hood, we wouldn't have to build a fire, and we could eat as soon as we got there."

"Gregory that's the most ridiculous thing I've ever heard."

"I swear Brother Hansen does it all the time with burritos."

"Sorry, Gregory. I'm not willing to risk having battery acid or oil grease as a condiment on my dinner."

"Oh, brother."

After we ate our hobo dinners, we messed around. We found some cattle wandering around and threw rocks at them. It was boring. Cows are lazy. They ran about five steps and then just turned around and looked at us, like they'd forgotten we threw the rocks in the first place. We also found a shedded rattlesnake skin. It looked like the world's biggest pork rind. Kyle Hewson jumped up and down on it like a crazed jackrabbit and ruined it, though. Kyle was a big fat kid that we sometimes called Shamu because at his baptism, just as the accordion doors hiding the font were pulled back, he slipped on the steps as he descended into the baptismal font, overcorrected, and then belly flopped into the center of the font. He completely soaked all of the little kids sitting Indian-style in the front row.

Dad told bear stories around the campfire after it got dark, while everybody roasted marshmallows. He did the same thing every year. His tongue and gums were still black from the black licorice he had eaten, and it made his teeth look really white.

From across the campfire the only thing on his face you could really make out were his glossy white teeth.

Dad started off by telling about the time when he went to Yellowstone with his family when he was a kid. His mom left the groceries in the car overnight on accident, and when she had Dad go get them out of the car the next morning, there was a bear trapped in the car. The bear had eaten all of the food and torn up the seats in the car. I think it was an Oldsmobile—which, like most cars back then, had different door handles than now. All you had to do was pull the handle down. The bear must've smelled the food, got up on his hind legs, and then knocked the door open with his paw. Dad said there was Cream of Wheat and Ovaltine all over the car—and all over the bear.

All the little kids loved the bear stories, but what I really looked forward to was Brother Montgomery's scary stories. He told one every year. They usually scared the crap out of me. I think they even scared Gregory, because he always acted like he was really busy roasting marshmallows and making s'mores during Brother Montgomery's stories—like he was too busy to listen. I know he listened, though, because he was always really talkative when we were all trying to go to sleep after we'd get back to the car.

That year Brother Montgomery told the story of the Mogollon Rim Monster.

"Boys, I think it's only fair that I tell you a little something about the place we're camping tonight. Most of you don't know this, and I don't think the bishop knew this when he picked this campsite, but about thirty years ago, in 1951, there was a terrible tragedy up on the Mogollon Rim—about forty miles from here.

I had been working as a game warden that summer after my first year in college, and it just so happened that I was assigned to the Payson substation of the Arizona Department of Fish and Wildlife. The crew I was on was assigned to patrol the Mogollon Rim. It was our job to generally keep an eye on campers and others who were on state lands. Most of the people on the state lands were weekend campers from Phoenix, but there were also quite a few cattle ranchers who got permission to graze their cattle on the grassy meadows above the rim. These ranchers would hire crews to keep track of the cattle during the few weeks of grazing."

He paused and gazed steadily at the group and then continued. "One summer night, kind of like tonight—a night with a million stars and a breeze swaying the pine trees—there was a young Mexican boy named Pedro Morales keeping watch on the rim. Pedro had been brought up to the rim from Nogales with his three brothers to watch over a herd of about two hundred cattle that had been brought to a large meadow just above the rim to graze on the summer grasslands. The four brothers took shifts watching the cattle at night. Juan, the oldest, watched from 7 p.m. to 10. Mateo was on from 10 p.m. to 1 a.m. Pedro had the loneliest shift, from 1 a.m. to 4 a.m., and then Jaime came on from 4 a.m. until 7 a.m. They each had a bedroll, but there was only one coat. It was really just a hooded shawl. It had black and reddish horizontal stripes. You can still find these little woolen ponchos in the markets in Nogales for about ten dollars or so.

"When each shift ended, the next brother was awakened and handed the shawl. Pedro was particularly sleepy on this night. He began his shift standing just outside the light of the flickering campfire, but soon he became cold and bored. The night was strangely silent, and it made Pedro even sleepier than he already was. He found a large boulder next to the campfire and perched up on top. Far in the distance, miles away, he picked out the sound of a muffled moan. One of the cows in another herd must be calving tonight, he thought. Minutes later another muffled moan. Two calves in one night. Pedro thought to himself how grateful he was that he didn't have to help deliver calves on a night in which he was so tired.

"Pedro's legs soon began to tire from remaining in his squatting position. He could feel the sensation of needles in his legs as they began to fall asleep. He slid down the boulder and sat leaning his back against the face of the boulder. The smooth surface of the rock had been warmed by the fire, and soon Pedro began to doze, drifting in and out of sleep. He would awaken, slightly startled, every time his head began to bow and nod into his chest. He would raise his head with a jerk and look out toward the cattle; then slowly his head would begin to droop and nod again. Over and over and over.

"Pedro began to dream of sitting in the warm Nogales sun and smelling the fresh tortillas his grandmother would make for him. He unconsciously smiled and sniffed the cool mountain air of the rim as he slept—as if he were really in his grandmother's house in Nogales.

"Then!" Brother Montgomery's voice lowered to a whisper, and everybody jumped. Some of the dads laughed.

"As suddenly and as innocently as he had fallen asleep, Pedro heard it for the first time. Breathing. Heavy breathing. Panting."

Brother Montgomery panted like a cornered Doberman.

It was so quiet you could hear the hum of the campfire. Every once in a while a piece of wood would crack and pop, and all of the little kids would jump. Most of them were sitting in their dads' laps by then. Gregory was busy with three coat hangers, roasting three marshmallows at one time.

"It sounded like a dog—but it couldn't be a dog, could it? Pedro's mind raced. The tone was much too husky for a dog. It was something else—a bear maybe? No, it couldn't be. It almost sounded human—like a very fat man who had just climbed a flight of stairs. The breathing became closer and closer and closer. Pedro was now fully awake. His eyes were wide open. His adrenaline was pumping through his body. He stood bolt upright and looked toward his brothers, who were sleeping soundly under the stars. The breathing continued. It wouldn't stop. Closer, closer, closer! Then, suddenly, it began running in a full sprint. Fallen twigs and branches cracked and snapped as it stomped through the brush and trees. Pedro frantically bent over, grasping for a rock near the fire's edge to throw at the thing. But just as he grabbed hold of a stone, he was tackled from behind. A razorlike swipe cut inches into his back. The force of the blow sent Pedro face first into the fire. He let out a frantic blood-curdling scream."

"AAAAAAAAAAAGH!!" Brother Montgomery screamed. Everybody spasmodically jumped. Gregory dropped one of the coat hangers and stared at Brother Montgomery. The other two marshmallows he was roasting caught on fire, but he didn't even notice.

"Now Juan, Jaime, and Mateo were awake. They jumped to their feet and instinctively rushed toward their little brother's scream. But by the time they reached the campfire, Pedro's fourteen-year-old body lay bleeding to death and burned from head to toe. His thick black hair was gone. So were his eyebrows and eyelashes. He looked like a sea lion—bare skinned, bald headed, and with eyes wide open. The beast had nearly cut his torso in half with its swipe. Pedro began to gasp like a hooked fish brought out of water for the first time. The only movement he could make was to open his eyes even wider in an expression of the horror that he felt. He remained suspended between life and death for a few seconds longer and then passed away into the cool Mogollon night. The brothers quickly threw every log, stick, and twig they could find onto the fire. Soon it was nearly six feet tall.

"Each brother took a flaming branch from the fire and held it. The brightness of the fire blinded them to distances more than fifteen feet from the fire. They couldn't see, but they could hear the cattle begin to stamp nervously then stampede into the woods. Only minutes later, they heard steer after steer, ten in all, desperately moan and wail. Then the noise stopped and they were left until morning. Only when the sun came up did they realize the carnage that had occurred. Most of the cattle had returned, but just on the edge of the forest lay the ripped-up hides of ten steers. There were no bones, no head, nothing except blood splattered on the dirt and pine needles and ripped-up cowhide. A butcher could not have been more efficient if he had tried. Pedro is buried up on the rim. His brothers went home to Nogales with the shreds of Pedro's poncho and never returned to the rim.

"The beast that killed Pedro and the cattle that night was never caught. It turned out that five head of cattle from a different herd had been butchered on the same night about a mile away from Pedro's campsite. All of the game wardens from the Payson substation were called in to try to track and trap it, but we were never successful. An old Yavapai legend has it that a few hundred years ago, Walking Bear, the strongest and fiercest Yavapai warrior, was banished from the tribe for stealing the ceremonial coat of the chief—a coat that some say contained red and black stripes across its back—and wearing it and mocking the chief while he slept.

"The young warrior was cursed by the tribe's medicine man to live out his namesake. He was left alone in the forest to wander as a lost bear; yet he had the mind and memory of a man so that he would never forget the mockery he had made of the chief and the sacred ceremonial coat. We never found the beast that killed Pedro and the cattle, but we did find some petroglyphs on the canyon walls up on the rim that show a very large bear body with the head of a man. A walking bear."

After he was done, everybody made their way back to their campsites. You could hear some of the younger kids whining about wanting to go home. I wouldn't have been surprised if some of them wet their pants. We walked back to the Suburban, and I, for one, was secretly relieved we were sleeping in it instead of outside under the stars or in a tent.

Gregory said that Brother Montgomery was lying—that he'd told the same story as the previous summer at Scout camp, but it had been about the "Camp Geronimo Monster." I asked Dad if Brother Montgomery made the story up. He said he didn't know. He was grinning, though.

We got ready for bed, and Gregory asked Dad if we could turn on the radio and listen to the Dodgers game. They were playing the Braves. Dad shrugged, flipped back the ignition, and Vin Sculley's voice crackled a play-by-play lullaby that floated across the Mojave desert, over the Colorado River, through the

Valley of the Sun, and up into the cool piney heights of the Mogollon Rim. Gregory was asleep within minutes. It took me a while. The Dodgers won five to two on Fernando Valenzuela's complete game victory.

The next morning we ate pancakes, eggs, hash browns, and Dutch-oven biscuits. In the mornings at the campouts everyone smelled like smoke, and all the dads had messed up hair and hadn't shaved. It made it easier to imagine that they used to be boys once.

After breakfast we had gunny sack races, two-legged races, and an egg toss. Gregory and Dad won in Gregory's age group. We came in second in mine.

After helping clean up the campsite, we drove home. When we pulled into the garage, Mom was sitting next to the door on the wooden toy chest that Grandpa Carter had made.

I wondered how long she had been waiting for us. She looked pale and sick. She walked out onto the driveway with Dad while we unloaded our sleeping bags. A few minutes later, they both came back into the garage. Dad was holding her hand. I'd never seen them just stand and hold hands before. Mom was leaning on his shoulder like she was about to fall over.

"Grandpa died this morning, boys," Dad said reverently. "Mom's going to fly to Utah tonight. We'll drive up early tomorrow morning."

Mom said nothing and went inside. Dad watched her go and then looked at us again. His lip started to quiver.

"Todd, I need you to clean out the Suburban. Gregory, I need you to mow the lawn and then clean the pool. It needs chlorine, too."

He went inside. We looked at each other, said nothing, and hung our heads in unison.

21

Take Me Home

Mom flew to Utah that night, alone. Grandma had no idea that Grandpa had passed, and we were under strict orders to say nothing on the subject in her presence.

Dad came into our rooms at 3:00 a.m. the next morning and woke us up. He's a morning person—he always gets up a 4:30 a.m. to get the newspapers. But it was early for him too. I barely remember him coming in. He had put the middle seat in the Suburban down and made beds for all of us. The girls and I lay on sleeping bags where the floor and the middle seat usually were, and Gregory slept on the backseat alone. Grandma was in the front passenger's seat with her afghan and a neck pillow.

What seemed like only a few minutes later, I woke up. It took me a minute to realize what was going on and where I was. I looked out the window. We were in Kanab getting gas at Chevron. Then I remembered. Grandpa was dead. The heaviness in my chest and the dull gnaw in my stomach that struck when I heard the news in the garage the day before returned like jabs to the body. Dad was tired. Grandma was slumped forward, sound asleep. She did not look comfortable. As we continued north, every so often Dad would gently reach over and push her head back against the seat. She would stay there balanced for a few minutes, but then her head would slump forward. What remained of her frail neck muscles would attempt to slow the headlong descent, but it was useless. She would snort and sometimes mumble, but she never came close to waking up. Gregory and the girls were still asleep. I got to my knees to peer over the front seat and saw the sun rising. I yawned, and so did Dad. He knew I was awake.

Dad kept his left hand on the steering wheel and stretched his right arm out along the top of the front bench seat, then extended his hand, signaling me to give him five. Some dads hug, some dads even kiss; Dad gives us five. Dad will walk past you and stick out his hand as you pass him. That means you're supposed to give him five. I slap him a five real hard when we're joking or when he's in a good mood. But usually it's just a soft five, and then he squeezes my hand real fast—as quick as a heartbeat.

I gave him a soft five, and he squeezed my hand, but he didn't let go. He held it for a while. After a few moments, he asked, "Wanna help me stay awake?"

He curled up his hand into a fist and stuck out his pinky. I grabbed it and squeezed. He didn't say anything more, but I squeezed his pinky as we snaked alongside the East Fork of the Virgin River and then the Sevier—past Mt. Carmel Junction, through Orderville and Glendale, past the dusty salmon- and ochre-hued knolls.

We continued on past the sculpted dead-end hollows and box canyons with their juniper and piñon pine and the varicose veins of cottonwood scrub tracing every gully and wash that had a trickle of water, through the quiet farms of Hatch and Hillsdale and the comparative bustle of Panguitch's Main Street.

Just before we reached Circleville, the birthplace of Great Grandma Willey, Dad shook loose his pinky from my grip and pointed to a ramshackle ruin of a log cabin just off the road. In tones much too enthusiastic for someone who had been fighting the hypnotic force of an empty road since three o'clock in the morning, he told me how Great Grandma Willey knew a young boy who had lived in that shack, the oldest of thirteen children, named Robert LeRoy Parker.

Leroy was a boy who loved his mama and tolerated his dad. By all accounts he was a fine boy. Mormon pioneer stock. He even planted a grove of poplars behind the homestead for his mama. When he turned eighteen, he was so bored with life on a small town farm that he left his mama and Circleville for the lure of adventure and freedom. It wasn't too long before the folks in Circleville read in the newspapers about the kind of adventure Robert LeRoy Parker had found—robbing banks as "Butch Cassidy."

Dad raised his eyebrows. "His most audacious job was at the Castle Gate Mine. I bet you didn't know that."

"The same Castle Gate that was in the letter?"

"Same one. In those days, miners were paid in cash. A special train brought the payroll into town on payday. The mining and railroad companies were so nervous about train robberies that the dates of the paydays were only known to a select few. Not even the miners knew. Butch Cassidy and his gang—they were called "The Wild Bunch"—knew a payday was coming soon, and instead of robbing the train they decided to steal the payroll after it was delivered to the mine's paymaster. They stayed in Helper for a few days trying to be as inconspicuous as possible, pretending to be working out their horses for horse races. When the payroll came to town, they stole it from the paymaster and dashed out of town. One of the bunch had already cut all the telegraph lines in and out of town, so they had a major headstart and disappeared into the Utah desert. They had hideouts all over Utah. The most famous hideout was a series of remote slot canyons called Robber's Roost. No one could track them."

I didn't see Dad yawn after that.

We got to Uncle Charlie's in Provo around lunchtime. When we saw Mom, it was pretty clear she'd been crying. She was wearing an apron with ducks on it. She kissed us. Uncle Ted, Uncle Charlie, and Aunt Charlotte were there too. Dad brought Grandma inside. She recognized Mom but paid no real attention to Uncle Charlie and Uncle Ted, even though they hugged her, kissed her on the cheek, and called her Mom. Grandma quietly stood next to Mom like a shy and unsure kindergartner being introduced to her teacher on the first day of school.

After lunch, all the adults went into the living room. I sat in the kitchen, pretending to eat. Grandma sat next to Mom on a leather couch, where they made small talk about the weather and about how we'd made such great time driving. The funeral was discussed superficially and vaguely, in the way parents sometimes talk about certain things in front of their kids, thinking they won't understand. When it comes to Maggie, Mom and Dad have even resorted to spelling what they're talking about. They think they're experts at conversing this way, but they're not. We heard this little exchange once:

"So, Bob, what do you think?"

"About?"

"About what I told you on the phone earlier."

"Sorry, babe, I can't remember."

"It involves the fourth one?" Mom leads.

He gives her a confused I-have-no-idea-what-you're-talking-about squint and tilt of the head. Meanwhile, all of us are following the volleys of parent-speak back and forth like spectators at a tennis match.

". . . And taking up temporary residence this evening for the next twelve to fourteen hours at the dwelling of a close acquaintance?"

He squints harder. She resorts to spelling.

"S-L-U-M-B-E-R?"

Still squinting. Head still tilting.

"P-A-R-T-Y?"

"Oh. Yeah. That. No, I'm not in favor of that. Not tonight, anyway."

"That's no fair, Dad!" Maggie protests. "Everyone else gets to spend the night at their friends'! Why can't I?"

They fooled no one. Not even Maggie, and she was only five then.

In the living room, Uncle Ted, the oldest, started the conversation that they all knew they needed to have but no one wanted to start.

"So everything's ready for tomorrow?" he asked, looking at Mom and then Uncle Charlie.

"Yes. The Relief Society is preparing the Relief Society room so people can come early and say hi and *view* everything. The chapel is ready. The music is ready. The programs are ready. The guys from the mor—M-O-R-T-U-ary," she half spelled, "seem to have everything under control. His bishop will conduct, you guys will share some memories, and *this* bishop (motioning her head in Dad's direction) will give a talk. And one of mine will give a quick Article of Faith."

"What about you?" Charlie said, looking at Mom.

"I can't do it. I'll never make it through. Plus, there is someone I need to sit with," she said, glancing at Grandma for all to see.

Ted began to fidget. He around looked anxiously. Grandma sat quietly, looking at her clasped hands, oblivious.

"How should we . . ." He paused and looked fearfully at Grandma. She was still staring at her hands. "Break the news?" he continued. "Or, do we even need to break the news?" he reconsidered.

"Of course we need to," Mom said.

"Are you sure? What effect is that going to have on her—and, maybe more importantly, on *you*?" Charlie asked.

"I'll be fine. I can deal with whatever happens—*if* anything happens. It probably won't even register."

"Well, it's up to you. I'll do whatever you think is best."

Uncle Ted is a wuss, I thought as I eavesdropped.

"I think we should get it all out right now," Mom suggested.

"Okay. Why don't you go ahead, then, Linda."

Uncle Ted is a total wuss. Maybe the biggest wuss on earth.

Dad clenched his teeth but said nothing. His jaw muscle flexed and bulged on either side of his face. He had a grim look on his face. You could tell he was thinking to himself, *Linda has to worry about her and care for her twenty-four hours a day, plan the funeral, make all the arrangements, and you—her oldest son—can't*

*even be the one to tell your own mother that your dad, who she can
no longer remember anyway, has died?*

He was annoyed, but he said nothing. He reached over and
gently grabbed the top of Mom's hand.

Mom looked at Ted for a couple of long seconds—like the
ones at the end of a tied-up basketball game, but she didn't say
anything either. She already had one arm around Grandma. She
turned and slightly dipped her head to look at her, trying to make
eye contact, to get her attention.

"Mom?" She said gently, almost like she was trying to wake
up a sleeping child.

"Mom?" she repeated.

Grandma looked up and turned her head, expressionless.

"Mom. There's something that we need to tell you. All of us."
Mom looked around the room at everyone and paused.

"There is something very sad that we need to tell you." Pause.
"It's about Dad." Pause. "Mom? Okay, Mom?"

Grandma said nothing, but she continued to look at Mom.

Mom readjusted her sitting position, pulling her arm from
around Grandma's shoulder. She kneeled on the floor in front of
the couch and directly in front of Grandma, then put both hands
on her shoulders. She looked Grandma directly in the eye, locked
in pupil to pupil. Mom's eyes welled. Grandma's didn't, but she
continued to stare into Mom's eyes with a flicker of interest.

"Mom, Dad passed away on Saturday. His heart stopped
beating. He had a heart attack."

"But he didn't suffer," she added.

"He's gone, Mom."

Dad's jaw muscle was flexing rhythmically. He was trying
to hold back tears. Tears streamed down Mom's cheeks, but she
managed to smile and cup Grandma's cheeks with her hands. She
kissed her on the forehead.

"He's fine, Mom. He's just fine. He's in a better place."

When Grandma still didn't respond, Mom repeated in a
whisper, "He's in a better place."

Everyone else was in tears. Uncle Ted sobbed. Grandma continued staring into Mom's eyes.

22

Please Don't Go

Grandpa's funeral was held on a Tuesday in Grandma's ward building. There was a viewing in the Relief Society room before the funeral. At first I couldn't look at Grandpa. It was too weird. He looked like wax, like a candle with his face carved into it, or one of those stuffed animals that you see in museums. He looked only half real.

He was dressed in an outfit that I'd never seen him wear before. Dad said it was his temple clothes. He looked goofy being dead and wearing those clothes. He looked best in his blue jeans and his hat. He's the only grandpa I ever saw that wore blue jeans. He used to sit in his jeans and hat out on his yellow porch swing and look at Timpanogos.

Rock, squeak, wheeeeeze.

Rock, squeak, wheeeeeze.

Rock, squeak, wheeeeeze.

I'd like to hear that again.

I sat on the swing next to Mom yesterday, but she rocked it different. The rock was too quick and the squeak wasn't there. Neither was the wheeze.

Grandma didn't go to the viewing. Mom thought it would be too bizarre for her. All of the extended family combined with people from her ward who hadn't seen her for so long would make it too difficult and too unpredictable.

After the viewing was over they closed the door to the Relief Society room. Only family was allowed. That was when Mom brought Grandma in. Their arms interlocked and they shuffled to the front of the semicircle that formed around the casket. Uncle Ted said a prayer. Mom took the wedding ring off Grandpa's finger and handed it to Grandma. She looked at it curiously and said to Mom, in her normal speaking voice, "Who's he?"

"That's Dad, Mom. Isn't he handsome?"

Mom was remarkably composed. Grandma made no reply. Uncle Ted sobbed. Dad stepped closer and took Grandma's other arm.

Mom took a step forward and started to cry softly as she stroked the hair on Grandpa's head three times and then kissed him on the cheek. Uncle Ted came forward and clutched Grandpa's now ringless left hand. A tiny strip of snow white skin was visible where the ring had been, a contrast to the tomato-tending tan he had earned in his garden.

Uncle Charlie took his turn, quickly leaning in to kiss Grandpa on the forehead. His nostrils flared and his chin quivered, but he didn't cry. Uncle Ted closed the casket, and Mom buried her head in Dad's chest and started to cry again. Dad stood tall, with an arm around Grandma, who emotionlessly studied the ring.

We moved the casket out of the Relief Society room and up to the front of the chapel. I was an honorary pall-bearer. So was Gregory. Gregory and I walked in front while Uncle Charlie, Uncle Ted, Dad, my cousins Bill and Kelly—Ted's boys who were at college—and one of Mom's cousins carried Grandpa into the chapel.

Grandpa's bishop conducted. His name was Bishop Tanner. There was a prayer and a song. Then Aunt Charlotte played the harp. After that Uncle Ted shared memories of Grandpa. He said he remembered that Grandpa was a hard worker and honest and loved to laugh. Uncle Charlie shared memories too and said that he would always remember how much Grandpa loved Grandma. He told about how when Grandma moved to Arizona, Uncle Charlie would meet Grandpa in front of Grandpa's house each morning for an early walk. Grandpa would be sitting on the porch swing waiting, sometimes whistling. As they slowly zigzagged the streets named for different varieties of trees, Grandpa would constantly scan the cracks in the sidewalks and the creases in the gutters. Whenever he saw a stray daisy sprouting from a crevice, he would carefully bend down and delicately snap its stem as close to the ground as he could. He would carry it and twirl it between his thumb and index finger for the rest of the walk. He picked every one he saw. Uncle Charlie had finally asked him why he picked all the daisies.

"Why do I pick them?" he had responded. "Because they're beautiful," he had replied, answering his own rhetorical question.

"Well, why do you keep them, then?"

"Like I said. They're beautiful."

"Why daisies? We pass plenty of other flowers."

"They remind me of your mother. She loves daisies." He had emphasized the present tense.

They'd kept walking. For all Uncle Charlie knew the conversation was over. After a few quiet moments, as they rounded the corner and began the slight ascent up another street named for yet another variety of tree, inching closer to the foothills that would soon dead end into the low benches of the towering Wasatch peaks before them, Grandpa had continued his explanation, unsolicited.

"I can't see her Charlie. Obviously, I'm not around her much anymore. But I know she is *delicate* and *precious* and *alive*," he'd said with growing emphasis.

"And I know that someday she is going to sprout and bud and bloom and smile, just like those lonely, forgotten little wild daisies quietly blooming by the roadsides. She'll be as beautiful and happy and feisty as she ever was. *That's* why I pick them. They remind me."

Up to that point, Uncle Charlie had never noticed, but he began to notice whenever he went in Grandpa's kitchen that there were always two or three of the daisies in a water glass on the windowsill above his kitchen sink.

Gregory and Lisa exchanged slack-jawed glances at each other. There was no more doubt, if there ever had been any. Grandma was Daisy Petal.

After Uncle Charlie, it was Dad's turn to talk. He talked about how the first time he took Mom out on a date, Grandpa was mowing the lawn and asked Dad to help him out. Mom came outside, and there was Dad raking grass in a shirt and tie. She hadn't even known he was there yet. Dad also told how Grandpa would always walk with me and Gregory down University Avenue to 7-11 to get cherry Slurpees and Cracker Jacks. He loved Cracker Jacks. Dad also told about how Grandpa was so poor that he dropped out of BYU and worked in the coal mines before he got married. He saved every penny to pay for the ring that he had bought to give to Grandma—the one that Grandma still wore but had no idea why. He wore the ring on a leather string around his neck for a year while she was at BYU learning how to be a teacher, even though she never taught at a school. He had worn that ring while he made dark, smelly rides down the mine shafts, while he ate alone in the dark stoop of the intestinal caverns that snaked underneath the mountains of his boyhood, and while he laid the bodies of the dead on the dance floor at Castle Gate.

I looked out from the stand and saw Mom; she was crying again. Grandma sat up straight and was surprisingly alert if not emotionally engaged, like she was at a movie.

Then there was a song. "Abide with Me!" The bishop stood and gave some "remarks." I don't think he knew Grandpa very well. He just read a bunch of scriptures.

Then it was my turn. When the bishop was done, Dad squeezed my shoulder. My cue. I stood up and walked over to the pulpit. I was nervous but sad too. The bishop lowered the microphone.

I cleared my throat.

"We belie—"

I cleared my throat again.

"'We believe that through the Atonement of Christ, all mankind may be saved, by obedience to the laws and ordinances of the gospel.' This is the third Article of Faith. I love you, Grandpa. I love you, too, Grandma. Name of Jesus Christ, amen."

"Amen," the audience responded.

I walked back to my seat and sat down. Dad put his right arm around me and put his left hand, palm up, on my left thigh. He stretched it out. I gave him a soft five. He held my hand.

I looked up and out into the audience and saw Grandma. She looked at me attentively with a faint expression of satisfaction, almost pride. Then I looked at Mom. She wiped her eyes and looked up at me. She nodded and made a point to mouth "amen" again so that I could see. She was smiling.

VIII

It's clear long before I say "amen"—it will be over soon. Gregory's blessing is resolute. There are no questions, only inevitability, finality.

We will soon be parentless. It is stark and real, but still somehow unimaginable.

The self-loathing realization that I have not lived up to expectations—that sharp cut of semifailure and dull gnaw that lingered for months after Dad suddenly died of a heart attack (only three years after retiring and before getting the opportunity to fulfill his dream of learning a foreign language and serving a mission with Mom in some remote jungle)—is now reintroducing itself. Much has been given, much has been required, but deep down we know that not much has been done for anyone but ourselves. Her death will bring on another period of self-wonder, self-assessment and self-recrimination. For a time, we will pray more earnestly and resolutely. We will turn off the music in our cars, put our iPods away, and ponder, meditate, reflect. We will demonstrate a temporary intolerance for frivolity. There will be no appetite for romantic comedies and sitcoms. We will worry ourselves with the tragedy and reality of wars, famine, earthquakes, homelessness, and hurricanes that twenty-four-hour-a-day cable news provides and quietly wonder to ourselves what we can possibly do. But, ultimately, we will talk and fret but do nothing. We will look in our mirrors and wonder how our mother got to be eighty-two and how we got to be forty-something, we will acknowledge finally (and maybe reluctantly) that the real heroes in life are the Robert LeRoy Parkers of the world and not the Butch Cassidys. We will be sickened and repulsed by our vanity, our pursuit of things *over unheralded and determined* experience, *and our preoccupation with beach resorts, shoes, the latest can-you-believe-she-said-that gossip, fluorescent white teeth, subtle tans, augmentations, 10K times, Sunday football scores, and all the other things that wordlessly scream the stark and painful reality that, underneath it all, maybe we are only theoretical believers of everything she taught us.*

23

What a Fool Believes

"Tony Dorsett," Gregory said slowly, out of the blue.

"What?"

"Tony Dorsett."

"What about him?"

"Number 33."

"Yeah. I know. So?"

"So, you're number 33 too."

"What're you talking about?"

"Thirty-three days, man. Thirty-three days until your life changes. *For-e-ver.*"

"You're a freak, Gregory."

"Thirty-three days," he said again and laughed mischievously.

Every time he said thirty three, he flashed three fingers with his left hand and then three with his right hand.

"So, big deal," I lied.

"No big deal? Nice try. Are you kidding? Listen to Mr. Seventh Grade Stud!"

"Why do you have to be so annoying?"

"It's my job, young grasshopper. It's my job. Actually, it's the job of every ninth grader—to teach you discipline and the mysteries of Mangas Coloradas Junior High."

Gregory and I shared the backseat the entire way home from Utah. This was his way of taking the opportunity to remind me of what I was mortifyingly already aware of—there were only thirty-three days until school started. Seventh grade. My first year of junior high.

I kept telling him to be quiet, but he wouldn't stop. There would be peace and quiet for fifteen minutes or so, followed by bursts of warnings and propaganda.

"You know you gotta take a shower after PE every day? Right?"

Gregory said the PE coaches had a rule that if you didn't take a shower after PE, they wouldn't let you go to your other classes.

According to Gregory, even the coaches would call you a wuss when they took roll if they found out you weren't taking a shower after class was over. He demonstrated:

"Adams!"

"Here."

"Baker!"

"Here."

"Brown!"

"Here."

"Wuss!"

No one answers.

"Oops! Did I say *Wuss*?! I mean *Whitman*! Has anyone seen Todd W. Wuss Whitman? Oh, *there's* Wuss—I mean Whitman. Sorry, Whitman, I didn't see you back there. Doesn't that W really stand for, 'Sorry Coach, I *will* take a shower next time"?'

Then, Gregory said, everybody in your PE class would laugh, and the whole seventh grade would call you a wuss for the rest of your life. Even the girls who went to other elementary schools who you didn't even know would giggle when they saw you, he said.

"Look, look! That's the one who's afraid to take a shower with the other guys in PE."

"Him?

"Yeah, him. He's the wuss!"

According to Gregory, everybody would even sign your yearbook "Dear Wuss . . ."

"Dear Wuss, math was a blast, hope we have prealgebra together next year."

"Dear Wuss, stay cool and cute. Give me a call over the summer."

"Hey, Wuss, too bad you're such a wuss. Ha ha. See you next year."

"You're basically marked for life," he said, warning me.

Gregory said that all the ninth graders would make fun of the seventh graders in PE. "They call you hairless, and ask if you need a microscope and tweezers to help you take a whiz." He also said that on the first day of PE all the ninth graders would wait around the corner from the showers while the soaking-wet, naked seventh graders lined up to exit the showers and get their standard-issue, industrial-scented, crusty locker-room towel. Each seventh grader, he explained, would take a towel from the PE aide and peek around the corner, like a frightened wildebeest reluctantly preparing to cross a rain-swollen, crocodile-infested river.

"Hurry up already! Get outta here!" the aide would yell.

The line would start again. The seventh grader would dart around the corner into a gauntlet—a birth-canal-like aisle of orange lockers lined with zitty metal-mouthed ninth graders laughing and screaming the F-word, snapping towels at your bare butt as you ran past them. Some of the meaner ones, Gregory said, would make rat tails—soaking wet towels rolled up as tightly as possible—and aim for your wiener as you instinctively cup yourself and waddle as fast as you can through the chaos. When snapped correctly, a rat tails sounds like the crack of Indiana Jones's whip.

Gregory says that some rat tails even drew blood. He told me one kid supposedly even had his sack ripped open by a rat tail.

I stared out the window as Dad decelerated through Richfield's main drag, trying my best not to pay attention. Gregory nudged me and said that the previous year one kid came out of the shower and was running to his locker on his tippy toes, trying not to slip on the wet, polished concrete floor. Just then, Albert Taufa—the insane Maori foreign exchange student from New Zealand and reigning ninth-grade heavyweight wrestling champ who walked around the locker room stark naked— jumped around the edge of a row of lockers doing a Haka war dance, screaming in some Polynesian dialect. He was slapping the top of his legs, sticking out his tongue like Gene Simmons, and making different deranged faces. The kid started running the other direction, and Albert Taufa chased him to a dead end. The kid turned around and started begging and offering him money. Albert kept doing the Haka—slightly crouching, eyes bulging out of his head, methodically slapping his quads, swinging his legs forward in sweeping rhythmic steps, and sticking out his tongue and screaming. The kid kept begging. He offered Albert his lunch, his homework, even his bike. Albert made no acknowledgment of the offers. He just kept Hakaing and then, with a wide-eyed psychopathic stare, he snapped a dripping wet rat tail. The crack was so loud, Gregory said, that you could practically *hear* the sting of its bite. The edge of the towel caught the kid's inner thigh. The kid cried with resignation, "I am a dead man!" and crumpled to the floor as if he'd been shot. Gregory said the kid had a blood blister the size of a silver dollar pancake for two weeks after.

"And that's not even the worst of it," Gregory continued. "PE is nothing. Just wait until the Hello Dance. Talk about sheer terror and panic." He laughed.

"The what?"

"It's gonna be awesome!" he proclaimed.

I'd never danced before. My face must have given away my concern because he laughed again and said that there was "nothing to worry about"—which only confirmed that I should definitely worry about it.

"I'm telling you, Todd, don't stress it. Just do the deacon shuffle."

"The what?"

"The deacon shuffle. It's a simple as that."

"As simple as what?"

"Listen, don't *worry* about it. You'll either figure it out ahead of time or it will come to you as natural instinct."

I was speechless. *What a weirdo*, I thought.

"Dances are a form of institutionalized mating ritual. And all mating rituals are foolproof. If somebody doesn't tell you what to do, at the last minute and in the right situation your natural instincts will take over."

There was a definite possibility that he had been sniffing Maggie's magic markers or something.

"Listen, young grasshopper. Always remember two words: *Deacon. Shuffle.*"

"How can I *remember* something when I don't know what it is, idiot? Does it have something to do with passing the sacrament?"

He smirked.

"What does passing the sacrament have to do with the Hello Dance?" I tried again, with a hint of desperation in my voice.

He just grinned and repeated, "Deacon shuffle." Then he put on his Walkman, made a few mocking disco twirls with his hands, like a basketball ref making a traveling call, and closed his eyes with a wide smile.

"And one other thing," he said, pushing the left headphone back off of his ear, "you'll need a jockstrap, too."

He readjusted the headphones, smiled, and closed his eyes again. I stared at him for a few moments. I could hear the faint blare of Van Halen escaping from his spongy, black headphones. I stared at him for a few moments in utter confusion and watched his smile fade into a deep, worriless sleep.

24

He's the Greatest Dancer

After the funeral, Grandma's nighttime visits started to increase in frequency. Her daytime wanderings halted for the most part, replaced by nighttime visits to my room, and who knows where else. It was too hot to wander anywhere in the daytime, and it was probably too hot for her to sleep at night. Even though she couldn't remember it, her body's need to sleep was likely being upset by its conditioned craving for nearly eighty Utah summers worth of cool Wasatch evening breezes that had been harvested every night by her open bedroom window.

It was possible she was wandering into Lisa's room and Gregory's room, too, but I doubted it. Her wanderings there would have been very short-lived.

Gregory would have lain in bed and yelled downstairs in an irritated tone.

"Mom! Dad!"

"Mom!"

"Dad!"

"Mom and Dad! Can you come get Grandma out of my room? She just woke me up, and she's sitting here staring at me!"

Mom would have eventually heard him and raced upstairs.

Lisa would have gently walked Grandma back to her room and then told Mom about it in the morning.

Either way, the wanderings would have been over.

I don't know why, but I never said anything. I guess I wanted Grandma to have the freedom to roam around if she wanted to, as long as she was safe. And, once I got used to waking up and getting over the absolute, although momentary, terror of not knowing what was going on in my own room in the middle of the night, I actually liked the fact that she picked me, that she felt safe and wanted and comfortable in my room.

I also didn't want Mom to worry. She was constantly worrying about Grandma and was still mourning Grandpa. Nighttime was her only escape from all of it. If she knew Grandma was wandering at night, she would lose her nights too. She would probably move a recliner into Grandma's room and sleep there. She would never sleep soundly again—which would make her days even worse. Dad was gone most nights doing doctor stuff or bishop stuff, and oftentimes doctor-bishop stuff combined. People had a tendency to use Dad as a free resource for unloading their medical problems, not just their personal problems. They concocted reasons to see him as bishop and then used it as a free consultation for their back pain, throat ailments, and flu symptoms. He began keeping a prescription pad in the bishop's office, and it became as important as his temple recommend book. Dad didn't seem to care, but it bugged Mom.

The point was, Grandma wasn't hurting anybody and Mom didn't need to know.

There were several nights that I woke up and saw Grandma sitting at my small desk, as prim and proper as a schoolgirl, my aluminum desk lamp illuminating her book of remembrance as she slowly turned its pages, gazing at each picture for several seconds. Sometimes she squinted, sometimes she only stared blankly, lost in time and space, trapped in a black hole of displaced context and unrecoverable memory. Sometimes she mumbled to herself, sometimes she "harrumphed," and sometimes she sighed. Every once in a while she would touch a page and gently brush her fingers across a photograph. Sometimes she tapped on a photograph as if she had discovered a small pilot light of memory and was trying to ignite a broader, more robust flame. Once she even stuck out her tongue at a photo, flicked it with her middle finger, and said out loud, "Serves you right!"

At first, I pretended to be asleep, watched her for a few minutes, and then eventually fell back asleep. When I woke up in the morning, my sheets were always pulled up to my chin, my bedroom light was off, and the wet swimsuit and dirty clothes that had been strewn on my floor were folded in a neat pile on my desk.

Things changed one night, though, when Grandma stood up abruptly from my desk and began to bob and twirl with her arms tightly wrapped around the album cover. Her white cotton floor-length nightgown whizzed and billowed. Her eyes were closed, and she had a slight crack of a smile on her face. I had been pretending to be asleep, but the sight of my Grandmother slow dancing with a Saturday Night Fever album cover in my room at two o'clock in the morning made me giggle. She clearly heard me, but without pausing she continued her bobbing and twirling. Her eyes remained closed and she said, "Haven't you ever danced before? Haven't you ever held your lover in your arms?"

"Actually, uh, no. Definitely *no*," I said. The sentence started hesitantly and ended more emphatically than I had intended.

"Sounds to me like you've got something to learn *and* something to hide."

"Whatever," I said defensively.

She laughed. She actually smiled and tilted her head back and laughed.

"Young man, if you haven't danced, you need to learn. And don't fool yourself, everyone has a love."

I ignored her and tried to go back to sleep, but it was no use. After about five more minutes, the music in her head must have stopped, because she slowly wound to a halt, collected the book of remembrance on my desk, then turned off the desk lamp and slowly exited my room.

The next night I awoke to her sitting at the desk, book of remembrance wide open. But this time she was lost in thought, staring at my poster of George Gervin. The "Iceman" was wearing a silver sweatsuit and sitting, legs crossed, on huge blocks of ice with two silver basketballs at either side.

"Grandma?"

She looked over at me.

"I have a question for you."

She continued looking at me.

"How did you learn to dance?"

She ignored my question and said, "What does this say?"

She handed me an ancient-looking greeting card with a cartoonish picture of large yellow sunflowers on the front and the word *Darling* preprinted in gaudy gold cursive.

I opened the card, and the same gaudy preprinted text continued. *You are my sun. You are my flower.* Opposite the preprinted message, there was a handwritten note in slightly smudged blue ink.

I looked up at her.

"Read it to me."

I cleared my throat, squinted at the tiny text, and began.

November 18, 1960

Dear Gail,
I have been thinking about what more I can possibly say that I have not tried to say already. These past few months without you have been the worst of my life. I have found myself under the rubble of a deep mine shaft that has collapsed as a result of my own shoddy workmanship and carelessness. I see rays of your sunlight beaming from above the caved-in walls, and there is nothing more that I want than to return to the warm embrace of the force that is you. I can be a better man and a better father than I have been. And I will be. I will do my best to live worthy of your embrace. That is my simple, solemn promise to you. I understand if you cannot accept this, but it does not change and will never change my love for you.
—C

P.S. Sunflowers were the closest things to daisies I could find.

I couldn't look up at Grandma when I finished. I knew this was serious, and I was too embarrassed to look at her. I don't know what happened between them, and I didn't want to know, not even one little bit. I had no desire to rubberneck and watch her relive the journey. All I knew is what I had seen over the years—they loved each other, they loved my Mom, and they loved me. No questions asked. Their lives were quiet, modest, and dedicated. They had no riches—other than evening strolls alongside creeks and weeping willows, earnest conversation on creaky, rusted porch swings, simple gratitude for fresh picked raspberries and sugar snap peas, and the comfort and purpose found in milking, shoveling, pruning, and gathering. I instinctively knew that whatever happened in 1960 was a fork in the road that had affected the trajectory of lives, including my own. I was grateful that she had let him come back, that she had swallowed hard and forgiven, or at least tried.

She was demented, there was no doubt. She wasn't always sane or rational, but I trusted her—completely. And something deep inside that I couldn't explain was telling me that even though she was completely crazy and probably didn't know who I was and didn't care what I asked or didn't ask, Grandma deserved my trust, the trust to know that I wouldn't ask, "What happened between you and Grandpa?" or stare and stammer, "Why are you crying, Grandma?" I didn't want to know the details, and I didn't need to know. I already knew everything I needed to know. I had almost twelve years of experience with them both to back that knowledge up.

I admit, in hindsight, I was slightly curious to know why after twenty years she'd told him it was like 1960 all over again when he left her in Arizona. Maybe that was her desperate swing for the fences to shame him into taking her home with him. Or maybe she had kept that pain, nursed it, and cared for it for all those years, waiting for the perfect opportunity to throw it back in his face. That couldn't be it, though. Watching her solitary, silent midnight dance with a tiny cardboard apparition of her Dancer, her lover—the husband lost in her malfunctioning mind—I had to think that the most basic and most fundamental human emotions were taking over. Yes, she was demented. Yes, she was lost and stuck in the maze of her memory, a puzzle she would never solve. But she loved him. She loved the Dancer. He confused her, and he preoccupied her. He kept her up at night. He was her reason for living.

On top of it all, I *couldn't* know. I couldn't know something like this, something that maybe Mom didn't even know about her own mother. It wouldn't seem right or fair. All I knew was that somehow Grandma had been wronged, terribly wronged, even by Grandpa's own admission. So wronged, she would have been justified to not let him come back. But somehow she found a way to let go, to get on with it, to trudge along until she regained solid, stable ground. And by doing so, she had saved her family. If sacrificing yourself to save something of value means you're a hero, then Grandma certainly qualified.

Mom had probably never seen the card that changed the course of Grandma's life, her life, and the chain link to untold posterities. Maybe Mom didn't even know that they had been separated. Maybe a story of work trips or illness had been concocted. But, in the end, it didn't really matter.

Somehow she had moved on, maybe even forgiven him. There was no crumbling cabin on the side of the road left for all those that passed to casually comment on the price of being seduced by the fool's gold of far-flung freedom and adventure. He was Robert LeRoy Parker. A man of poplar groves and solid, dignified, small-town living. To his credit, Grandpa was no Butch Cassidy.

It was a lot to chew on. Grandma remained silent. I heard sniffles but didn't look up.

I purposely fumbled with the card and turned it over, looking at the plain but glossy white back of the card, then flipped it over, pretending to be fascinated by the sturdy-looking yellow petals and gigantic brown irises of the sunflowers.

"Young man," Grandma finally said.

I slowly lifted my eyes looked up at her.

A frail, almost skeletal hand, spotted with age and slightly trembling, rose and wiped the sockets of both eyes. I looked back down, embarrassed, not knowing what to say but for some reason thankful that I was there.

"Yeah?"

"Do you still want to know how I learned to dance?"

"Sure, I guess so," I said politely. What else could I say?

She slowly scooted the desk chair back, careful not to catch the back legs in the carpet, and rose, bracing her weight on the scratched wooden surface of the desktop, knees cracking.

"Come here," she said, standing in the middle of the room.

By this time I had mostly gotten used to being half naked, clad only in my tight, white Fruit of the Looms, in the presence of my Grandmother. So, without too much hesitation about my appearance, I slowly kicked off the single sheet covering me, stood up, and met Grandma in the center of my room.

Grandma extended her right arm, shoulder high, directly to her side. My fan oscillated to and fro, providing a gentle breeze and a slight hum. She nodded at me and made a point to elegantly twist her wrist, placing her palm down so it faced the ground.

"Take my hand," she said firmly.

I reached for her left hand, the one hanging at her side.

"No, *this* hand." She nodded toward her extended right hand, signaling with another elegant twist of her right wrist.

"Oh," I said.

I took her right hand with my left. She rested her palm in mine.

"Now, place your other hand on my back, just beneath my shoulder blade, elbow extended."

I reluctantly extended my hand toward her hip.

Sensing my discomfort, she impatiently grabbed my hand and put it in its place.

"There." She sighed pleasantly.

I was looking straight into her eyes. I'd never really realized it until that moment, but I was almost her exact height. I noticed the texture and complexity of the web of wrinkles that shot out from the corners of her eyes and then curved and twirled in their own unique patterns down her cheekbones and across her jaw.

I shifted my gaze to look at my feet. She rested her left hand on my right shoulder and said, "This is how my mother taught me to dance. Just like this. Down by the river bottoms under the box elder maple tree that anchored her laundry line."

She moved her right foot back.

"Follow me," she said. "But you must be *smooth*. You must be *fluid*. Not herky-jerky. Can you do that?" she asked encouragingly. This was the old Grandma Carter speaking. Confident and direct.

"I don't know. But I'll try," I said awkwardly, looking down and beginning to feel subconscious about the briefs slightly wedging upward in my crack.

"*This* is called the fox trot." She smiled and began, slowly stepping backward, pulling me forward in her wake.

"Two, three, four," she counted, jerking me forward, to the side, then backward, to the side, then forward

"And five, six, seven, eight . . ." she continued, yanking me forward a couple of paces in her imperfect square.

25

Good Times

Oranging season for Gregory and his buddies usually ended in mid-February. And the season almost always unofficially ended with a grand finale that rained spongy, overripe oranges down on to the heads of unsuspecting fourteen- and fifteen-year-olds at the Valentine's Day stake dance.

By the end of February all of the oranges are gone, harvested or fallen to the ground, too fat and ripe for the branches to support. The bushy, fruitless orange trees are fertilized, irrigated, and receive fresh coats of white sunscreen on their trunks, readying them for the warm spring days and scorching summer to come.

By the middle of March, tiny snowflake-sized buds appear briefly and then pop into small puffs of popcornlike blossoms, eventually expanding into thousands of tiny, white starfish-shaped flowers. The rate of joggers and couples out on evening walks increases dramatically during the short-lived burst of citrus fragrance. Bumblebees and hummingbirds appear from nowhere and spend a spring break hovering and harvesting sweet nectar from the blossoms before they dry up and fall to the ground.

By mid-May, small marbles of green begin to take shape, slowly expanding and rounding into taut golf-ball-sized green oranges that continue to swell until they become the size of baseballs and sometimes freakishly large softballs. The cooling nights of late October and November eventually release the sugars that soften the inner flesh and turn their green skins a dull yellow. By mid-December, even the heartiest have turned a deep sunset orange and are ready to be picked and shipped to the most citrus-starved reaches of the country.

During the oranging off-season, especially the summer months, Gregory and his band of aspiring juvenile delinquents would incubate and then experiment with new acts of mischief. Although nothing could truly replace the efficiency of the instantaneous adrenaline rush that only oranging supplied, that summer they tried a wide variety of substitutes. There was "pool hopping" (which consists of doing a cannonball in a neighbor's pool in the middle of the night, then hopping the fence and doing the same thing in the next neighbor's pool, and so on and so on, until the light in every master bedroom in the neighborhood is on and every dog within a mile is barking), waterskiing in the canal (pulled by a motorcycle, ATC, or a truck), and "Mutual of Omaha-ing" (which consisted of perching in trees over front doorsteps and documenting romantic advances as older high school boys returned their dates home; Ben-G called this "observing the mating rituals of the species indigenous to this ecosystem, like Marlin Perkins would").

Although these activities created bursts of excitement every so often—like when Jericho's heel was bitten by a Rottweiler as he scrambled over a brick wall during a midnight pool-hopping run (he lost one of his brand-spanking-new white Stan Smith Adidas tennis shoes in the process and had to convince his mother that a drunk Indian hanging outside the Westwood Cinema had for some unknown reason made him surrender one shoe "as a remembrance of the sins of the Mormon pioneer bastards who stole my land in Lehi" or die). Or like the time Ben-G lost his balance and fell out of a tree while Mutual of Omahaing the blossoming sophomore-to-be Sara Thornton and the rising senior left tackle for Mesa High, DeWayne Kwycezki, just a few feet from their sloppy front porch make-out session, setting off a chain of events that included a blood-curdling scream from Sara, a fifteen-minute chase on foot down alleys and across University Avenue, and Ben-G pretending to shop for tampons while hiding out in the feminine hygiene products aisle at Skaggs drugstore.

But of all their paltry substitutes for oranging, the only thing that even came close for them was fake fighting.

The premise of fake fighting is simple: Several boys pretend to beat the living crap out of one boy, usually at night on a lonely corner, as a solitary car approaches. As the car approaches, the driver notices a vague commotion in the distance, just beyond the illumination provided by his headlights. The driver flashes his high beams and cautiously continues, slows, and notices a group ahead and what appears to be a scuffle. The driver taps his breaks and slows to a crawl as he passes the small mob scene. As he rubbernecks past the group, he notices that they are boys and that one of the boys is lying in the gutter on his back pleading in muffled, desperate tones, while several other boys punch and kick him. At the same time, one of the punchers looks up, points at the car, and sounds the alarm, "Car! Car! Get outta here!" The pack of boys scatters. By now the driver has rolled past the scene and is engaging in a should-I-or-shouldn't-I-go-back battle with his conscience while he watches in his rearview mirror as the victim struggles to his feet and bends over, one hand on his knees while the other clutches his side, and attempts to catch his breath.

If Gregory and his friends are lucky, the driver has passengers, and that driver and those passengers are collectively shocked and outraged that such a heinous assault on a lone victim could take place in their peaceful neighborhood. One passenger hops out of the car to check on the victim while the others make a furious vigilante chase in pursuit of the bullies.

In the summer and fall, Gregory and his friends talked incessantly about fake fighting, but they rarely did it, primarily because none of them had the guts to be the victim. Although the adrenaline rush for the pretending bullies is intense, especially when chased, there is nothing quite like the combination of fear, anxiety, and the absolutely blank canvas of the unknown for the person pretending to be the victim. Anything can happen.

And he is alone. If he is found to be a faker, he's left alone to defend himself from what could be a "why, I oughta kick your ass!" lecture, a call to the cops, or even a real beating. In those cases, the victim is left to his own devices and discretion about if and when he should pull the ripcord and attempt an escape—for which, unlike the bullies, he has no help and no headstart. Otherwise, the victim has to do a convincing enough acting job to persuade the wannabe Good Samaritan(s) that it's okay to go on their way, that he is fine, that it was no big deal, that, yes, he really should find new friends, that thanks, but no thanks, he doesn't need a ride home, that no, no, really, there is no reason to call the police, trust him, that would only make things worse at home, and that yes, of course, he will tell his parents all about it.

One night, just before school started, Gregory came into my room. I was looking at the baseball cards I had just purchased with my allowance—Ron Cey, Alan Trammel, George Brett, Keith Moreland, Joe Beckwith, Dennis Lamp, Pete LaCock, Jack Clark, Carl Yastrzemski, Joe Charboneau, John Tudor, Larry Parrish, Sixto Lezcano, Rick Honeycutt, and Tug McGraw—and had just started chewing the crunchy sheaf of chalky bubble gum that came in every pack when Gregory walked in.

"What are you doing?" he asked, noticing the baseball cards.

"Wait, who'd you get?" he continued before I could answer the first question.

I fanned them out in front of my chest to show him, like I was playing a fifteen-card hand of poker.

He plucked a card from the fan. "Who the heck is Sixto Lezcano?"

"I have no idea," I said.

He read the back of the card, commenting, "Cardinals. Outfielder. Eighteen home runs last year. Not too bad. But only hit .229. Only played in one hundred and twelve games. Never heard of him," he summarized.

He turned the card over again, examined Sixto, and harrumphed, satisfied that he had learned something new.

He grabbed another card from my hand.

I sighed impatiently.

"Wait. Pete LaCock? *LaCock!?* Is this for real?" He started laughing. "Pete LaCock? This has to be a joke."

I waited patiently for him to continue the unsolicited commentary I knew was coming.

"Would you look at this guy?" he said, flipping the card over and showing me the photo of Royals first baseman Pete LaCock. He looked like the Brawny paper towel guy, only with blond hair that had been stuffed unsuccessfully under a blue baseball cap.

Gregory examined the statistics on the back of the card. "Geez, a first basement hitting .205? Royals fans are gonna start calling him Pete *LaWeenie* if he doesn't start hitting."

He flipped the card back over and looked at both Pete LaCock and Sixto Lezcano. "Hilarious," he mused.

"Can I have them back now?"

He handed them back to me. And fake stretched. "Well, like *sixto* of my friends are downstairs and wanna go fake fighting."

"Good one," I said, acknowledging the lame pun.

"So."

"So, none of them want to be the victim."

"So."

"So, I told them they were wusses and that my little brother would do it."

"Yeah, right."

"I'm serious."

"Why would you say that? I'm not doing it."

"Why not?"

"Why don't *you* do it?"

"C'mon. Seriously. I told them that you have the rare combination of balls and ingenuity to do it," he said, blatantly dodging my question.

Balls and ingenuity. It was one of his catch phrases that he thought was flattering. I was pretty sure he had stolen it from Coach Rory Rawlings. I'd heard it before.

"C'mon. I'll even promise to start calling you Todd LaCock if you do it. Or Sixto Whitman. Your choice.

I said nothing.

"Seriously, you'll be a legend!"

"Uh—I thought I already was," I said sarcastically.

"Exactly. That's why they believe me. They think you'll do it just for that reason. C'mon, seriously. It will be awesome," he tried again.

I don't know why, but I gathered my cards, stacked them in a neat pile, picked up my shoes, methodically double-knotted them like I was Mr. Rogers, and then stood up.

"Thattaway, *Sixto*!" Gregory exclaimed.

26

Street Life

It only took the first car. Except for a solitary streetlight about thirty yards in the distance, it was nearly pitch black, a moonless summer night. A monsoon dust storm had swept through at dusk and left a vague stench of musty dirt. There were sporadic aftershocks of wind gusts, and a few storm-severed palm fronds scraped along the road like phantoms. It had been dark for at least two hours, but the gritty black asphalt still retained some of the blistering heat of the afternoon.

"Car!" several of Gregory's friends announced in unison as they saw approaching headlights in the distance.

I assumed the position, kneeling down in the gutter and slightly burning my knees, then lying down and curling into the fetal position in the middle of the circle of suburban teenage hyenas.

The road smelled of melted tar and wet dirt. I wanted to sneeze.

I lifted my head slightly and could see the headlights approaching through the mob's bare legs. I noticed that Barry Friedman had exceptionally hairy legs and was wearing drugstore flip-flops. He was in serious trouble if there was a chase, I thought.

As the car came closer, some of the boys took their acting jobs too seriously. They must have thought that the occupants of the car had bionic ears. So, they actually started making up impromptu reasons for beating me up. They began yelling in ridiculously shrill tones the spontaneously fictionalized grievances that warranted their vigilante butt-kicking.

Some of them were so hyped up that they were actually punching and kicking me.

"Why'd you push my sister, you little bastard?!" screamed Jake Nelson.

"Yeah, why'd you push his sister? You think you're some kind of tough guy picking on little girls? Huh? *Huh?*" they jabbed for added emphasis.

"This is *fake* fighting you idiots! Cut it out, you're really hitting and kicking!" I protested.

As usual, Gregory was the director. So I appealed to him. "Gregory, seriously, tell them to act like they've done this before!" But he was too absorbed in the strategy and clock management of the choreography. By then, the car was nearly right there.

"Staaaay. Staaaay. Staaay. Keep punching. Keep punching. Okaaaay . . . NOW!" Gregory ordered.

He turned and pointed directly at the car, feigning surprise, "Oh, crap! CAR!" he yelled, sounding the fake alarm, moving his mouth and lips exaggeratedly so the car's occupants could read his lips.

A station wagon abruptly stopped and jerked into park. The hyenas scattered toward the nearest fences and alleys.

The driver's side door swung open almost before the car stopped. The figure of a slender woman emerged and hurried around the front of the idling engine. The heavy door rocked on its hinge, but swung back out and remained wide open. I slowly arose from the gutter but remained bent over, facing the ground and clutching my side, not wanting to make eye contact with the Samaritan.

"Oh my goodness!" the driver said as she approached.

Avoid eye contact. Do not look up, I reminded myself. Out of the corner of my eye I noticed that the station wagon was a wood-paneled, yellow Caprice Classic with spoked hubcaps. I instantly became nauseous.

I glanced up. There she was, peering out of the window on the passenger's side.

Jenny Gillette.

"*Sonofa* . . ." I groaned under my breath.

My recon glance had only lasted a split second, but in that instant, as she recognized me and I recognized her, the wide-eyed look of curiosity on her face was wiped away with a disappointed furrowing of her brow.

I ducked my head back down toward my knees. My stomach dropped with it.

"Oh, no," I muttered to myself as I saw Sister Gillette's brown leather huarache sandals and burgundy toenails come into my view of the asphalt.

"*Todd?*"

"Todd *Whitman?* Is that you, dear?"

27

Ain't No Stoppin' Us Now

Although I didn't fully comprehend it at the time, I realized later that there are certain moments in life when you have to "follow through on your commitments, stay the course, and *endure to the end,*" as Dad would say (each phrase gradually increasing in religious intensity). This included choosing when to sacrifice for a greater cause, even when you didn't necessarily completely believe in the cause, even when you didn't really like all of the people who backed the cause, and even if you sometimes wondered what would have become of your life if you had never been cajoled, coerced, or coaxed into joining the cause.

I knew if I came clean with Sister Gillette right then and there that she would be confused, slightly appalled, probably disillusioned, and maybe even angry with what we were doing. On the other hand, maybe she would admire our thirst for excitement and applaud our creativity. After all, we weren't really hurting anyone or anything. It's not like we were shoplifting, spray painting playground equipment, or harassing teenage girls with whistles and catcalls.

If I confessed on the spot, she would have, at best, considered me a strange and maybe even cute budding teenage boy trying to deal with the new spurts of testosterone coursing through my veins. At worst, she would have considered me a deceitful juvenile delinquent, a psychotic in training for greater crimes—with fake fighting acting as the gateway drug to an eventual career in bank robbing. Either way, whatever existing impression she had of me (if she had one at all) would be tainted forever. At that moment, my secret dream, now five years off, of posing for prom pictures in Jenny's living room while Sister Gillette giddily snapped photos of me trying to pin a corsage on Jenny's dress, seemed fantastical and ridiculous, lost forever.

Confessing on the spot would have other downsides as well. Gregory would never forgive me. I would be like a jailhouse collaborator, worthy of total mistrust, unending mockery, and random beatings. My caché as a ballsy preteen trickster and mischief-maker would be gone forever. When I was thirty years old and I ran into guys from the neighborhood, I would still be mercilessly reminded of "that time" when I narked on everyone and got everyone grounded for two weeks.

So, as I stood crumpled over, faking like I had broken ribs and internal bleeding—and, strangely, taking note of the fact that Jenny's mom had a tiny, sterling-silver toe ring on the second toe of her right foot and that each of her burgundy big toes had a golden cursive monogram of "GG" (for Georgia Gillette)—I made the easiest decision of my life. It was nearly instinctual. To appease Sister Gillette, I had to pretend that I had been jumped by some unknown teenage thugs. But, it was as equally imperative that I somehow clarify for the record, for Jenny's sake, that I was not some victimized wusscicle that had been beaten up.

Jenny's Mom insisted that she drive me home. I resisted and made excuses. If she took me home, she would insist on walking me to the door, and there was no way I could act my way out of this in front of Mom or Dad. I would be dead.

"Thanks, but my parents aren't home. I'll just walk."

"Well, if you're parents aren't home then you need to come to our house until they get home."

"No, they said I needed to be home by 8:00 or else I'm in big trouble."

"I think they'll understand. I'll explain everything. It'll be fine. Get in." She felt responsible now. She wasn't screwing around. There was no use protesting, however politely. I obeyed and got in.

I was in the backseat next to Jenny's four-year-old brother, Gus. He was strapped into a hand-me-down booster seat with navy blue velour that was splotched with milk stains and ground-in animal cracker shards. Directly in front of me was the back of Jenny's rich chocolaty brown hair resting against the beige cloth headrest. I could see a red barrette with roses on it clipping her bangs over her left temple.

Jenny said nothing. She didn't even turn her head. It was as if I didn't even exist in her universe.

I think the fact that I had just had my butt kicked was, in Sister Gillette's mind, somehow endearing. Maybe it was because she liked underdogs, or maybe it was because she didn't have any older boys of her own, or maybe it was that she was just gullible. It's not like there were street gangs wilding in our neighborhood.

The rest of the short drive was spent in absolute silence. Gus sucked his thumb quietly. His head remained in perma-lock, slightly cocked to the right, cautiously staring at me the whole time as if I were the most interesting creature on earth. Sister Gillette turned off the radio and every so often glanced at me quizzically in the rearview mirror. The only sound was Gus's rhythmic thumb sucking over the vague drone of the station wagon's engine.

Thankfully, the ride was less than three minutes. Just as Sister Gillette hit the garage door clicker and started up her driveway, she asked, "So, Todd, who were those hooligans?"

"I don't know. I think they might have been a bunch of ninth graders. I've never seen them before," I stammered.

"Well, whoever they were, you should stay away from them. And you shouldn't be out by yourself after dark."

I didn't answer.

"Well, here we are. Let's go inside and take a look at you."

Jenny led the way into the house. Gus and I trailed her, giving me a perfect view of Jenny's deep blue, form-fitting jeans. The cursive "Gloria Vanderbilt" stitched in orange on the right back pocket rhythmically swayed with each stride.

Jenny plopped down at the kitchen table in front of a mess of scrapbooking supplies. Gus continued into the family room just off the kitchen and immediately started dexterously playing with colored building blocks scattered across the floor with one hand and continued sucking his thumb with the other.

"Have a seat, Todd," Sister Gillette said from behind.

"Oh, I'm fine. I'll just stand," I replied tentatively.

"Don't be silly, you just got beat up. You need to take a seat."

I glanced at Jenny, and she smirked as she looked through a pile of photos.

"Well, I wasn't really beat up. I mean . . . it didn't really hurt," I stammered. "There were just so many of them that I had to curl up on the ground for protection," I said lamely.

I glanced at Jenny again. She continued to smirk while she wrote something in her three-ring binder.

"Well, we're just glad we drove by when we did. Otherwise you might be in an ambulance right now. Now hop right up here," she said, patting the countertop.

It was worse than I thought. She wanted me to sit up on the kitchen counter like she was going to put a Winnie-the-Pooh Band-Aid on my knee and give kisses to my boo-boos.

But I didn't have the guts to resist, so I obeyed like a good little boy.

Jenny watched silently from the kitchen table. She was no longer faking like she was scrapbooking. She genuinely thought this was funny now.

Sister Gillette saw my scraped knees and insisted on "cleaning them up."

I wasn't sure what she was going to do. I watched warily as she wadded up a paper towel and found some rubbing alcohol in one of the kitchen cabinets. She carefully removed the cap from the bottle, delicately placed the paper towel over the mouth of the bottle, and poured.

She had treated the alcohol with such care—like it was nitro-glycerin or something—that I expected her to gently dab the scrapes on my knee. I was wrong. Her cheery demeanor quickly turned to the no-nonsense mien of a hardened emergency-room nurse as she began matter-of-factly scrubbing my scraped-up left knee. She scrubbed like she was using an SOS pad on a gritty frying pan. The pure, unadulterated rubbing alcohol on my fresh scrapes felt like a fistful of needles was being pressed into my flesh. I thought I was going to wet myself and then pass out. I yelped like an injured coyote. My eyes began to involuntarily fill with water. Jenny raised her eyebrows and went into the other room with Gus.

Complete defeat.

"That should do it. I don't think it will get infected," Sister Gillette said, satisfied.

Just then, Brother Gillette, a thin, prematurely balding insurance agent with a pointy nose, perma-grin, and neatly groomed mustache, came into the kitchen, slightly alarmed.

"Who's crying? What's wrong?" he asked, surveying the kitchen.

"*Nobody's* crying," I said instantly and a little too forcefully.

Seeing me sitting on the counter with my legs dangling over the kitchen floor, he wrinkled his forehead in confusion. He looked at me and then Sister Gillette.

"Todd Whitman? What's going on?" he mumbled toward Sister Gillette.

"Hey, Brother Gillette," I said awkwardly.

"What's going on, my friend? What brings you to my kitchen counter?"

"He was jumped by a bunch of older boys and was getting beat up. Thank goodness we drove by when we did," Jenny's mom said before I could answer.

"Beat up? That's terrible. What happened?"

Here we go again, I thought. "Well, I'm not really sure. I was walking home from the Croshaws. Ben-G and I had been trading baseball cards, and then all of a sudden these guys came out of nowhere and were saying that I said something mean to one of their sisters or something. They all started yelling and freaking out. Pretty soon, they pushed me to the ground and surrounded me and started cussing and kicking and punching me. The next thing I knew, they started yelling, 'Car! Car! Get outta here!' And then they all took off. That's when I saw your station wagon and Sister Gillette and Jenny and Gus."

"Do you know who they were?"

"No, not really. It was pretty dark. I think they were a bunch of ninth graders, but I'm not sure. I think I saw a couple of blue corduroy jackets, so they were probably FFA kids."

"Jackets? In this heat?"

He was right. The story made no sense. I tried not to panic.

"Yeah, it was pretty weird," I managed.

I bent over and blew on my newly raw kneecaps.

"Man, it really stings," I softly and pathetically whined, desperately trying to change the subject.

"Well, we need to call your mom and get you home," Sister Gillette said, reaching for the phone. "What's your number, Todd?'

"You can just take me home. Or I can walk. It's not very far."

"Don't be ridiculous. We can't have you walking around with those ruffians still out there."

There was no point in protesting. I was screwed. I gave her the number. She dialed, then put the receiver up to her ear and smiled at me.

"Hello, this is Georgia Gillette. Is your mom there?"

"Hmm. Is Bishop Whitman there?"

"He's not?" she repeated back to whoever was on the other line. "Hmmm . . ."

"Is this Gregory?"

"Hi, Gregory. It's Georgia Gillette."

"I'm fine, thank you, dear."

"Well, Todd is here at our house. A bunch of older boys ambushed him and beat him up."

"Yes, it is scary. I saw the whole thing."

"Sure, if you want to come pick him up that would be just fine."

"Do you have someone to drive you?"

"Okay, then. We'll see you in a few minutes."

Five minutes later, Gregory was at the Gillettes' front door being extra polite and extra charming, making small talk with Brother and Sister Gillette.

Out on the curb, Jake Nelson sat nervously in his mom's idling Suburban.

As I walked through the family room, I glanced over at Jenny as she helped Gus stack a red block at the top of Gus's skyscraper.

"Hope you feel better," Jenny said with a Cheshire grin.

"Oh, thanks," I said sheepishly.

"Be sure to tell Gregory, Barry, Ben-G, Jericho, and—let's see . . . who else was there?—oh yeah, Jake Nelson and the other guys that ran off, hi for me too." She flirtatiously smiled.

I got the hell out of there without saying another word.

IX

I sit across from Philip Boettcher, grandson of the original D of D. Boettcher & Sons Mortuary, in his wood-paneled office on the opposite side of his shiny mahogany desk, with a slab of plate glass on top. He smiles kindly. He is wearing a dark suit, crisp white shirt, and boring solid maroon tie. I can't help wondering how many dark suit funeral ensembles he owns.

After it is all said and done—the kind smiles, the gentle whispers, the subtle direction, and the crash course about the protocol of death and burial from the mortuary staff—it is, like everything else, just a business. He presents an invoice on ivory colored parchment paper that describes the "bronze package" promising "full services" with "the utmost dignity" we had selected. There is a description and itemized price for everything—embalming, professional cosmetology, hairdressing, posing (whatever that means), a daily refrigeration fee, two registration books, a memory book, a "cashmere beige" bronze casket with "desert champagne velvet" interior and a "millstone gray" polished granite marker. I give him my credit card. He smiles gratefully and says, "Thank you. Forgive me. This will just take a moment." He swivels in his chair and swipes the card on the keyboard of the computer on his credenza. The burst of static and hiccupping screeches of his dial-up modem makes the signal. Payment accepted. Transaction complete.

28

Take Your Time (Do It Right)

Asking her how she learned to dance somehow unlocked some forgotten time capsule buried in Grandma Carter's malfunctioning mind. From that night on, she visited my room nearly every night. I didn't wake up every time she came in. And, thankfully, she didn't come in my room, flip on the lights, and say, "Wake up! Time to dance!" It was nothing like that. I could tell she was glad on those nights when I did wake up, but she never purposely woke me.

One night I woke up and saw her standing in my room, not in her nightgown but in a slip. She was holding a dress in her hand. The zipper was stuck and she had it in her mouth, using her teeth to try to unlock its grip on the flowing red taffeta fabric.

"Oh, dammit all!" she sighed under her breath in frustration.

It made me laugh.

Most nights that I woke up, I just lay in my bed, rested my head on my elbow, and watched her stammer, giggle, and twirl. Sometimes she had one-sided conversations with some imaginary person I couldn't see. They talked about magazines, dresses, and hair. They talked about boys—their looks, their mannerisms, and their slights and small but seemingly apocalyptic acts of indifference or rudeness. There were passing references of hopeless crushes and dreamy admiration. There were responses to parental inquiries about chores and school work, which were filled with matter-of-fact yes sirs and no sirs and yes mamas and no mamas. There were challenges to parental decrees about the perceived vulgarity and immorality of some of the types of dancing that she loved.

"Touching cheeks on the dance floor is *not* 'public love-making'!"

"You are overreacting, Mother. A couple dancing the Toddle does *not* need a marriage license!"

"Oh, Mother, be serious. The road to hell is *not* paved with jazz steps!"

"My dress is fine. Yes, a million times, *yes,* I have done as you have asked. I have 'striven for simplicity and charm and a complete absence of all conspicuousness,'" she said in a mocking tone, requoting some piece of instruction that her mother had read and reread to her out of some etiquette handbook.

One night, she sat on the edge of my bed, staring yearningly at the Dancer as he posed on the Saturday Night Fever album cover in her lap, and recounted a trip with the Dancer and a group of the "BY gang" to Salt Lake City. They rode the Salt Lake, Garfield & Western Railway out to Saltair, a huge resort built on stilts over the top of the Great Salt Lake, and danced in what was advertised as the world's largest dance floor to the songs of R. Owen Sweeten's "Jazziferous Band." She said the Dancer told her that one time there were so many dancers packed onto Saltair's massive dance floor that they prohibited the Charleston because they were afraid that all those people stomping their heels so hard on the downbeat would shake the whole pavilion into the lake below.

Some nights, noticing that I was awake, Grandma asked me to dance. On others she gave me no choice. Still others, she stood by silently and shyly, as if she were waiting for me to ask her to dance. On those nights, I volunteered by asking her a question about a particular step she was doing or by asking her politely if she needed any help.

Depending on her frame of mind and mood, I might be the pupil she taught and lectured, the roommate she giggled with and confided in, the teenage best friend she gossiped with, or the nonthreatening second-string boy she gratefully but somewhat reluctantly danced with while she kept one eye on the door, anxiously wondering if and when the Dancer might show up.

We always started with the Fox Trot. It was her warm-up dance, the scales she played before moving on to more difficult and lively dances. I never really mastered the Fox Trot, but she didn't give up on me.

Our Fox Trots usually began with simple instructions, which were nearly identical each time. I was never sure if she was repeating the instructions because she couldn't remember that she had recited them verbatim almost exactly twenty-four hours earlier or if she was purposely teaching by repetition.

"The gentleman always encircles his partner with his right arm, but not too far, only about halfway," she would always begin, taking my right hand in hers. "You see, the gentleman then lightly lays the palm of his right hand just slightly below her left shoulder blade," she would say as she placed my right hand in in its proper place.

"Yes, that's right. Right there," she would confirm, looking directly in my eyes. "Now, with his left hand, the gentleman takes his partner's right hand and stands at arm's length in a position that is happily between that which is most formal and that which is most comfortable." (I never really got that part.)

"The gentleman must take special care not to hold his partner's arm in an awkward or uncouth position." (I also never understood how clasping someone's hand and extending it outward could be considered uncouth, but she admonished me on that point every night.)

"The gentleman's face is always turned slightly to the left. His partner's will face directly in front or maybe ever so slightly to the right."

At this point, she would make a point to make eye contact with me, to make sure I was paying attention and following her instructions.

"The gentleman must now lead. He must lead with grace and authority. His partner must follow him and not try to lead the dance herself."

Another look to confirm I was keeping up with her. I would nod, and she would give me a slight tug forward and say, "Now, begin . . ."

On those nights that I played the role of student, I was the foil to the Dancer.

"No, no, no. The Dancer does it *this* way."

"Yes, that's right. That's just about the way the Dancer does it. Very good."

After a couple of weeks, my Fox Trot seemed passable, although not fluent. Her prelude of instructions became tedious, even to her, and the comparisons of my Fox Trot to the Dancer's became fewer and fewer. I sensed a growing boredom in her with the methodical, flairless moving square of my Fox Trot.

She moved on to tangos, waltzes, and square dances. She giddily jabbered about (and sometimes gave creaky demonstrations of) the Charleston, the lindy hop, the camel walk, the shimmy, the toddle, the grizzly bear, and the turkey trot. For all she knew, she was in the dancehalls of Price, Provo, and Salt Lake City, reliving them all.

My favorite was the black bottom.

"Imagine there's been a huge summer rainstorm—a real gusher," she said with enthusiasm. "Imagine that there is thick, pasty, tarlike mud everywhere in your daddy's pasture," she continued, eyes twinkling. "And imagine that you see his finest milk cow murmuring and mooing in the middle of the pasture. She's stuck, and her udder is nearly bursting. She needs to be milked, but there's not much you can do. So, it's up to her. How will she get herself out of this fix?"

With that introduction, in the middle of my room, she rocked and strutted in place, like her daddy's finest milk cow trying to work her way out of the sticky, ankle-deep mud. She rocked and swung. She stamped and tramped. Her steps became progressively faster and wider. She had worked her way out of the imaginary mud. She stretched out her arms. They swayed breezily, like tree branches, to the jazz riffing in her brain as she continued rocking and strutting in that square. She smiled ecstatically the whole time.

There was the Shag, the cat step, the castle walk, and the cake walk. I couldn't keep them all straight—and sometimes neither could she—but it seemed like there was a different one each night. Most of the time I just lay in my bed and smiled and watched her dance, clutching the album cover against her chest and smothering John Travolta in her bosom. Then, after an undetermined amount of time had passed, she would abruptly stop, pack up her book of remembrance, turn off the light, and walk out of the room. It was like someone had yanked the plug of the record player in her head from its socket.

29

Heartache No. 9

During the day, the hopelessly in-love, teenage dance-a-holic version of Grandma did not exist. She was old. She was ornery and even mean much of the time. If she wasn't sitting in her spot on the end of the couch watching TV, she was with Mom running errands—to the grocery store, to the post office and the fabric store, to Maggie's ballet lessons or Lisa's piano lessons, to our practices and church activities, to visiting-teaching appointments, to Mom's book club, or even to lunch with Mom and her friends.

Grandma was Mom's constant companion. She always sat shotgun in the new Suburban. Mom had whichever of us was sitting behind Grandma make sure that her door was locked when she got in, since Grandma sometimes got angry for no apparent reason and tried to open the door and step out of the car, even though it was speeding down the road. One time she almost succeeded.

"Blast it all, I'm getting out of this thing."

"What's wrong, Mom?"

"Open this door, right this instant. I want to get out," she demanded, trying vainly to open the door.

"Todd! Put your hand on the door lock! Hurry, Todd!" Mom instructed while she attempted to find a place to pull over amid the traffic.

I scrambled up behind Grandma and stretched my arm through the narrow space between Grandma's front seat and the door. I put my index finger on the door lock, pressing it down into the doorframe as hard as I could, until my first knuckle turned white and the tip of my finger was bright red. Grandma reached across her body with her left hand and tried to pry my index finger off the lock while she furiously tried to open the door latch with her right hand. I thought she was going to break my finger.

"Ouch, Grandma! Geez, stop it already! Do you want to fall out of the car?"

"Mother! Look at me! Stop! This is crazy!" Mom implored Grandma.

Mom was finally able to pull over to the side of the road to try to talk sense into Grandma, but she just kept trying to break my finger. I was yelling, "Ouch!" Maggie was crying, and Mom eventually gave up and started driving for home like a maniac.

After that, whoever was in the car with Mom and Grandma had to ride directly behind Grandma and keep his or her finger on the lock as a precaution. When Mom and Grandma were alone and there was no one there to risk their index finger for Grandma's health, Mom drove below the speed limit and in the right lane at all times so that she could slam on the breaks and pull over if necessary.

Sometimes Grandma would cry and moan in the car, "Let me out of here! Let me out of here!" and pound on the window. Sometimes Mom would sniffle, and we could see her crying in the reflection of the rearview mirror. It would make us want to cry too.

During the day, Grandma rarely had anything to say, and if she did it was most likely either negative or embarrassing—and it was probably both, especially when nonfamily was around.

Whenever Mom had carpool duty last year, first picking me and Maggie up from William Ellery Channing Elementary School and then heading to pick up Gregory and Lisa at Mangas Coloradas Junior High, we would arrive at Mangas Coloradas a few minutes early and wait for the final bell. The bell would ring, and kids would stream out of classrooms and funnel into the parking lot and the bike racks while Grandma would stare out the passenger's side window at the instantaneous chaos. There was the arrival of a caravan of yellow buses, clumps of kids waiting for carpools to arrive, bike riders imbalanced by overloaded backpacks dodging the pedestrian traffic and swerving to find optimum cruising balance, and carpooling moms jockeying for position in the parking lot and side streets. Grandma scanned the parking lot and sidewalks and provided monotone bursts of commentary like a patient boxer jabbing, jabbing, and then uppercutting.

Long-haired skateboarders were "morons." The acne-faced ninth-grader freaks wearing Black Sabbath T-shirts and lighting up cigarettes on the sidewalk just off school property were "abhorrent little demons." And immodestly dressed girls were "hussies" or "shameless" or "Jezebel" or any combination of the three.

"Why, what a shameless hussy that Jezebel is," she would say, directing her gaze at any girl who dared wear a tank top or a halter top.

The boys who rode their bikes and toted a saxophone case or trumpet case in front of them across their handlebars, like a machine gun mounted on a World War II jeep, always elicited a comment.

"Well, would you look at that? I hope that ignoramus crashes and scrapes his face on the road. That'll teach him."

When we carpooled with Ben-G and Jericho, they said their favorite part of the entire day was riding home with Grandma Carter. Sometimes she called them idiots, imbeciles, or nitwits. She had no filter and she didn't care if they heard her.

"So, we have to take the two idiots home today, I guess," she would say as we all piled into the Suburban. Ben-G and Jericho laughed every time. They thought it was hilarious. When we dropped them at home, climbing out of the car they would always singsongily say, "Thanks, Sister Whitman. See ya, Todd. See ya, Gregory. See you later, Grandma Carter."

"Nitwits," Grandma would say, with them still in earshot. Ben-G and Jericho would stagger up their driveway laughing the whole way.

Lisa's friends, on the other hand, were scared to death of Grandma Carter. Sue Wheeling started bawling her head off one time when Grandma Carter jerked around in her seat and hissed, "What're you looking at, you little hussy!"

Mom had to walk Sue up to her front door to talk to Sue's mom and apologize for a few minutes while Lisa made sure the car door stayed locked. The whole time, Grandma repeated over and over, "I don't like the way that little hussy looks at me. She *should* be crying. Serves her right."

When Gregory's friends rode in the car with Grandma Carter, Gregory often announced, "All aboard! The Crazy Train is now departing Mangas Coloradas Junior High School!" Every single time, Mom said, "Enough Gregory. That's enough." Although Grandma Carter never caught on to Gregory's joke, she resented the rambunctiousness that occurred in the backseats as Gregory and his friends recounted the day's events. And, true to form, she let them know about it.

"Those boys ought to be gelded," she once said to Mom loudly during the drive home, like a rancher dispassionately sizing up a herd of young stallions. "They are obnoxious and without means of releasing their energy in any positive way." Grandma had no volume control on her voice either, and it carried. She was like a kid with a Walkman in his ears who talked too loud, overcompensating for the sound blaring in his ears. Gregory and his friends heard every comment, and Gregory engaged.

"What does *gelded* mean?" he asked, smiling expectantly and holding back a laugh.

"Castrated. Their testicles should be cut off straightaway, so they can focus and live productive lives," Grandma said, turning in her seat and glaring. Gregory and his friends howled with laughter.

Mom had her own difficulties with Grandma. Book

clubs and lunches became next to impossible to emerge from unscathed.

In the middle of a discussion at a book-club luncheon hosted by Mom's friend Claudia Johnson, while eight ladies were speculating about whether the romantic portrayal of Joseph and Mary in *Two from Galilee* was realistic, Grandma stood up and frantically yelled, "Where did this mud come from?! Who put mud on this couch?! My dress is ruined! They've ruined my dress!" and started to sob. She had no idea that she had pooped her own pants. Even when Mom took her into Claudia Johnson's bathroom and stripped her down, washed her back, buttocks, and legs with a washcloth, and finally got her to calm down, she still insisted that Claudia had somehow negligently allowed someone to track mud into the house and onto the couch.

"That woman has no house-cleaning skills, and her children are like little varmints tracking dirt and mud and vermin everywhere," she bawled in frustration as Claudia stood there helping Mom clean Grandma Carter up. They threw away the dress and her garments in a double-wrapped black Hefty bag, and Mom borrowed a white Mickey Mouse sweatshirt and gray sweatpants for Grandma Carter to wear home. Mom called Dad and told him he needed to come home, then went and rented a steam cleaner and returned to Claudia's house. She stayed at Claudia's and shampooed the couch and carpet and scrubbed out her shower. She didn't get home until after dinner.

After that, Mom had to force Grandma Carter to wear an adult diaper whenever they left the house. Mom convinced her it was a "new-fangled" device to protect against sitting in mud. The diapers didn't get much use, however, because Mom gradually stopped leaving the house unless it was to pick one of us up or to grocery shop or to run to the drugstore for a prescription refill. Preparing Grandma to leave the house was worse than bundling up a young baby on a wintry day. A baby couldn't slap your face or dig his fingernails into your arms in protest or say hurtful things like, "You're an evil woman!" or "I loathe you!" or "I would prefer not to be seen in public with someone as homely as you." Although a baby could cry uncontrollably, a baby couldn't rip his own clothes off, kick in the dashboard of the Suburban, or rip the sun visor from the roof of the car while he bawled comfortlessly. A baby couldn't say to a neighbor you bumped into at the grocery store, "Be careful. This woman is from Salem. She is a *witch*!" or contemptuously demand to know, "Who are *you*?!" or bawl to the cashier at Goldwater's, "This woman stole all my money! Please call the police! You must call the police!"

So, Grandma gradually began spending even more of her time in the house, blankly watching TV in her spot on the couch and occasionally trying to slip outside with her book of remembrance and her Saturday Night Fever album cover firmly in her grasp.

Mom rarely wavered in her dedication to Grandma. She was always attentive. Always helping her take her medicine, making sure she wasn't hungry, checking to make sure that she wasn't too hot or too cold, providing comfort for every irritation, trying to plan in advance for the proximate cause of any inconvenience, and silently absorbing the body blows of every hurtful comment.

We didn't say anything, but we knew that all of this was taking its toll on Mom when Dad took us school shopping that year and began coming home later than usual on Wednesday nights because he had gone grocery shopping after bishopric meeting. He sometimes even came home for lunch and started working half days every other Friday so that Mom could be alone to shop or just drive aimlessly, by herself. So that she could somehow at least attempt to forget for a few hours that at age forty-five she was mothering a toddler who would gradually become an infant.

30

Make That Move

The Saturday night before school started, during one midnight visit, I asked Grandma Carter if she had ever heard of a dance known as the "deacon shuffle."

"The *what?*"

"The deacon shuffle."

"I'm afraid I'm not familiar with that one, young man, although I do know how to shuffle."

"One, two," she said shuffling her feet from side to side like a malfunctioning robot. "One, two," she continued creakily.

"I don't think that's it, Grandma Carter."

"Is it done by deacons? Or," she said, thinking aloud, "is it an imitation of a deacon?"

"I have no idea. Gregory told me that I'll need to know how to do it."

"Why?" she asked quizzically.

"Because there's a school dance coming up."

"A school dance?" Her eyes lit up. "Oh, what will I wear?" she crooned like a boy-crazy teenager.

She began to describe every dress she owned, every dress her older sisters owned, and every dress her friends owned. For the next ten minutes, she wondered aloud about what she would wear and what her friends ought to wear.

Then, interrupting herself, she said, "What is the theme of the dance, young man?"

"The what?"

"The theme," she said impatiently. "The theme. There has to be a *theme*."

"I really don't know. It'll be my first dance, so I have no idea."

"Oh, don't be ridiculous, there has never been a dance that has not had a *theme*," she protested, giving emphasis to the *E* sound.

"Then it's probably terror. That's my theme for it," I said, trying to make a joke.

Completely missing my attempt at humor, she quickly retorted, "You are being ridiculous. A school dance is a gay, happy affair. No school dance would ever have a theme of terror. You must ask your teachers. They will know the theme."

"They supposedly call it the Hello Dance," I offered.

Apparently satisfied with that answer, she moved on. "When is this Hello Dance?"

"I'm not really sure about that either. It's supposed to be sometime during the first week of school, but it's supposed to be a secret. No one really knows when it will be."

"Not even the angels in heaven nor the Son of Man Himself knows when He will come again. Did you know that?" she asked, completely out of the blue.

"Yeah, I think I've heard that before. Actually, Brother Croshaw thinks he knows when it will be. But he won't tell anyone when. He studies that stuff quite a bit."

"Oh, that's ridiculous."

"Yeah, it is," I agreed. I didn't know how to bring Grandma Carter back to earth, so I gently added, "And, oh, by the way, Grandma, I don't think you're invited to the Hello Dance."

"Oh, don't be ridiculous. The Dancer may be there."

"Uh, it's only for seventh graders, and I think the Dancer already graduated from high school. So he would be way too old for this dance. The teachers would throw him out if he showed up. He'd probably get arrested or something, too."

She wrinkled her forehead and tilted her head back as if to say, *Why on God's green earth would anyone ever want to throw out the most handsome and beautiful dancer in all of Castle Valley?*

"I bet he'll probably be at a different dance," I said casually, trying to soften the blow.

"Yes," she replied slowly. "You may be right. There's a subscription dance in Price next weekend. That's surely where he will be."

"What's a subscription dance?"

"Well, young man," she said, ignoring my question, "if you've never attended a dance, you need to be on your best behavior. We call this good dance *etiquette*."

"What do you mean?"

"What do I mean? I mean, how will you ask a young woman to dance? What qualities will you look for in a dance partner? Which young women will you ask to dance? What conversation will you make as you dance? You must be an astute and empathetic conversationalist."

"I don't plan on dancing."

"Now *that* is ridiculous, young man. Why wouldn't you dance? Have you no ideals or dreams? Dancing is merely an artistic means of expressing what you aspire to be. And, what's more, as a gentleman, you have a *duty* to dance. You do not stand around allowing young ladies who have made the time and effort to prepare for a dance to feel awkward and uncomfortable. You are a gentleman, aren't you?"

Not caring to hear any answer from me, she continued, uninterrupted. "And why would you deny yourself the joy and satisfaction of sharing wholesome recreation in the terpsichorean arts with a lovely young woman? And, for that matter, why would you deny *any* young woman the same?"

"I really have no idea what you're talking about, Grandma. But, for one thing, I don't know how to dance."

"Oh, hogwash. You are a fine enough student of the Fox Trot."

"That's not really the kind of dance that kids do these days."

"Oh, don't be ridiculous. The Fox Trot is the bread and butter of all dances. It is done at every dance. It is the artistic antidote to the vulgarity of the impulsive gyrating of free-form dances to which the hooligan generation seems to gravitate."

I rolled my eyes and said, "Like I said, I've never been to a dance before, but I really don't think there will be any Fox Trotting, Grandma."

"The Fox Trot will demonstrate every quality that you want to impress upon a young lady—dignity, grace, charm, poise, leadership. Aren't those all qualities that you want to demonstrate to your young lady friends?"

"Sure, I guess, but I don't really see . . ."

"Let's take it step by step," she said, interrupting again.

"First, how will you ask a young lady to dance?"

"That's *irrelevant*, because I won't be dancing—"

"You certainly will be," she said authoritatively. "You will be unable to contain yourself when you see the fresh, florid faces of your young female peers."

"I doubt it."

"Well, let's pretend anyway. How will you ask?"

"I don't know. 'Wanna dance?'" I ventured.

"*Wanna dance?*" she repeated in a gruff voice, mimicking me.

"No, absolutely not."

"Stand up right here in front of me," she said pointing to the carpeted bedroom floor.

I sighed and kicked off the single sheet and stood up, clad only in my underwear.

"Now, you pretend you are the young lady. I will pretend I am the young gentleman."

This is a new level of creepy, I thought, *pretending to be a girl while standing in my room in the middle of the night in only my tighty-whiteys.*

The goofy role-play began.

"Excuse me, miss," Grandma said firmly, smiling brightly at me. "May I have the pleasure of your hand in this dance?"

"Why, I would be delighted," I said enthusiastically in a high-pitched voice, mocking the exercise.

In princely fashion, Grandma gave a slight nod while dramatically extending her right hand, palm upturned. The signal was clear. I was to place my hand in hers. I complied. "Thank you," she said clearly, nodding again and continuing to maintain eye contact with me at an uncomfortable level of intensity.

I shivered as the fan's manufactured breeze oscillated across my back. I wasn't sure if it was the slight change in temperature or the sheer eeriness of the situation.

She held my hand and took two steps as if to lead me out to the dance floor and then stopped.

"Now, that is how you properly ask a young lady to dance."

"Okay. Thanks, Grandma. That was really helpful," I said facetiously.

"Now, you will take your position in the Fox Trot and lead her gently, with poise and dignity, through your dance steps. You must be firm. You must be pleasant. And you must make interesting conversation."

I scratched my bare stomach and sighed.

"Well, what will you talk about?"

"Probably nothing. I have nothing to say."

"Of course you do," she said impatiently.

"No, I really don't."

"You do. Maybe you're just too enamored of your dance partner to think clearly. That sometimes happens. The first time I danced with the Dancer, I was tongue-tied and embarrassed. He asked me several questions, and I don't recall even answering."

She looked thoughtful for a moment and then continued. "You can make conversation about a number of topics. The Hero method is good for beginners."

"What's the 'Hero' method?"

"H-E-R-O," she spelled.

"I know how to spell *hero*, Grandma."

"The *H* stands for health or hobbies. The *E* stands for education. The *R* stands for relatives. And the *O* stands for organizations."

"I don't get it."

"These are all excellent topics of conversation. What is the name of a young lady that you yearn to dance with at this Hello Dance?"

"I don't know," I stammered, lying.

"Of course you do. There must be at least *one* young woman that you fancy, at least a little bit," she pressed.

I said nothing.

"Young man, your silence is telling. She must have a name."

Gregory and Lisa weren't around. There was no risk. "Jenny," I said hesitantly.

"Okay. Jenny, then."

She cleared her throat and took me in the Fox Trot position. Then, looking directly in my eyes, she said, "Why, Jenny, you look lovely this evening; what do you do to maintain such robust health?" She tilted her head to the side. "Tell me, Jenny. Of which hobbies are you most fond?" She released me from her Fox Trot grip. "See, it's simple."

I tried, once again, to change the subject. "Thanks, Grandma. That will be *really* helpful. So, what's a subscription dance, again?" I asked, emphasizing the "again," even though she never explained it the first time.

"It's a series of dances organized by a local charity or club to which one may subscribe."

"Like a magazine?"

"Yes, it's similar in nature, I guess. Subscription dances are a series of dances held periodically—say, for four weeks in autumn—that allow young people to act gay and mingle with dignity and grace in a wholesome environment supervised by a committee of chaperones. Depending upon the rules of the subscription, a subscriber can invite a certain number of friends."

Ben-G and Jericho would have jumped all over the acting-gay description. It would be one of those comments that they would refer to over and over again for years.

"I'm so looking forward to acting gay at the homecoming dance. Aren't you, Todd?" I imagined them asking in several years.

Gregory probably would have too. I snickered under my breath at the way it sounded, but let it pass.

"So, you have to pay?" I asked.

"Yes, generally the subscriber pays a subscription fee. That's why it's called a subscription dance. The proceeds go to the organization sponsoring the dances—like the Daughters of the Utah Pioneers."

"So, do you think the Dancer will ask you to the subscription dance next weekend in Price?" I asked tentatively. There was something tweaking my conscience as I asked. Was it fair to egg her on? To ask her about something that was clearly not reality?

It was sort of like when Maggie falls asleep on the couch watching *Mister Rogers* or *Sesame Street* and starts to talk in her sleep, Gregory will try to ask her questions or provoke her into some pretty funny conversation. Sometimes she goes along with it. Sometimes she doesn't. I have to admit, it *is* pretty funny. But this was different; this wasn't a few muttered unconscious phrases from a dream about ponies or puppies—this was a real conversation, with real emotions, real feelings, and with actual consciousness. Whether it was real or not hardly seemed to matter.

I wanted to know. And she wanted to tell.

31

Let It Be Whatever It Is

In Arizona you get gypped. School starts in mid-August, the most hellish part of the Sonoran summer, when you can get first-degree burns just from grazing your inner thigh on your bike seat. For the first few weeks of school, there are heat warnings, so you can't even have recess. You play outside and swim all day long in the summer, and then school starts and suddenly you can't play outside. It makes no sense. Dad always said it was because of "the liability." I asked him what that meant once, and he said it was because of the lawyers and the people who want free money when their morbidly obese child faints on the playground. That made no sense either at the time, so I dropped it.

It didn't matter anymore anyway, though. I was in seventh grade. No more one-classroom, one-teacher, flapping-a-parachute-in-PE and three-recesses-a-day kiddie stuff. This was junior high school—seventh grade. We were thrown in with the eighth and ninth graders. The eighth graders were actually nice and somewhat sympathetic. They seemed somewhat humbled by their frizzy hair and standard-issue orthodontia. They were mostly just really enthusiastic that they weren't seventh graders anymore. The ninth graders had newly sprouting muscles, boobs and acne, and perfectly straightened teeth. A few even had peach-fuzz mustaches, and when the boys wore tank tops, it was intimidating; nearly all of them had bushy clumps of hair under their arms. Some of the ninth-grade boys and girls even paired off and held hands or walked with their arms around one another and a hand in each other's back pocket. These were all terrifying symptoms of their burgeoning adulthood.

Mom insisted on driving us to school on the first day. She pulled into the poorly named "kiss and go" lane (couldn't someone tell the principal we weren't kindergartners anymore?), and we scrambled out of the Suburban. Gregory, the ninth-grade legend in his own mind, Lisa the peppy eighth grader full of school spirit—"Red Sleeves Pride" as they called it—and me, the fresh but terrified seventh grader, putting on a brave, confident face, scanning my new surroundings for some recognizable, friendly seventh-grade face. Gregory and Lisa both led the way through the adobe arch that welcomed all to the "Home of the Red Sleeves!" and the inner plaza of the outdoor campus of Mangas Coloradas Junior High School. In the middle of the plaza there was an ornate fountain with four carvings at each point of the compass signifying the "Four Rs of Red Sleeves Pride." From the plaza there were four broad pathways to other adobe-style buildings. The pathways were known as the "Corridors of the Four Rs." The corridors of "Respect," "Responsibility," "Recreation," and "Rigor."

I had prearranged to meet Ben-G, a fellow seventh grader, at the fountain. Lisa recognized several friends and said, "See you later, Todd. Good luck." Then she walked over to meet them so they could compare their different colored must-have LeSportsacs. Gregory continued walking, then turned around, took a few strides walking backward, pointed at me, and laughed uproariously.

A few kids from William Ellery Channing walked past and were almost too nervous to say hi. They muttered, "Hey, Todd," almost inaudibly and kept walking, looking down at their schedules and scanning the scene for their classrooms. Pretty soon, Ben-G and Jericho, now an eighth grader, approached.

Jericho pointed to the Corridor of Respect and said, "That's the way to Chorus, Orchestra and Home Ec. In other words, that's where the finest ladies will be. Tread carefully, young men. Tread carefully." And then he left.

Ben-G and I had seventh-grade English first, our "home room." We both had the same teacher, Mr. Salmon. He wore bell-bottom jeans that were too snug and creeped up his crack, a silky, spread-collared sky blue shirt and shiny black dress shoes with heels that seemed to be made for stomping small rodents. He had a manicured tight perm of brown hair with gray flecks, a pointy nose, almond-shaped brown eyes with long, curly eyelashes, and a dramatic air. He pranced around the room and proclaimed, "Welcome!" to each student that entered the classroom, outstretching his hand toward a random open seat, like one of the *Price Is Right* girls presenting a washer/dryer combo to the studio audience bidders. He placed Ben-G near the front on the far side of the room, next to the wall and underneath a portrait of Mark Twain. He put me in the second-to-last row near the door.

After the second bell rang, he walked purposefully to the front of the class room and wrote "Mr. Salmon" with a flourish on the chalkboard. He half pirouetted to face the class and melodically chirped, "Welcome to seventh-grade English, where you will learn the science of proper grammar and the art of written expression—with help from her muse, introspection, of course." He smiled, closed his eyes, and deeply inhaled through his nostrils, like a middle-aged woman taking in the fragrance of Magnolia blossoms, before continuing through the mundane routine of the first day of school—class rules, calendar, grading, and a dogmatic lecture on the four Rs of Mangas Coloradas Junior High.

I listened carefully, trying to catch all of it. Even before school started, the whole morning had been full of newness, nervousness, and faking like I knew exactly what I was doing. In reality, I was teetering on the edge of panic and constantly worrying about doing something that could be construed in any manner as uncool or as a dead giveaway of the greenhorn status I was unmistakably marked with.

The bell rang, and I raced to put everything back into my backpack, like I was part of Richard Petty's pit crew.

Textbook in backpack. Zip.

Pencil and eraser in pencil bag. Zip.

Nondescript, black, three-ring binder, and spiral-bound notebook with Dallas Cowboys logo in backpack. Zip. Zip.

I stood and waited between my desk and the door for Ben-G. He was talking to some girl who must have gone to William Lloyd Garrison Elementary. I'd never seen her before. Then he started to talk to Mr. Salmon. What a brownnoser. I started to get impatient. Was I going to be late for my next class? Should I wait for Ben-G? Would I be a total loser if I walked alone? Was Ben-G cool enough to walk with anyway? Was I cool enough for him?

Thoughts buzzed inside my head like caffeinated bees. *Geez, now who is Ben-G talking to? How do I know that kid? This is ridiculous. Is Ben-G going to completely blow me off even though I'm standing here waiting? Where is my next class? B-234. Where the heck is room B-234? It's through the Corridor of Recreation, right? I remember that at least. Will I be mocked if I ask an eighth grader or a ninth grader where it is? How do I get to the Corridor of Recreation? Should I take a pee now? I don't really have to go, but wait, there's a boys' bathroom right outside Mr. Salmon's room. Should I take a preemptive pee even though I don't really have to go, or wait until later and risk not being near a bathroom or being near a bathroom but not knowing where it is? What's the fastest route to my locker? Wait, should I even go to my locker? Is Ben-G going to his locker? Am I supposed to go to my locker? Doesn't everybody hang around by the lockers and flirt and gossip—should I do that? How do I even do that? What if I can't remember my locker number? What's my locker combination? Preston Pearson (RB, #26), Rafael Septien (K, #1), Gary Hogeboom (QB, #14)? Or, wait, is it Everson Walls (CB, #24)? Am I a geek if I don't have my locker combination memorized already, if I have to unzip my plastic pencil-holder baggie and pull out the tiny sticker that came plastered on the lock? What if the sliding locker latch gets stuck and won't open? Geez, what is taking Ben-G so long? Should I stay away from the lockers altogether? I heard ninth graders try to stuff seventh graders into their lockers on the first day. Oh, screw it, should I just carry everything around in my backpack? But what will I do with my backpack during PE? Is*

*it true the PE lockers are too small to hold a backpack? Holy crap,
B-234, that's PE. PE is next hour. Will they make us dress out today?
Will we really have to shower today, on the first day? No way. No
possible way. What if I don't shower? Is Gregory totally full of it about
the whole not-taking-a-shower thing? Are they really going to call me
hairless? Man, I am so stinking hairless. When am I going to grow?
Dad thinks I'm going to be 6'5". I think he's on drugs. Will I look
like a total weenie if I wear a swimsuit in the showers? Will they
really make some of the seventh graders do butt slide races across the
open shower floor? Holy Moses, will you hurry up already, Ben-G?
I wonder where Jenny is right now. Will I bump into her? If I do,
what should I do? What should I say? Should I say anything? Should I
ignore her and act like I don't care? Do I have the guts to say anything
even if I want to? Is it cool to say something or is it cool to act like I
don't know who she is? There's no time to go to my locker now anyway.
Wrap it up, Ben-G, seriously! Thank goodness. Finally! Holy cow, it's
about time.*

"Hey, you going to your locker?" Ben-G asked as he finally
came to the door of Mr. Salmon's room.

"Not now. Are you?"

"Yeah, I guess."

"Who was that?"

"Some kid named Eric. He played on Jericho's baseball team
last year."

"Not him. Who was that girl you were talking to?"

"I don't know. Adrian, I think. Yeah, Adrian." He was faking
short-term memory loss. He knew her name. He just wanted me
to think he didn't care enough to remember her name. I wasn't
stupid.

"So, from now on, are you gonna say, 'Yo, Adrian' whenever
you see her?"

"Yeah, that would be pretty funny, huh?" he said.

32

Plain Out of Luck

The first day of PE was, in fact, horrific, but for reasons completely unexpected. There was no dressing out, no showering, and, therefore, no butt slides, snapping towels or rat tails, no gauntlet, no calling out the "wusses" in the roll call, and no comparative catcalls about the relative state of a pupil's progression through puberty. The horror was in the form of Coach Rory Rawlings, the lazy summer basketball-camp coach with a knack for insults. To the severe disappointment of the few of us who knew him, he had been transferred from Arroyo Vista Junior High to Mangas Coloradas—belly, polyester sport shorts, and all.

"Good morning, ninnies," he said, grinning like a cartoonish evil scientist while bovinely chomping on a wad of Big Red. "Our first and only order of business today is to introduce you to my collection of animals. Those of you in the nerdy honors classes might even call it a 'menagerie,'" he laughed, amusing himself.

No one else laughed. We all exchanged confused glances that said, "This is PE, right?"

He looked down at the roll for thirty seconds or so, scanning it from top to bottom.

"Ah . . . here we go . . . One of my summer basketball camp mongoloids. " He looked up and squinted. "Whitman!" he called out. "Where is Miss Todd Whitman?"

The adrenaline of sheer terror spiked through my veins. Instantly, my arms tingled, set fire with apprehension.

Why me, Lord? I thought as I stepped forward.

"Hi, Coach," I nervously offered.

"*Hi, Whitman,*" he said in falsetto, mocking me.

Everyone else was too scared to laugh. Their faces collectively expressed gratitude that they were not me.

"Whitman here is going to impersonate each of my animal friends. These animal friends will visit you when you are *TARDY!* When you are *NOT LISTENING!* When you are being *DISRESPECTFUL!* And when you are smarting off or otherwise *ACTING LIKE A JACKASS!*" His voice rose with the end of each sentence.

"Oh, no! Coach Rawlings said *jackass,*" he said, using the falsetto again. "Yes, ladies, that's right, I said *jackass,*" he continued, switching back to his normal voice. "You can take it up with your mommies if you like. If you dare."

He stared at us then asked, "The bell rings at what time, ladies?"

No one replied. Everyone was caught in the no-man's land between shock and terror.

"Whitman, the tardy bell rings at what time?"

"9:30?" I said tentatively.

"Yes, that's right," he said in his normal voice, then, "*9:30!*" in falsetto. "If you walk through that door one second after that bell rings, and it rings at . . ." He paused.

"9:30," we all replied in unison.

"That's right, *9:30,*" he repeated in falsetto. "If you walk through that door one second after that bell rings, you will get to know the snail. That's right *the snail,*" he repeated slowly. "Lie down on your stomach, Whitman." When I didn't react immediately, he added, "C'mon, hurry up, Whitman; the polished cement floor won't bite. You might get a fungus, but it won't bite."

I lay down on my stomach obediently. The floor was actually nice and cool.

"Okay, now, Whitman, I want you to act like a snail. How do you do that, you say? Well, it's quite simple. You stretch your arms all the way out in front of you. Go ahead, Whitman, you can do it. There you go. Good boy," he said, acting like he was a father encouraging an infant to grasp a rattle. "Now, come up on your knees, sliding them forward on the floor. No, Whitman, no. Keep your arms straight and stretched out on the ground while you bring your knees forward. There you go. Keep going. Keep going. Now, ladies, take a look at Whitman. Keep going Whitman. Did I say stop? Take a look at him and imagine doing that across the gym lengthwise. One trip across the gym like a snail for every minute you are late."

He surveyed the group watching me snail my way down a narrow aisle of lockers.

"Okay. Get up, Whitman, and come back. So, ladies, if you're late, you're what?"

"A snail," we all replied in unison, silently covenanting that we would never dare be tardy.

"All right, Whitman, on your back. C'mon let's go," he said impatiently.

I dropped back down and lay on my back, arms at my side in anticipation, like I was getting ready to do a snow angel. Coach Rawlings stood at my head, and the rest of my fellow plebes huddled around me. Some stoner kid with bangs drooping down over one eye crouched behind Coach Rawlings and flipped a bird right between Rawlings's knees while closing his eyes, head banging, and sticking out is tongue like Gene Simmons. Some of the kids started to laugh. Rawlings thought they were laughing at me. He had no idea.

"Okay. Stick your arms straight up in the air."

I complied.

"Now your legs."

I complied, or at least thought I did.

"C'mon, Whitman. Straight up in the air! Arms and legs straight up in the air!" He snorted. "Good. Now hold them there. C'mon Whitman, keep 'em straight up."

This cement is going to cause permanent spine damage. It's going to wear down the knobby parts of my vertebrae, I thought.

"Now. What does Whitman look like?" Rawlings asked. Then, without giving time for any answer, he continued. "A dead bug. To be more precise, a dying cockroach. So, therefore, my lady friends, this is what we call the *dying cockroach*."

My stomach muscles were on fire, and my back was killing.

"When you are disrespectful to me, another coach, or one of your fellow sorority sisters, you will impersonate a dying cockroach for some untold number of minutes, maybe the entire hour. Got it?"

The group nodded, and the stoner popped up and nodded seriously just in time for Rawlings to turn around to make sure those behind him were nodding too.

"Good. You're not done yet, Whitman. Not even close."

I sighed, resigned to my guinea-pig status.

"Stand up, Whitman."

I complied.

"Okay, Whitman. Act like an elephant."

"Uh . . . I don't really know what you mean, Coach."

"An elephant, Whitman. You know, big, gray, wrinkled skin, trunk, big ears? Ring any bells? It's not difficult."

"Um. I'm not—"

"Good gravy, Whitman! Bend down!"

I thought for sure he was about to kick me.

"Bend down, Whitman! Why do I have to repeat everything fifty times?"

I bent down and touched my toes.

"Okay. Hold it right there."

I held and waited for his white Converse All Stars to address my butt cheeks.

"Don't worry, Whitman, you're gonna be fine. Now, instead of touching your toes, bring your palms together."

I did as I was told.

"Well done, Princess Ugly. Now, keep your hands together and sway your arms back and forth loosely and slowly. Think like a grandfather clock—tick, tock; tick, tock; tick, tock. Yes, that's it."

This is total insanity, I thought.

"Now stay just like that. Just like that," he said quickly, like a photographer who had just gotten everyone's heads perfectly tilted in a family photo and was racing back to his tripod. "And walk."

"Walk, Whitman, walk! Yes, that's it," he said excitedly. "Now walk in a circle around this group."

I walked slowly in a circle around the group, with my arms swaying like an elephant's trunk, like a complete moron.

"Now, Whitman, on every fifth step, I want you to lift your trunk up and trumpet like a bull elephant."

"Coach, I really don't know—"

"Trumpet, Whitman! Make a trumpet sound, a bugle sound, a growl, a grunt—anything! Anything at all!"

"Vooooo-oooooooh! Voooo-oooooh!" I blurted lamely.

"Now keep going! One step, two, three, four, five and . . ."

"Vooooo-oooooooh! Voooo-oooooh!"

"Okay, stop, Whitman. Gather 'round."

He looked at us with a smirk on his face. "Girls, when you don't listen, that leads me to make conclusions. It leads me to conclude that you don't have ears, or your ears are too small. You must need bigger ears. Who has big ears? Yes, that's right. Elephants have big ears."

The hour was more than half over. The showers and gauntlet were starting to seem not so bad.

"If you fail to listen, you will be consigned to do the elephant walk in the gym, in front of the entrance to the girls' locker room, for ten minutes. Got it? I'm sure all of your little girly peers will just love to see your big swinging trunks and hear your love calls."

He allowed this to sink in then added, "Now, young ladies, the catch-all. Down on your hands and knees, Whitman."

I got down in position, like I was getting ready to crawl.

"If you want to act like a jackass, I will be happy to turn your dream into reality. You will spend the rest of the hour acting like a real-live jackass."

Everyone turned to look at me in anticipation.

"Okay, Whitman, start in the push-up position—palms on the ground, and knees and stomach off the floor. Now keep your palms on the ground and bring your toes closer and closer to your palms until your butt is perched high in the air, like the Matterhorn."

He nodded his approval. "You see this ladies? Are you paying attention? This is the starting position. Now, Whitman, keep your palms on the ground and then kick both of your legs up and behind you. C'mon let's see it. Let's see the jackass in action."

I did a few kicks. The blood was rushing to my head, and my arms were starting to quiver.

"Now when you kick, Whitman, you're gonna yell, 'Hee-haw! Hee-haw!'"

There was no point protesting.

"Hee-haw! Hee-haw!" I kicked unenthusiastically.

"C'mon, Whitman! With *spirit!*"

"Hee-haw! Hee-haw!" I yelled, overcompensating on both the kick and the yell.

"All right, Whitman, back on your feet. Now, you ladies excuse me for a moment, while I get one of my friends. He went into the windowed coaches' office and opened the bottom drawer of a metal desk. He pulled out what looked like a large gray Christmas stocking.

Coach Rawlings returned, holding the stocking in front of him, like he was about to unveil King Arthur's sword. "Now, my little debutantes, our last and most dangerous animal."

We all crowded around to get a glimpse of what was in the stocking.

I dropped to the back of the circle, trying to disappear into the crowd.

Rawlings slowly removed the stocking and unsheathed a heavy wooden paddle with spongy, grayish blue tennis-racket-grip wrapped on the handle. A small hole had been drilled through the handle, and a pink baby rattle was hanging from a leather string. Coach Rawlings smiled admiringly and held it high for all to see. **Rusty the Rattlesnake** had been engraved in gothic script on to the face of the paddle with a wood-burning kit, probably by Rawlings himself.

Everyone took an involuntary step backward, like it was kryptonite.

The stoner kid whispered to no one in particular, with a combination of awe and terror, "This guy's a friggin' maniac."

"Calm down, girls. Take it easy. Whitman? Where's Whitman?" My shoulders sank. "Clear out. Make a spot for Whitman."

The group parted, and I reluctantly approached Coach Rawlings, desperately hoping the stoner kid was wrong.

"Well, hello, Whitman. So nice to see you again. C'mon up. Don't be shy."

He gestured to the gym floor. "Assume the jackass position again, Whitman."

I kneeled down, got into push-up position, and then inched my toes closer until my butt was raised high in the air.

Dear Lord, please let this end happily and without permanent damage, I silently prayed.

"Now, chiquitas, what happens to a jackass when, no matter how hard you try, no matter how patient you are, he just won't learn? That little jackass is just determined to kick and hee-haw himself into exhaustion. Do you know what happens to a little jackass like that?"

Rawlings put his finger over his lips. "Shhhh! Shhhh! Everybody quiet! Very quiet," he said. He continued shushing until he was gradually hissing at whisper level. Then just when the hiss was barely audible, he raised the paddle over his head and began to shake it violently, like he was a psychotic witch doctor. The baby rattle came to life with a terrifying clamor.

"*Beware!* Rusty the Rattlesnake is *out of his cage!*" Rawlings rapturously cried heavenward. It looked like his eyes might roll back into his head.

"*Holy mother.* This guy *is* a complete maniac," the stoner whispered with certainty and genuine fear.

"A jackass that won't learn will ultimately feel the bite of the *rattlesnake!*" he proclaimed.

And with that, he swung the paddle down and connected the 𝕽𝖚𝖘𝖙𝖞 𝖙𝖍𝖊 𝕽𝖆𝖙𝖙𝖑𝖊𝖘𝖓𝖆𝖐𝖊 imprint squarely across my flaccid buttocks. I didn't even have time to clinch in defense.

The loud slap of the swat—solid oak on tight denim—was followed by a collective, almost nauseated, gasp. I shrieked on impact and crumpled back into the push up position. The stoner turned ashen and looked like he was going to pass out. I almost passed out.

There was no way on earth I thought he would actually do it. I figured my chances were way better than Isaac's on Mount Moriah—and he survived without a scratch, and probably got a post-trauma hug and mutton feast as rewards for his patient submissiveness.

"Now," Rawlings continued solemnly, "for those of you who feel the natal urge to go home and tell your mommies all about PE and what a meanie Coach Rawlings is, and your mommy or daddy happens to call me or pay a visit to Mr. McGee, you will spend the rest of the week running up and down the bleachers with a pacifier in your mouth and carrying a bottle of milk."

From the gray stocking, he pulled a well-worn pacifier with a tiny picture of Big Bird on the nub and a baby's bottle with Elmo on the side. There was no doubt he was serious.

I slowly rose to my feet, buttocks throbbing with white-hot heat, feeling like I had a steel brush lodged in each butt cheek, and rejoined the group. They cleared more than enough space, like I was a homeless Vietnam vet in front of them in the fifteen-items or less check-out line at Basha's. I was toxic.

Just then, the bell rang. No one lingered to make small talk. Everyone speed-walked for the door.

From behind, I heard Rawlings deeply bellow, in all sincerity, "Nice job today, Whitman! Nice job!" as if I had scored the winning touchdown against Arroyo Vista.

33

Touch and Go

I spent the rest of the day trying to think of ways to alleviate the sting and burn of my posterior. It felt like I was sitting on hot coals. I daydreamed of desk chairs made of ice blocks and wished I had a small inner tube to sit on, so the interior of my buttocks could be elevated off the surface of the heavy orange plastic chairs. I fantasized about laying stomach-first on the utilitarian grayish brown carpet under my desk. I could barely pay attention in math. No matter how many times I shifted my weight or crossed my legs to give one butt cheek a rest from the pressure, they both burned equally hot.

My math teacher was Mr. Sturgess, a short balding man who wore gray proletariat slacks, a short-sleeved white shirt, and a wide, brown and beige striped clip-on tie. The polished cul-de-sac developing on the crown of his head was framed by shortly cropped gray hair and sideburns. He walked with a lazy stride and had the slouchy posture of a man clinging to the prospect of retirement and the public school pension that goes with it. He wearily announced that our class marked his twenty-sixth year teaching prealgebra to Mangas Coloradas Junior High students. He joylessly told us it was a joy to work at such a fine school, a school that, thanks to Mr. McGee's efforts, had never had a finer faculty and staff.

He sat at his metal desk with its Formica faux-wooden top at the room's front-and-center and robotically listed and then described by rote the class rules, "behavioral expectations," and an outline of "our year together." He showed slight signs of enthusiasm when he gave the seemingly mandatory lecture about the Four Rs, describing in excruciating detail how it was his idea eighteen years earlier to establish a set of guiding principles for the school. He exhaustively chronologized how the Four Rs came to be, and told of his part in making them "the foundation of everything this terrific junior high school stands for and their legacy for generations of Mangas Coloradas students and alumni to come." Those who weren't nodding off rolled their eyes or yawned.

Just when we were all nearly comatose, he announced we were having an impromptu test. Our slouches disappeared instantaneously as we all sat up straight in anticipation and groaned in unison. I instinctively uncrossed my legs and quickly slid my butt backward, momentarily letting the fear of a first-day math test overpower the raw nerve endings on red alert on the surface of my gluteal nether regions.

"Don't worry. This test is merely evaluative in nature," he announced in monotone as he licked his thumb and stood on the front row counting out copies of the test to be passed back.

Only two or three kids seemed to know what that meant, and they were probably the ones who wouldn't have anything to worry about anyway.

I breezed through long division, decimals, and fractions, and then fell into the abyss of directed numbers—positives plus negatives, negatives minus negatives, negatives plus positives—I thought my head was going to explode.

In the silence, Mr. Sturgess sat at his desk and clipped his fingernails over a tin trash can. Then he carefully fogged his glasses with deeps breaths and shined each lens with a handkerchief. When he was finished, he pulled out a *Popular Mechanics* magazine and soon became fully engrossed in its contents.

After ten minutes, he abruptly called, "Time. Pencils down. Push your tests to the upper left-hand corner of your desks. You may sit at your desk quietly contemplating your goals for the year until the bell rings."

We all watched the long red second-hand needle on the clock mounted above the blackboard take its sweet time moving around the dial three times, until the bell sounded and we gathered our things and scattered out the door.

As I made my way through the throngs streaming out of the classes leading into the plaza, I noticed T. J. McKay approaching from my left. He lit up with an admiring smile when he saw me. I stopped and waited for his path to merge with mine.

"Holy crap," he said, with a dude-I've-been-looking-everywhere-for-you expression. "I heard you got swatted by Rawlings!" He laughed in disbelief. T. J. was the only kid I knew that could laugh and talk at the same time.

"Who'd you hear that from?"

"I heard it in social studies from some kid named Danny who went to William Lloyd Garrison. He sits next to me. He asked if I knew a kid named Todd Whitman, and then he told me. After that everybody was talking about it. Everybody's in there."

"Like who?"

"Well, there's a bunch of William Lloyd Garrison kids and a few from Frederick Douglass in there too, but Ben-G's in there. Jericho's in there too."

"*Jericho?*"

"Yeah, I guess he flunked the class last year and has to retake it or something. It's pretty funny that he's in there with Ben-G. When the teacher realized there were two Croshaws she almost started to cry."

"Curtis is in there . . ." he continued, trying to wrack his brain. "Jeff Mangum, David Somerset . . . I forget who else. Oh yeah, Heather Simmons, Lisa Esposito, Jenny Gillette. There's a bunch."

My stomach knotted. Jenny had heard. "What did he say?" I asked trying keep a blasé expression.

"Who—David Somerset?"

"No, not David Somerset, idiot. The kid from William Lloyd Garrison—Danny or whatever his name is."

"Oh, he said Rawlings made you act like an elephant, a donkey, and I forget what else, insects or bugs or something. And that he nailed you, *hard*—with a huge paddle he calls Rusty the Rattlesnake."

I felt distinctly nauseated now, but I knew there was nothing I could do.

"What did he say about me? About how I reacted, I mean? Did he say anything?" I asked too urgently.

"He said you took it like a man. I think he's secretly in love with you."

We started walking again amidst the masses of bubbly students. I had to take small, delicate steps. When we had gone only a few feet, T. J. flicked his head back and said, "Hey, Danny," as the bird-flipping stoner from PE bisected our route.

T. J. nudged me. "That's him. That's Danny. Your soon-to-be love interest."

Danny the stoner glanced over and flicked his head in acknowledgment, then did a quick double-take. Recognizing me, he stopped and came over to us.

He flicked his bangs to the side with a neck snap and asked, "Dude, not to be gay or anything, but how's your *ass?*" He seemed to be genuinely concerned.

T. J. burst out laughing and gave me an I-told-you-so elbow to the ribs.

"Fine, thanks," I said meekly, and immediately regretted my words. How big of a dork could I possibly be? *Fine, thanks?* I repeated in my head.

"Well, that guy's a nut job, man. Who sits around and makes his own paddle—and then *names it?* Seriously?" he asked, walking away.

"That kid's just as nutty as Rawlings," I said watching Danny bounce away. He was a tippy-toe walker.

T. J. was still laughing. I punched him in the shoulder and he laughed even harder.

We parted ways as T. J. headed to the Corridor of Recreation, toward PE.

"Keep laughing," I called after him. "You better hope you don't have Rawlings."

"I don't. I already checked. I have Coach Staff," he called back, walking backward and holding up his schedule in triumph.

"'Staff' is who everyone gets!" I called back. "That just means they didn't know which coaches would be teaching which classes when they printed the schedules. So, you don't know who your coach is yet. Mine says staff too," I said, displaying my schedule and pointing to the second-hour row.

T. J. stopped laughing and came back to personally examine my schedule. An oh-my-gosh-he-could-be-right look fell down his face, and he turned and hastily headed toward the Corridor of Recreation.

While T. J. made his way to PE, I headed to my locker for the first time. Locker 3131. I found it without too much effort and was able to successfully fake like I knew what I was doing. I entered the combination as I had been tutored by Gregory the night before. Turn the dial twice to clear it. Right—Preston Pearson (RB, #26). Left—Rafael Septien (K, #1). Right—Gary Hogeboom (QB, #14). It wasn't Everson Walls (CB, #24) after all. The lock clicked open without a problem. My love for the Dallas Cowboys had never been greater.

Ben-G called out, and he and Curtis walked over to me. We all had first lunch together. I dumped my books in the locker, and we headed toward the cafeteria. They wanted to know all about what had happened in PE. Curtis confirmed that essentially the same thing had happened during his first-hour PE class, except that one kid watching was so freaked out that he paced up and down the aisle of lockers with his hands clasped on top of his head muttering, "Feeling sick, feeling sick," and then ran to the toilet and puked.

We walked into the cafeteria, not sure what to expect. The noise was deafening. There were tables everywhere and four separate lunch lines. There was a "hot" line, a "cold," line and two "fast-food" lines. There were three or four kids in each of the hot and cold lines and about fifty in each of the fast-food lines.

"We're gonna spend the whole lunch period in line if we do fast food," Ben-G observed. "What do you wanna eat?"

"I don't care," I replied. I really didn't. I just wanted to find a place where I could stand in peace. I didn't want to sit down, on account of my injured rear, and I didn't want to walk any farther than I had to.

"Let's go "hot," then," he said without even consulting Curtis.

Turkey a la King was the day's fare. It looked like Thanksgiving in a blender—or, in a word, disgusting. The hairnetted ladies plopped heaping scoops of the muck on our trays, smiled and, staying on script, said, "Welcome back," in their second language, not realizing we were seventh-grade rookies in every sense of the word.

We made our way over to a table where a group of boys we all knew from William Ellery Channing were sitting. It was so crowded that some of the kids were sitting on the floor Indian-style with their plastic margarine yellow cafeteria trays in their laps. I opted to place my tray on a corner of the table and stand up. It was perfect cover for the strangeness of standing and eating. It looked like I was purposely maintaining the link between the group on the floor and the group at the table. Everyone wanted to know about Coach Rawlings. All of the guys inched closer as I told the story. I was like an inmate in the prison yard telling my gang of fellow convicts how the warden was a no-good-you-know-what and how they better watch their backs. When I finished, everyone was muttering, "holy crap" to themselves and expressing gratitude that they didn't have Coach Rawlings for PE. The ones who did have Coach Rawlings compared the experiences of the poor guinea pigs from their PE classes and nodded in silent appreciation for what I had been through.

"Did it hurt?" Jeff Mangum asked.

"Not really," I lied nonchalantly. "But I think I have some welts on my butt," I added truthfully. They thought I was joking and laughed.

Just behind us was a table full of William Ellery Channing girls. Jenny was one of them. There were so many of them huddled together that they had two squeezed on every seat.

They would have looked like Eastern European children on an immigrant ship approaching Ellis Island if it weren't for all of their perfectly curled and feathered first-day-of-school hairdos and new outfits. If they were anything like Lisa, they had stayed up late the night before trying on every article of new school clothing, tirelessly testing each combination with countless poses in the mirror, and finally deciding that they hated all of their clothes and needed more and going to bed angry with their mothers for not letting them buy that one special pair of jeans or shoes that they were denied. And, ironically, for all of their prepping and primping, the only clothes and hairdos they noticed were their own. No one else cared what they were wearing.

As they sat insecurely at the lunch table, they all put their heads forward to hear some whispery piece of summer gossip or the supposed inside scoop on some teacher or class or boy and then all threw their heads back in laughter, like the tide lapping up on shore and pulling back out to sea. At one point, they all turned around and looked at me in unison, then huddled together over their trays for a few seconds and threw their heads back uproariously. I stole a glance and caught Jenny's eyes. She raised her eyebrows at me as if to say, "Really?" and then stuck her head back in the huddle, leaving me to torment myself for the rest of the day about what that look meant. Was it a sympathetic and admiring, "Really? You poor thing. I can't believe how tough you are," or mocking disgust, "Really? Just like I thought, you are *such* a geek."

34

Beginner's Luck

Thankfully, fourth and fifth periods occurred without incident. Fourth period was Woodshop, which showed up on our schedules as "industrial arts," apparently to satisfy the inferiority complexes of the Woodshop teachers. My teacher was Mr. Rushdale, a tall muscular guy with an unnaturally dark tan, dark hair, and a full, trimmed mustache, like Burt Reynolds in *Smokey and the Bandit*. He wore a short-sleeve, white T-shirt with red sleeves that said "MCJHS" in black letters on the front, blue jeans, and work boots. The red sleeves on his T-shirt fit tightly over his biceps and he stored his protective goggles over his left bicep when he wasn't using them. The overly tanned and humongous biceps were a dead giveaway that he was some kind of weekend-warrior body builder. Before he even said one word to us—and there were none of the usual first day pleasantries like "Welcome to Woodshop," or "C'mon on in, I'm Mr. Rushdale"—he turned off the lights and played a movie called, *Safety in the Industrial Arts*. It showed dramatizations of kids dorking around in Woodshop classes, welding classes, and auto-body classes. Every time there was a "safety breakdown," evil out-of-tune violin music screeched and the camera zoomed to an extreme close-up of a careless shop student with a look of abject horror on his face just as he realized he had dismembered a finger, pulverized his feet with a heavy object, or blinded himself with a blowtorch. The film didn't show any actual blood or dismemberment, but we could visualize what happened when the music shrieked. Fingers were cut off, arteries were hit, blood spurted to the ceiling, the teacher applied a tourniquet while the fastest runner in the class ran to the front office and the weirdest kid in the class searched on the sawdust-covered floor for the raggedy missing fingers half of the class started sympathy barfing and passing out, the next fastest runner was sent to the nurse's office to retrieve an ice pack so the dismembered digits could be kept ripe, sirens came blaring down the street, and after three surgeries and a gazillion stitches and a couple of days in the hospital, the kid came back to school with a huge bulbous white bandage wrapped over his entire right hand that required him to scribble in hen scratches with his untamed left hand for the rest of the year.

The movie ended in silence. Mr. Rushdale turned on the lights and then passed out a laminated, bright yellow piece of paper to each class member—the class rules. We took turns reading them aloud like they were scriptures, and then Mr. Rushdale took us on a tour of the shop. The class buzzed with unspoken excitement when Mr. Rushdale removed the goggles from his hulking left bicep, our signal to put on the plastic eye goggles that had been placed on each of our desks. He powered up the band saws, miter saws, radial arm saws, table saws, jig saws, and disc sanders. The deafening hum of the savage machinery made us feel like men. We were elated. We could practically feel shots of testosterone shooting through our veins and arteries. We reviewed the class rules at each stop on the shop tour. Although they were numerous, we took them deathly serious. We self-policed one another; anyone who was perceived to be daydreaming or whispering to his neighbor as Rushdale explained the rules or demonstrated how to use some piece of equipment was harshly told by another one of his neighbors to "pay attention!" or to "shut up and listen!" It was one thing to worry about detention in English class; the prospect of having your fingers sucked in and mangled by a radial arm saw was an entirely different level of punishment. Elementary school was over. Forever.

After we returned to our seats, Mr. Rushdale removed his goggles, slid them up snugly around his left bicep, and announced matter-of-factly that we would have a test on the class rules and safety instructions the next day and, if necessary, every day thereafter until every single student achieved 100 percent on the test. No one would be able to use the equipment until everyone had scored perfectly on the safety test.

This was one test that the all-male pubescent population of the class would, without doubt, take seriously. The bell rang, and as we filed out of the classroom and into the Corridor of Responsibility, the chatter was boastful and proud. We had visions of building skyscrapers, riding motorcycles hard and fast, flirting with older girls, and other supposedly manly things dancing in our heads.

Fifth hour was science, and it was, in a word, brutal. I didn't know a single person in the class. With the Turkey a la King settling like a brick in my stomach, the cranked-up air conditioning humming hypnotically, the post adrenaline letdown following the exhilaration of Woodshop, and another droning lecture about class rules and the Four Rs from our teacher, Ms. Zimmerman, who dressed in the latest teenage fashions like she was trying to impress her female audience with her hipness, had me nodding off and fighting to stay awake. I wanted nothing more than to lay my head down on the sturdy black-topped lab table and nap it all off. The fifty-three minutes of class time dragged on endlessly until there was a rumble of excitement and competing hisses of disgust when Ms. Zimmerman described in painstaking detail the future prospect of dissecting pig fetuses marinating in formaldehyde-filled baggies—but only if we were well-behaved and made sufficient progress throughout the semester, as if carving up aborted piglets was some kind of treat. Mercifully, the bell rang before she could finish.

My last class, sixth period, was choir. It was entirely made up of seventh graders who would a be a performing choir known as "Seventh Heaven."

Mom was surprised I had signed up for it. I was surprised I had signed up for it. Ben-G had signed up for it too. We did it wholly based upon the insistence of Gregory and Jericho that it was the greatest class of the entire seventh grade, and maybe the whole school. This was because it was a little known fact that all of the cutest seventh-grade girls, and the ones destined to be most popular, for some reason instinctively took choir, just as the swallows return to San Juan Capistrano every year. "And," as Jericho described, "almost no guys—and certainly no cool guys—sign up for it. So, you have the run of the house. And it'll be your own fault if you don't come out of there friends with all the chicks that make going to school worthwhile."

"Trust me," Jericho had said.

"Trust me," Gregory had repeated, practically as an amen.

We trusted them, but I was having a severe case of second thoughts. As I made my way down the Corridor of Respect, I thought seriously about heading to the nurse's office and faking ill. I had to give Gregory credit. He had been pretty much right about everything—except that the intensity of everything he described had actually been even more acute and more real. Science was more boring, and PE more humiliating. But I could only imagine how horrific a choir class would be for someone who had no desire or propensity to actually sing and was in it solely to attempt to associate with seventh-grade girls who were supposedly most likely to achieve the status that we all secretly sought.

I came in just as the tardy bell was ringing, the last one in the door. By now, the news of my PE experience had been published far and wide, and I had been hearing murmurs of, "Yeah, that's Gregory Whitman's brother," and "Yeah, he's Lisa's little brother," from the eighth and ninth graders I passed between classes and locker stops. So it was no surprise that when I walked in and every head turned to see who else was in their class, that the low rumble of pre-class conversation spiked and was even punctuated with a few giggles.

The room was a small elevated amphitheater of four ascending, light green carpeted rows. Plastic, stackable chairs were loosely arranged throughout the room. The teacher, or "director," as we were instructed to refer to him, was Mr. Laughlin. He had longish thinning hair that he combed straight back to cover the signs of premature balding and a coiffed Wolfman-Jack beard. He literally sang opera as I walked in, belting out, *"Welcome! Welcome! You were nearly laa-aaaate, young man!"* directing his gaze and bass-alto at me. He turned in a sweeping motion to the rest of the class, continuing, *"Welcome! Welcome to aa-aaa-aaa-aalllll!"* And then he bowed dramatically, his wispy comb-over flopping in front of him.

Ben-G had saved me a seat next to him on the back row. I took my seat and quickly scanned the room, I counted six boys and twenty-two girls, including Jenny Gillette tucked in on the far left front row. Four of the six boys were likewise scanning the room, taking stock, quickly analyzing whether they had made the right decision, whether the advice they had received from their older brothers or friends had been legitimate or a bad joke. Only a few of the girls scanned the room. They all hung on every word that Mr. Laughlin spoke or sang. He had a tendency to break out in song midsentence for no apparent reason.

"Ladies and gentlemen, it is my absolute pleasure to teach and direct you this semester," he said, transitioning into song. *"Together, we are "The Seventh Heaven!"* he sang, and began walking over to the piano as if this was all choreographed (and it probably was). He sat down at the piano and began pounding a familiar tune, something my mom listened to on the radio in the car, although I couldn't place it.

He called out to the crowd between songs like a cheesy cabaret singer, "You see, this semester, we will *all* get a turn to sing, just like I am. As soloists. And as a choir. It is terrifying and it's exhilarating, and it's *MUSIC!*"

Ben-G leaned over and said, "Did he say *'soloist?'*" Goosebumps of terror instantly appeared on our forearms and shins.

"Together, we are 'The Seventh Heaven!'" he cried, bursting into song once more. The girls started clapping with the bass

line, Jenny as ringleader. Laughlin ate it up. He pushed the piano bench back and stood up, playing, rollicking and belting out a Captain and Tennille song with exuberance. I felt sick to my stomach. I was pretty sure Ben-G did too.

X

Philip Boettcher hands me a single-spaced, 8½ x 11 three-page receipt (ivory parchment paper, of course) with two hands—Japanese salary-man style. I stand up and take it.

"There's one more thing," he says quietly. "The flowers."

"Oh, I thought the florist billed separately for those," I say, reaching for the wallet in my back pocket.

"No, no, you're right." He smiles. "The florist did bill separately for those, and she mentioned that your sister has already paid in full. It's not that. Nothing like that at all," he continues. "You see, well, this is a most unusual situation. In fact, I don't recall ever seeing anything like this before. No one here at D. Boettcher & Sons has."

"I'm sorry, I don't understand. If there's a problem with the flowers . . . How much do we owe you?"

"Mr. Whitman. I'm sorry, I'm not communicating very well, and I apologize." He pauses.

"I have four floral arrangements that were not delivered to the cemetery."

"Oh, that's no problem. There were plenty at the cemetery. Just donate them to the next funeral," I offer generously.

He smiles patiently.

"Mr. Whitman, they were purposely not delivered to the cemetery. We were pointedly instructed by the florist to not deliver them to the cemetery for the burial. The instructions were very specific."

He picks up his phone and pushes one digit. "Sheila, can you bring them in?"

He smiles and looks awkwardly at his overly shined black shoes.

35

To Each His Own

The night after the first day of school was one night that we could count on Dad being home in time for dinner, no matter what. He wanted the full blow-by-blow report of the first day of school. Classes, teachers, students, expectations, feelings, goals. It was brutal. Mom made sure to make a huge meal that everyone loved, so that we would be less restless and impatient and more willing to endure the questions. It wasn't an interrogation—there was nothing to be scared or nervous about—it was just boring and tedious.

The oldest kid went first. Gregory. And he was always the most difficult. Gregory's responses to nearly of all Dad's questions used either the word *weird* or *stupid* or both. This year he had obviously learned a couple of new words, although I was pretty sure he wasn't even using them correctly—*irrelevant* and *marginal.*

"So, Gregory, tell us about your first day as a ninth grader, as a big *freshman.* How was your last tour of duty through Mangas Coloradas?" Dad began, trying hard to be jovial.

"It was irrelevant."

"Irrelevant to what?" Dad asked. "Your first year of high school is, quite the contrary, very relevant—to a lot of things."

"Well, it was pretty stupid, then."

"How was it stupid?" Dad asked sincerely, undeterred.

"Everything was just stupid. I don't know, I can't really explain it. It was just stupid," he said, slightly irritated, between bites of prime-rib roast and mashed potatoes.

"Okay, I get it. Generally, you feel it was stupid. Let's get specific. Let's start with first hour. What do you have first hour?"

Everyone sighed. *Why does Gregory have to make this more painful than it already is?* we all thought, Mom included.

"Pottery."

"*Pottery?*" Dad looked at Mom incredulously. *He's taking pottery?* the look said wordlessly.

"Yeah, Dad. Pottery. And it's stupid."

"I got that part already. I didn't even know there was a *pottery* class," he said as if emphasizing the word *pottery* would somehow make it more believable to him.

"Well, now you know."

"What made you want to take pottery?"

"I don't know. It seemed like it might be something different or fun."

"And it wasn't different or fun?"

"It was different, but it wasn't fun."

"What made it different?"

"The pottery."

"What about the pottery?"

"It's different because you don't sit at a desk and read and take notes. You can walk around and check stuff out and do stuff."

"Well, that doesn't sound stupid to me. Why wasn't it fun? *You're* in the class, so I would think that it would be pretty tough for it not to be fun," Dad said, blatantly patronizing him in the hope that more robust answers would be forthcoming.

"The teacher's a weirdo."

"Why do you say that? What makes him weird?"

"It's a she. I don't know. She's just stupid."

"Well, there must be some rational basis for concluding on the first day of school that a teacher you've probably never met before is both a weirdo and stupid."

"She's goofy. She's a hippy or something. She was wearing a yellow sundress—that kind that you see in Nogales—and she was wearing flip-flops. She kept talking about touching things and feeling things and memorizing touches. She actually gave us homework on the first day of school. Nobody does that. We have to keep a "touch journal" for the whole semester. We have to touch five new things every day and write a paragraph describing each thing. She thinks that touching a bunch of different stuff will help us be able to 'connect on a deeper level with the clay,'" he said in a high and breezy tone, mimicking his teacher.

Mom was squirming in her chair. You could tell she was siding with Gregory on this one, but she acknowledged that this was Dad's thing, so she didn't say anything.

"Okay. It's definitely different, I'll give you that. But who's to say it's stupid? Different doesn't always equal weird or stupid. It's art, Gregory. Art is different from other subjects. In this class you get to actually create and discover, rather than learn about things that other people have created or discovered. Would you rather sit through an additional English class or math class?"

"That's irrelevant, Dad."

"Have you started your 'touch journal'?" Dad asked with a smile, clearly trying not to give away that he also thought it was ridiculous and weird.

Gregory was busy trying to saw through a piece of fat that was refusing to let go of the prime rib. Dad looked at Mom. She was frowning squeamishly about the prospect of a fifteen-year-old boy being encouraged to touch new things.

"Not yet," Gregory said without looking up, still working on extricating the fat from the roast on his plate.

"Why not? There are plenty of things you could write about right at this table," Dad suggested.

"Yeah," Lisa interjected. "How about your dinner? You're over there manhandling your meat. Just *touch* it already," Lisa said flippantly.

Mom nearly sprang out of her chair. Gregory stopped chewing. He was speechless.

"What? What did I say?" Lisa asked, genuinely concerned but unsure what her faux pas was.

"Nothing, Lisa. Bob, can we move on to second hour now? *Please?*"

"Okay, we'll move on to second period, but I assume that Gregory's goal for pottery is an A. Is my assumption correct, Gregory?"

"C," Gregory said as he took a massive bite.

"It better not be, or your touch journal will have some entries about the touch of my belt on your backside," Dad said, taking the bait.

"C," Gregory mumbled, and then opened wide and pointed to his mouth. It looked like a cement mixer full of ground-up mashed potatoes, meat and broccoli. "See!"

"Oh, Bob!" Mom protested. "Please, can we move on?!"

Grandma Carter even looked up abruptly and surveyed the table cautiously, like a deer eating grass on the side of a country road and stopping to watch a car slowly pass.

Dad moved on, and we heard all about how weird and stupid Gregory's classes and teachers were. The only exceptions were his journalism class—it was "marginal"—and the highly coveted sixth period PE class reserved for the ninth-grade football team, which was, predictably, "awesome."

To Dad's delight, Lisa, who went next, described every detail of life as an eighth grader in painstaking detail. Dad paid close attention and asked follow-up question after follow-up question, like he was an anthropologist from the future researching the lives of American teenage girls during the last quarter of the twentieth century. We heard about the outfit she chose to wear to school, why she chose it, and how it made her feel. We heard about the girls who were snotty and catty, the ones who were cute and *so sweet,* the boys who were foxy, cool, and even super cool, the boys who were lame, retarded, or total jerks. We heard about who she sat with at lunch and why and what they said. We heard about her locker and her plans to decorate it. We heard about her teachers, their mustaches and hairdos and clothes. We heard about her classes—English,

World History, Chorus, PE, Biology, and Home Ec and every requirement to get an A in each class and each major project for each class, including every major activity planned for Home Ec. This included taking care of a real live chicken egg for a week, cooking a four-course meal, preparing and living by a budget, and practicing conflict resolution, which Dad was especially curious about.

"What do you mean, 'conflict resolution'?" he asked.

"You know, like when you and Mom fight."

"Mom and I don't *fight*."

"Oh yes, you do, Dad. Don't deny it," she said playfully.

"Like when?"

"Like when you always get home later than when you say you will. Like when you won't just ignore the phone and let it ring. Like when you leave the newspaper on the bathroom floor. Like when—"

"Okay, okay, I think I get the point."

Mom smiled and nodded at Dad as if to say, "You see? She's right."

"Like when *that lady* steals money from my purse and tells me she didn't," Grandma said unexpectedly, pointing a shaking index finger at Mom.

Mom was used to it. She didn't say anything. Nobody did.

Grandma started to get up from the table. She was done. Mom helped her scoot her chair back and then walked slowly up the stairs with her, placing her right hand under Grandma's left elbow just in case Grandma started to slip. Grandma strangely had no problem with getting help from the accused purse snatcher.

"So, Lisa," Dad said watching Mom and Grandma ascend the stairs. "How should these conflicts be resolved?"

"I don't know yet. We haven't learned that yet. I guess you'll just have to stick around for the exciting conclusion that will come later this semester," she said cutely.

"Well, I will definitely look forward to that."

My turn was next.

"So, Todd, tell us about your first day as a junior high school student."

"It was good," I said blandly.

"Good? Or great? Maybe fantastic or stupendous? Or just good?" he said matching my blandness in jest.

"Incredible," I said with fake enthusiasm as Mom sat back down at the table.

"Okay, really, how was it?"

"It was *good.*"

No response from Dad. And everyone else except Mom appeared to be busy eating.

"What? Really, it was good," I said, addressing their silence.

"Wait 'til he tells you about PE," Gregory interjected out of nowhere.

"Don't interrupt. You had your chance, Gregory," Dad said.

"What do you mean?" Mom asked Gregory suspiciously at the same time, talking over Dad.

Dad continued his questioning. Mom continued looking at Gregory. And Gregory laughed and shrugged and looked down at his plate as he continued stuffing his face.

"What was your first hour?"

"English."

"Who's your teacher?"

"Mr. Salmon."

"I haven't heard of him before. Is he new?"

"I think he's new."

"He's new," Gregory interrupted again.

"How was he?"

"He seems pretty nice. We just talked about class rules, the Four Rs and stuff. Ben-G is in my class. I think it will be a pretty good class."

My strategy was to provide enough information to get by. If I was too excited like Lisa or too coy like Gregory that would only lead to more probing, more questions, more time. I was going to answer the questions asked, and that was it. I was going to bore him into submission.

"Okay, what about second hour?"

"It's PE."

"So, I'm guessing you probably liked it?"

"Yeah, it was fine."

"You are *such a liar*," blurted Gregory, smiling. Obviously he had heard about Rawlings and was waiting to spring this on everyone at dinner.

Mom and Dad turned to look at him. He looked at me, and I gave him a *seriously, c'mon, man* look that shamed him into silence, like when Michael Corleone brings Frank Pentangeli's brother from Sicily into the Congressional hearing room and Pentangeli changes his story.

"Gregory, you've had your turn," Dad gently reminded him, still not catching on that there was something more to my debut in PE.

"What's this all about, Gregory?" Mom asked him.

"Nothing. I'm just kidding. I'm just trying to give the little seventh grader some grief."

Mom turned to me.

"Seriously, it was just PE. Gosh, you guys are crazy."

Then Lisa sprang into action, as only an older sister could. She couldn't resist.

"*Well*, I heard that the PE coach has this paddle that he calls his rattlesnake. It has a rattle and everything. And he tested it out today—on Todd's bum. Todd got swatted in front of his whole class," Lisa announced with the smug self-assurance of someone well versed in the art of gossip.

"*What?!*" Everyone (myself included, testing a possible cover-up), exclaimed in unison.

Gregory's cement mixer choked and nearly spewed its contents in spasmodic laughter.

While Gregory tried to prevent a small floret of broccoli from shooting out his nose, everyone's gaze focused squarely on me.

"It's not that big a deal. He was just demonstrating. They were like love taps."

"*Not that big a deal?!*" Mom exclaimed, making it a big deal.

"Mom, seriously, calm down. It's not that big a deal."

"Linda, just a second—"

"No, wait a minute, Bob. Todd, are you telling me that your PE teacher has a paddle? And that he uses that paddle to hit his students?"

"No. Lisa is telling you that. Maybe you should ask *her* about it," I said defensively, glaring at Lisa.

"I'm just saying what I heard. Actually, what *everyone* heard. The whole school was talking about it."

"Todd, what happened?"

"Nothing. It's not a big deal. He was telling us that if we got too far out of line that he would give us a swat with his paddle."

"Bob, this is insane. You've got to call Mr. McGee and get to the bottom of this. First thing in the morning. Todd, you are not going to PE tomorrow. Not ever again as long as that man is the teacher. Neither is Gregory."

Gregory wasn't laughing anymore. "Nice job, Lisa. Seriously, what were you thinking? We don't tell everything we hear about *you!*" he said, joining the fray.

"Oh yeah, like what?" she replied, calling Gregory's bluff.

Dinner was delving into chaos. Mom stood up for no apparent reason and started clearing the dishes, even though we were all still eating. Maggie was asking when it was going to be her turn. Dad was speechless, still trying to figure out what just happened. Gregory was freaking out, saying there was no possible way he was not going to PE and completely blowing things out of proportion by announcing that he would drop seminary and secede from the Whitman union and move in with the Croshaws if necessary. Lisa sat back, silently wishing she could take it back, caught completely off guard by the insanity she had unleashed.

"Hold on, everybody. Hold on. Everybody, please calm down," Dad said calmly.

We all stopped and looked at him, except for Mom. She stood at the sink dumping uneaten broccoli and mashed potatoes into the sink and rinsing out the serving bowls. She didn't make eye contact, but she was listening intently.

"Listen, it was just a swat, and he said he'd do it only if the boys were getting out of control, right? So I don't think it's that big of a deal—"

"Not that big of a deal? *Are you kidding?*" Mom said before Dad stopped talking.

"Linda, when I was a boy, we got swatted for missing spelling words and not finishing our times tables in under two minutes. It's just discipline. If the boys are out of control in PE, then I have no problem if the coach gives them a reminder swat."

Gregory and I were taken aback. *Wait, is this* our *dad? Bishop Whitman, the generous and loving "father of the ward"? Doctor Whitman, the gregarious and loving family practitioner and pediatrician?* we thought, exchanging our own looks of incredulity.

"You *are* joking."

"No. Linda, I mean—"

"You cannot be serious, Bob. It's savage. It's medieval. It's . . ."

"Linda, I had teachers in school that would innocently ask us to place our hands forward on our desks and then smack them with a yard stick—*hard.* I had teachers that would write notes home to my mother on my forearms in permanent marker. I had one teacher that had a large sponge that looked like a piece of granite. She would throw it at us if she thought we were out of line. We thought she was throwing a real piece of rock at us. It was terrifying. We were only in second grade. It got us every time. One kid dove out of the way and gashed his head open on another kid's desk. His parents *thanked* the teacher for putting their son back in line. Another teacher would pull us up out of our chairs *by our sideburns* and walk us to the principal's office— still pulling our sideburns the whole way like we were on a leash. My parents knew all about it."

"Bob, I really don't care about the psychotic discipline techniques used in Post Falls, Idaho."

"My point is that if these kids are being disrespectful and screwing around, then the coaches should be able to remind them about being respectful—as long as it's reasonable. And I don't think a wake-up swat is unreasonable."

"Well, I *completely* disagree!" she said emphatically, standing in front of the sink, unconsciously gesticulating by shaking a dishrag toward the table. "It's corporal punishment. And it has no place in any educated society, much less in an educational institution. And certainly not in 1981!"

"I disagree, babe," he said calmly, shrugging, indicating that they were at an impasse. He thought calling her babe would help defuse the situation, but it was like a squirt of lighter fluid on hot coals.

"Don't call me *babe*, Bob! This is ridiculous and you know it. It's more of this weird sadistic wannabe macho stuff that all of these coaches are obsessed with. It's just like that baseball coach, Throckborden, and the athletic cups. They get their jollies by hazing unsuspecting boys, so they can laugh about it on Saturday nights at the bar with their buddies when they reminisce about one loser throwing a touchdown pass to another loser thirty years ago and console each other about how if it wasn't for that knee injury some other poor loser suffered he could've made it to the big leagues."

"Do you know how many times I was swatted with a paddle in school, Linda? I can't even remember, probably fifty—at least."

"That's Idaho for you," Mom said.

"You can knock Idaho all you want. We may not be the smartest, but you won't find a tougher breed than the Spud-niks," he said, raising his arms and flexing his biceps, trying again to defuse.

Maggie was still vainly asking when it was going to be her turn. Gregory, Lisa, and I got up and silently excused ourselves and snuck off to our rooms. Neither parent noticed.

I listened at the top of the stairs, waiting for a reply from Mom, but she was now fully engaged in dishwashing and ignoring him.

Dad gave in and said, "Answer me this. Do you think Todd or Gregory are going to get in any trouble in PE? I highly doubt it. They will understand that if you touch a hot stove, you get burned. There are consequences to certain actions. That creates discipline. That's all I'll say. If we think the discipline is getting out of hand then I'll personally go down and talk to Mr. McGee."

Mom continued doing the dishes.

It was quiet after that. I'm not sure what happened. But, I do know that Dad watched the 10:00 news in the family room that night instead of in his bed.

36

I Caught Your Act

I didn't have any homework, so there wasn't much to do in my room. I sat on top of my bed, resting my back against the wall, surveying the room. The door to the jack-and-jill (or was it jack-and-jack?) bathroom that connected my room with Gregory's room was closed. Paul Westphal and George Gervin hung above me. Across the room, Walter Davis smiled at me from a poster labeled "Sweet D," which showed him lying in a pile of candy and holding an oversized rainbow whirlybird of a lollipop in his hand. The oscillating fan made its tireless, recurring trip around the horn, every so often blowing in my face and making my bangs flutter.

I knew that tonight was not the night to aggravate or sass Mom, to appear lazy or helpless or needy. Tonight was all about self-discipline and responsibility. Any interaction would be serious and no-nonsense. There would be zero tolerance for messing around, wrestling with Gregory, or mocking Lisa as she tried on and posed in outfit after outfit in anticipation of school day number two.

I walked over to my bookshelf and picked up my book of famous Indian chiefs. As I did so, I saw a small pamphlet with a picture of the Washington D.C. Temple on it, entitled, "Articles of Faith," tucked between the book on Indian chiefs and *Amazing Sports Stories,* a book that I ordered in fourth grade from one of those monthly book order forms the teacher would send home with us. I had carefully chosen it over *Heavyweight Champions of the World.*

I smiled, pleased. The Articles of Faith would be the perfect cover. If Mom or Dad came in demanding to know what happened in PE, there I would be, sitting quietly on my bed earnestly trying to memorize the Articles of Faith. Surely, there would be no interrogation, no thoughts of calling the school, or meeting with Mr. McGee. The scared-straight instillation of discipline that Dad hoped for would already be bearing fruit.

I could picture Dad coming in to check on me, slightly cracking the door, and asking, "What'ya doing?"

"Oh, just trying to finish up memorizing the Articles of Faith."

"How're you doing? Everything okay?"

"Yeah, Dad, I'm fine. It really wasn't a big deal."

"All right, love you, bud." And then he would extend his hand for a soft five.

Dad would return downstairs and report to Mom, still working on the dishes and still ignoring him.

"Guess what Todd's up there doing?"

No answer.

"He's got the Articles of Faith out, and he's memorizing the ones he hasn't mastered yet," he would report proudly, as if the first-day-of-school swat was already teaching me the valuable life lessons that he expected.

I really only needed to polish the last three and I would be done, ready for passing them off to Sister Smiley and reciting one in sacrament meeting, when I turned twelve in October.

I grabbed the pamphlet and, forgetting for a moment that I had fresh butt-cheek wounds, sat down on the hard wooden desk chair. I sucked air through my teeth with the shot of pain reminding me of my injuries. I realized I was still was unsure how much damage, if any, had been done. I laid the Articles of Faith pamphlet down on my desk, carefully got up, and made my way to the bathroom door. I opened it tentatively. The coast was clear. Gregory wasn't in there, and his door to the bathroom on the opposite side of the double-sinked vanity was securely closed. I closed my door and locked it, then bent down gingerly to untie my shoes and unbutton my 501s. The button fly was new and awkward to me. Everyone in elementary school had zippers on their pants. Button flys were just another one of the small, strange changes that junior high school seemed to mandate. I took off my shirt to get the shirttail out of the way and dropped my jeans to the floor. Then I stuck my butt out toward the huge mirror affixed to the wall above the vanity. I stood on my tippy toes and looked back over my shoulder, trying to get a glimpse of my butt cheeks in the mirror. But the burn was coming from somewhere below the apex of the curve of my butt cheeks and the vanity was too high.

There was only one way to get a close up view of the carnage.

I climbed up on the vanity, straddling my sink, facing the mirror. I carefully pivoted one hundred and eighty degrees, like a right-handed pitcher checking the runner on second, until I was standing atop the vanity with my back to the mirror. I dropped my undies to my ankles and then bent down, toes hanging ten off the edge of the faux marble, off-white vanity, rested my elbows on my knees, and looked backward between my legs at an upside-down, up-close view of my salamander-white butt in the mirror. I forced my eyes away from the disgusting but somehow mesmerizing view of sack and crack and focused them right above the creases of where my butt met my hamstrings—where silver dollar–sized purplish pillows of blood blisters were branded on either butt cheek. The one adorning my left cheek had a purple blob, and the reddish outline of an ℞ tattooed underneath it.

I muttered, "Oh, my goodness gracious," to myself, and just as I reached up to touch one of the sizzling pustules, Gregory's door flung open.

"Oh my—what in the *HOLY*?" he exclaimed, ripping his Walkman headphones off of his head to stare at me peering through my legs at my own butt, naked, except for my calf-high tube socks and my drawers around my ankles.

"Get outta here!" I yelled, instinctively reaching down to pull my underwear up as fast as possible. But I was too quick for my own stocking feet. I slipped to the left, then slipped to the right on the slick vanity. I frantically waved my arms in a tight circular motion to get my balance, but it was no use. My heels slipped out from under me, my butt hit the edge of the vanity, and I tumbled down, face-planting on the floor. I woke up naked with a wet face and hair on the royal blue shag bathroom mat below my sink. As I came to, I found Gregory slapping my face and whispering loudly, "Todd! *Todd! Wake up!*" He had a dripping Dixie cup in his hand, the ones we used to rinse our mouths after brushing our teeth.

It only took a second to remember what had happened and why I was lying stark naked on my bathroom floor. Gregory was about six inches from my face and practically hyperventilating. I could see his flaking, chapped lips, a small grayish brown string of prime rib stuck between his teeth, and a painful-looking pimple on the interior wall of one of his flaring nostrils. He deeply exhaled his broccoli breath in relief. He was undoubtedly not worrying about me—he was afraid he was going to have to explain to the Maricopa County coroner why his dead younger brother was lying naked on the floor of their shared bathroom with his underwear around his knees.

"What were you doing up there? Are you some kind of freak?"

"What was *I* doing? What were *you* doing? Who just barges into a bathroom when the door is closed?"

"It wasn't locked. And I had to take a leak. And the natural place to do that is in the toilet—in case you forgot. But apparently you would rather climb up on the sink and watch yourself piss down the drain! You're a complete psycho!"

"I wasn't peeing down the drain, idiot. I was trying to see the blisters on my butt from Coach Rawlings!"

"You have *blisters*? On your *butt*? Are you *kidding*?" He asked sincerely, almost compassionately.

I was still sprawled across the bathroom floor. I lifted my butt in the air and said, "Look. It's hideous."

He stepped to the side and inched his head forward, but could barely manage a peek at my posterior. It was like he was at a gory movie peeking through the cracks of light between his fingers.

"Oh, my holy nastiness of all nasty!" he blurted and covered his mouth with his hand. "Your butt cheeks are bleeding! There is watery blood running down your butt cheeks!" He started dry heaving and laughing at the same time.

"It seriously looks like your butt cheeks are crying," he observed between coughs. "Wait, is that an *R*?"

I pulled up my underwear and started to walk toward my room, rubbing the new marble-sized knot just under the cowlick on the left side of my forehead.

"Oh, man, you have blood seeping through your underwear!" Gregory observed from behind, gagging as I closed the door to my room behind me.

"Is everything all right up there?" Dad called from the family room down below.

"Yes! Everything's fine!" I called back cheerily.

I sat back on my bed and was wondering how much more humiliating the day could possibly get, when Gregory walked in.

"Get out of my room, weirdo," I said. "You can't look at my butt anymore."

"Hold on—*you're* the one that asked *me* to look at your butt. Besides, I come in peace, Wounds-in-the-Rumpus," he said, bowing and christening me with an Indian name. He knew I thought the greatest Indian chief name of all time, other than "Crazy Horse" (of course), was "Rain-in-the-Face," a Lakota Sioux war chief who supposedly cut the heart out of Custer's younger brother at Little Bighorn.

"I'm not in the mood, Gregory. Seriously, what do you want?"

"I'm here to bind up your wounds and make you whole—to make your moon full again, Wounds-in-the-Rumpus."

"Please leave, Gregory."

"This is for you," he said seriously, unfurling a flesh-colored jockstrap from his clenched left hand.

"Why would I want your jockstrap?"

"Well, some may say you will never be able to *carry* my jockstrap, but I'm giving you the opportunity, for a limited time only, to actually *wear* my jockstrap."

"And why would I want to do that?"

"I'm being totally serious. And I'm trying to be nice. Really, I am," he said sincerely.

I said nothing. A signal that it was okay for him to continue.

"If your butt is bleeding and oozing whatever the heck it was just oozing, it's going to stick to your underwear, and then they're going to rip off. Hold on. I think I'm gonna dry heave again . . . Hold on . . ." He paused dramatically as if he would need to dash for the toilet, then gathered himself and cleared his throat.

"If I were you," he resumed, "I would put some extra-large Band-Aids over those purple prickly pears and wear this jock to school. The Band-Aids will protect the welts, and the jock will give you the masculine support that you need. But, then again, a peanut shell and a rubber band might work equally well in your case."

"Why wouldn't I just put Band-Aids on and then wear regular underwear? That makes no sense."

"It makes sense because you have no idea exactly when the Hello Dance is. But it'll be sometime this week. It's always during the first week."

"So?"

"So, let me put it to you this way. It's all about one thing—containment. You don't want a squirmer peeking out of your boy-kini's y-fly during a slow dance."

"Whatever, Gregory," I said, completely defeated by the day.

"I'll take that as a thanks-I'll-think-about-it-wise-older-brother and leave you two alone." He tossed his jockstrap in my lap. "Containment," he repeated, as he closed my door behind him.

37

The Real Thing

I couldn't sleep.

It was dark, it was hot, and for obvious reasons I lay on top of my sheets on my stomach rather than in my normal position—on my back with my hands clasped behind my head.

After I was confident that everyone was asleep, I crept downstairs, through the family room where Dad lay—still fully clothed, snoozing on the couch while Doc Severinsen was taking Johnny Carson to commercial break—through the kitchen and into the pantry where Mom kept all of our home medical supplies in a plastic Tupperware box. I found the largest Band-Aids I could find, took four just to be safe, and crept back upstairs and into my bathroom. This time I made sure my door was locked and Gregory's was too. I carefully took off my undies so as not to rip off any newly forming gluteal scabs and replaced them with Gregory's jockstrap. This time I made sure my socks were off, so my feet would have a better grip on the vanity. I carefully climbed back up on the vanity, reassumed the pose of a long snapper double-checking to make sure the punter is ready, reacquainted myself with the upside-down view of my juicy, coagulating welts, and delicately placed a large Band-Aid over each sore.

I unlocked Gregory's door to the bathroom and then returned to my bed, stomach first, wearing only the jock. It was still dark, still hot, and I was still uncomfortable on my stomach, although the fresh oscillating breeze on my nearly bare butt cheeks sent a refreshing shiver up my back the first few times it came around the room.

Sleep was impossible. My mind raced like I was in a Dr. Seuss story. I was trying to remember all of the class rules for Woodshop. I would not, could not, be the only guy in the class to not pass the safety test. I certainly did not want to draw any more attention to myself, especially in front of another all-male audience. Math was going to be brutal, I just knew it. I hated math. I dreaded it. I *loathed* it.

I started to replay the directed numbers problems in my head until I gave up, exasperated and forlorn. I started picturing equations in my head that I had no idea how to solve. Then I remembered PE. What would it be like tomorrow? Was Rawlings, at this very moment, lying in his bed too—scheming about more demonstrations, more humiliating experiments? Or would he cede the day-two rituals to the traditional hazings handed down by the ninth graders from junior high generation to generation.

Then I suddenly remembered that I would be required to sing. Alone. A solo. In public. In front of Ben-G. In front of Jenny and all of her friends. I had just about convinced myself that the whole choir idea been a huge practical joke by Gregory and Jericho. It had to be an elaborate ruse to humiliate us in front of all of the cute girls—the chosen ones, the trend setters, the opinion makers. The girls that could crush you with one reckless passing comment at their lunch table—without you even knowing that you had been crushed until two weeks later when you finally heard it from the kid who was the last to hear everything. Yet some spark of doubt remained. Was it truly an opportunity to find the preteen nirvana that they had sold us?

I tried adjusting my pillow. I tried lying on my left side, then my right, then back to my stomach. It was no use. I would not be asleep anytime soon, and it was well into the Roger Staubach (QB #12) hour. I turned on a small reading lamp with a mechanical arm that hung over my bed and found the "Articles of Faith" pamphlet tucked between *Great American Indian Chiefs* and *Most Amazing Sports Stories* on the neighboring bookshelf.

I lay down on my bed, elbows on my pillow, and held the small pamphlet in front of me. I read Articles of Faith eleven, twelve, thirteen, the last three, and tried to remember the correct order of "kings, presidents, rulers, and magistrates." I kept putting the president first. *We're Americans after all. Why wouldn't the president be first?* I thought. *And what's a magistrate anyway? Is there really any difference between "obeying, honoring, and sustaining the law"? Wouldn't you sustain it* before *you obey it?* Why did we need to honor it? Wasn't obeying it enough? I knew I had to obey Rawlings's ridiculous rules, but I certainly wasn't about to sustain them or honor them. I tossed the Articles of Faith off the side of my bed onto the floor in protest and pulled *Most Amazing Sports Stories* off the bookshelf. I'd read it probably five times. There were stories about Red Grange, Lou Gehrig, Sonja Henie, Sir Edmund Hillary, Jim Thorpe, and others. I was looking at a photo of Jesse Owens springing from his sprinter's crouch at the 1936 Olympics when Grandma Carter walked in.

She had never ever paid any attention to my attire before. In all the nights she had taken temporary dual occupancy of my room, she had never made a single comment about the fact that I was adorned only in my underwear. But that night, as she walked through my door, she immediately noticed my lack of attire.

"You've been injured."

"Yeah, I guess," I said, reaching back to grab the sheet to pull it over my butt.

"Wait," she said. "I see those bandages on your rump. Are you in pain?"

"Not really. It's not so bad anymore."

"What are those straps?"

I finally succeeded in finding the top of the sheet and pulled it up, covering the Band-Aids and the jockstrap.

"Oh, it's just a type of underwear," I said, trying to deflect any more questions. I didn't really feel like explaining to my grandmother the purpose and parts of an athletic supporter that was being used for an alternative purpose.

"Hmm," she said and moved toward my desk. "Were you injured at your Hello Dance?"

I couldn't believe she remembered our conversation about the dance.

"No, I wasn't injured at the Hello Dance, Grandma. We haven't even had it yet. And I'm not sure how I could get injured at a dance."

"Remember, you must be polite when you ask Jenny, your love, to dance. You must do so with confidence, grace, and dignity."

I couldn't believe she could remember Jenny's name either. I was baffled and embarrassed. I hope she didn't inconveniently remember this information at church or the dinner table. I said nothing, hoping her mind would wander into some other territory.

As she placed her book of remembrance and its companion, the album cover, on the desk, she glanced to the side and noticed the "Articles of Faith" pamphlet on the floor.

She bent down, creaking and cracking, until she grasped the pamphlet. She studied the front cover for a minute or two then handed it to me. "What are all these words on the inside?" she asked, squinting at the thirteen Articles of Faith.

"Oh, they're the basic things we believe."

She raised an eyebrow. "Like what? What do you believe?"

"Well, I believe in God the Eternal Father and His Son, Jesus Christ, and in the Holy Ghost, I guess. That's one of them. It's actually the first thing. And then there's Adam. We believe that men will be punished for their own sins not for Adam's transgression. And then there's Jesus. We believe that through the atonement of Christ all mankind may be saved by obedience to the laws and ordinances of the gospel," I rambled, impressing myself at my memorization skills.

"Um hmm . . ." she said, still squinting. I couldn't tell if she was really confused or if she knew exactly what I was talking about and was quizzing me to see if I knew them.

"Why do you keep saying 'we'? Who is 'we'?" she asked.

"I don't know, everybody in the Church, I guess."

She didn't say anything. She was still squinting at the tiny print on the inside of the pamphlet, so I went on. "You believe them. I'm pretty sure Grandpa believed them. My mom and dad believe them . . . I believe them too, I guess."

She closed the pamphlet and looked at the front cover. I couldn't tell if she was listening. "What is this building here on the cover?" she asked reaching over and handing it to me.

"It's the Washington D.C. Temple." I handed it back to her.

"Where is it?"

"Washington, D.C."

"I see," she said slowly, sitting at my desk and examining the picture of the six white spires, the massive body of the temple below sheathed in white Alabama marble, and the golden angel Moroni blaring his trumpet on top. "Why is it so large?"

"I don't really know. I've never been there. I guess people get married in there and stuff."

"Hmm."

She carefully placed the pamphlet to one side, placed the precious Saturday Night Fever album cover to the other side, and began her almost nightly ritual of flipping the pages of her book of remembrance, every so often glancing to the side to make sure the pamphlet was still there.

I lay on my bed and kept flipping through the pages of *Amazing Sports Stories*, looking at the photos and reading the captions. I paused at a photo of Jackie Robinson in a cloud of dust, spikes up, stealing home.

Breaking the silence of our impromptu midnight study hall, Grandma Carter said, "Young man, what is this? Is it the Washington D.C. Temple?" she asked, handing me two photos.

"Um, let me see," I said receiving the photos. She waited patiently, while I examined both of them.

The first was black and white, old fashioned, with white edges bordering the photo. It seemed ancient. Although the second one was in color, it too looked like an artifact that had bleached and faded over time.

In the black-and-white photo, a newly married couple stood beaming at the base of a large grassy hill. Behind it, atop the hill, stood the Manti Temple. I knew it because Mom and Dad had taken us there a few times to see an elaborate pageant that was staged for a few weeks every summer on that very hillside. The temple stood solid and palatial beneath a sky full of ominous, rolling thunderheads. The beaming couple was Grandpa and Grandma Carter.

She was slender and unwrinkled and bright. She wore a simple, silky, long-sleeved white dress that reached down to her ankles and wrists. A small strand of pearls adorned her left wrist, and a matching single strand hung comfortably just below her neckline. A simple veil was perched on her head like a lacy crown, and her dark, loosely curled hair draped down, grazing her shoulders. She stared directly into the camera, beaming expectantly, nearly bouncing with enthusiasm. Grandpa wore a charcoal gray, double-breasted, double-vented pinstripe suit, a crisp white shirt with a dark polka-dotted tie, and a black silky handkerchief peeking out of the jacket's breast pocket. He too smiled directly into the camera. His smile was firm and piercing. There was no gratuitous overindulgence or playful toothiness. His smile was joyful, but determined. His dimpled chin jutted forward confidently, and his unruly hair was brushed back, temporarily tamed. They held each other's hands in front of them, displaying their rings, although the jewelry was secondary. It was their clasp that stood out. It was firm and tight, as if they didn't want to let go, as if they wouldn't let go, ever. On the back of the photo, in smudged black ink was written, "WEDDING DAY, JULY 15, 1925" in capital letters.

The second photo, the color one, was taken in nearly the identical spot, at the base of the same grassy hill. It was summer. The grass was thick and rich. Large, blotchy cotton balls of clouds filled the otherwise bright and brilliant, almost periwinkle sky.

The Manti Temple stood prominent and proud, looking out over the Sanpete Valley, its cream-colored fortress of limestone radiating a warm, golden caramel glow, and its silver-topped chateau towers glistening in the late afternoon sunlight like reflectors. Grandma and Grandpa Carter stood in the same pose, a reenactment. Their hands were clasped tightly, but more comfortably. Their smiles were older, more mature and experienced, but equally vibrant and more playful. Grandpa seemed to be laughing, as if the photographer, most likely Mom or one of her brothers, were making goofy remarks while taking the picture. Grandma seemed to be concentrating her best on not looking at Grandpa, who was about to laugh. She wore a red knee-length linen skirt and a simple white cotton blouse, with what looked like the same single strand of pearls. He wore dark, nondescript slacks and a short-sleeved blue Oxford. The back of the photo was labeled in cursive pencil, "July 15, 1950." Their twenty-fifth anniversary.

"No, Grandma, this isn't the Washington D.C. Temple." Still on my stomach and propped up on my elbows, I reached over to hand her the photos. "They're both of the *Manti* Temple. It's in Manti, Utah—where you and Grandpa were married. The black-and-white one is your wedding day, July 15, 1925; and the second one, the color one, looks like it was taken on your twenty-fifth anniversary, on July 15, 1950."

"Who is this woman? What's her name?" Grandma asked, holding both photos in either hand, glancing back and forth at them.

"She's you, Grandma. She's Gail Pruitt Carter."

"She looks very happy."

"She was always happy," I quickly replied, immediately realizing I had used the past tense. It didn't register with her, but I instantly felt terrible and sick. I wished I could take it back. But before I could correct myself, she looked over at me.

"And who is this gentleman with her?" she asked, looking into my eyes.

I swallowed uncomfortably.

"He's the Dancer, Grandma."

A smile inched across her face.

"Your Dancer," I said. "He's Charles Pratt Carter."

She delicately tucked the two photos back into the swollen abdomen of the book of remembrance, carefully scooted the desk chair back, and rose to her feet. She momentarily balanced herself using the back of the desk chair and then confidently stepped to the center of my room.

She stared expectantly at my sliding closet door for a moment and then half curtsied. "Why, yes, I would love to, Mr. Carter," she replied to the empty space in front of her.

XI

A few seconds pass, and Sheila and another woman appear. They hold one floral arrangement in each hand. Four in all.

Each is simple and plain but elegant, expertly manicured and arranged in a thick rectangular crystal vase. Each vase bears only one type of flower. There is no baby's breath, ivy, or other cheap garnish or embellishment. Four crystal vases, four unique bunches of a single flower.

One arrangement is an overflowing gang of brilliant, almost electric purple hydrangeas. Another is a dozen perfectly firm and upright long-stem pink roses. In Sheila's left hand is a brimming bunch of wild daisies, each with a radiant golden iris and bright white petals.

"What are those? They're beautiful," I say, nodding to the vase in Sheila's right hand and its cluster of delicate cup-shaped yellow and white tapered flowers.

"Crocus," she says. "We don't see them too much in Arizona. They're from Southern Europe."

A small envelope is taped to each vase. Each envelope is labeled in her unsteady scrawl of blue ink:
"Ms. Lisa Whitman Rogers"
"Mr. Gregory C. Whitman"
"Mr. Todd C. Whitman"
"Ms. Margaret Whitman Wells"

38

Dim All the Lights

The annoying bray of the alarm clock came too early. I had fallen asleep before Grandma was done twirling and sashaying. I didn't remember her leaving, and I didn't remember falling asleep. I was tired.

I quickly woke up, however, as if I'd been given an electric shock as soon as I remembered all that was facing me—the complete unpredictability of the second day of PE, the results of my impromptu prealgebra test for which I would most likely be publicly condemned to remedial math in front of my entire third-hour class, the weighty anticipation of the Woodshop safety test, and the terror of mangling a solo in front of the only female peers I cared about. My innards were wringing themselves like Great Grandma Willey kneading a mound of bread dough. The impending dread was palpable, like the destroying angel prowling through the Israelite ghettos sprawled along the Nile, looking for firstborns that didn't follow instructions.

I had forgotten about the jock and the Band-Aids, but as I rolled over on my back, the sting of the resulting pressure applied to my buttocks reminded me of the previous day's nightmare. Too nervous that I would have another run-in with Gregory during my personal hygiene time, I elected to forego a morning shower. After blindly feeling to confirm the Band-Aids' adhesive integrity, I slipped on another new pair of 501s and my brand-new Kensington terrycloth shirt with blue and burgundy velour stripes. I wet my hands in the bathroom sink, dabbed at a few nighttime alfalfa-sprout growths, made a neat part down the middle of my scalp, and brushed my bangs back into place. I put my wallet and a red comb in my back pocket and made a goofy face at the mirror.

Breakfast, the morning carpool, and the preclass locker scene all passed without incident. English was no problem, and PE even went smoothly. After getting through the nerve-wracking first few minutes of roll call, it was like nothing had ever happened. Not even a smirk, smile, or smack on the butt from Coach Rawlings. Maybe he really was completely psychotic. We did layups and played H-O-R-S-E in the gym, loosely supervised by Rawlings, who sat in the bleachers and read the newspaper. In prealgebra, Mr. Sturgess announced that the results of our "evaluative tests" were "encouraging" and that we would not be given our personal results. The test was "merely for my own purposes and not for your consumption," he explained. That was fine with me. At lunch, I was again able to successfully mask my preference to stand rather than sit and further aggravate my still fiery buttocks by congenially standing at the table's edge and acting as the bridge to the competing conversations of those on the floor and those at the table. In Woodshop, to my relief, I achieved the manly score of 100 percent on the safety test, and nearly everyone else did too. And in science, I managed to stay awake and discovered, to my good fortune, that my neighbor and lab partner, Bridget Brown, was a brainiac who would effortlessly guide us both through the weekly lab assignments.

Choir, however, was an entirely different story. The unexpected smooth sailing of day two turned rough and choppy as soon as I took my seat.

"Ladies and gentlemen," Mr. Laughlin enthusiastically announced. "It is my distinct *pleaaaaa-surrrre!*" he sang, bursting into his opera voice, "to now escort you to a very special *aaaaaaaa-ssembaa-lyyyyyy!* That is . . ." he paused for dramatic effect, "ab-so-lute-ly. Pos-i-tive-ly. Most-assuredly. *Maaaaan— da—tooooorrrryyy* for all seventh graders—including each of *yooo- ooooo-uuuuu!*"

And, as dramatically as he started, he stopped. He took a few breaths to gather himself and calmly stated, "Okay, ladies and gentlemen, let's quietly and peacefully line up at the door."

Most of us knew what was happening. Knowledge of the Hello Dance was no secret. Gregory had warned me about it. And, likewise, other older siblings and friends had warned their younger brothers and sisters and friends about it. In fact, the female chatter at the lockers between classes was made up mostly of incessant speculation about when the day and hour of the Hello Dance would strike. The boys never mentioned it. It was some sort of instinctual male taboo. We did not talk about dancing. We all knew the girls were nearly obsessed with the anticipation of it all, but none of us acknowledged what was going on around us.

As Mr. Laughlin opened the blue metal door into the Corridor of Respect outside, we felt the familiar blast of sweltering Arizona heat in our faces. We were leaving one air conditioned faux adobe bubble, on our way to another. Some of the girls bounced on their tippy toes in anxious anticipation and nudged their friends. A couple of them even put their hands together under their chins and clapped with nervous excitement. Their hum of chatter was loud and blended into an unintelligible buzz. The six of us boys, however, self-selectingly formed an impromptu fraternity of dread and dragged behind the rest of the pack. Every few seconds, Mr. Laughlin would turn around and walk backward for a few steps and say loudly, "Gentlemen, keep up. Keep pace."

We streamed into the plaza and saw seventh-grade classes from each corridor making their way in similar packs through the plaza. For those of us who may have really believed we were on our way to "a special assembly," all doubt was removed when we marched right past the auditorium and approached the canopied picnic tables and small grassy area abutting the entrance to the cafeteria. As we passed the auditorium, several of the girls looked at each other, covered their mouths and noses with both hands in nervous celebration, and quietly cheered. We boys collectively slouched, shoulders drooping in a universally recognizable sign of despair, briefly closed our eyes, and slowly bent our necks backward and our faces heavenward as if to say, "Please, Lord, let this cup pass."

Our class was one of the first to arrive at the cafeteria's three sets of windowless, metal double doors. Mr. Laughlin pushed one set of doors open with both arms, and we were immediately hit by a gust of cold air-conditioned air. As we shuffled into the cafeteria, our eyes tried to transition from the overpowering brightness of the summer sun to the cavernous darkness of the cafeteria. Masses of seventh graders filed into the cafeteria behind us. Like insects in a darkened room, we naturally migrated to the only part of the cafeteria that wasn't pitch black—the space directly beneath a twirling disco ball illuminated by a blue spotlight.

As soon as each teacher had confirmed his or her arrival to the cafeteria by checking in with Ms. Herriman, the student council advisor, the doors were slammed shut in unison, and there was a moment of anxious bewilderment.

Just as I thought to myself, *What in the hell is going on here . . .* a shock of music that made half of us twitch in terror blasted forth and the cafeteria began to pulsate rhythmically with the thumping, heavy beat.

It was still nearly pitch black. We were still temporarily half blind, stumbling and groping in the dark amidst a crush of nervous and giddy twelve-year-olds just beneath the orbit of splotchy, twirling, blue light reflecting off the disco ball. Separated friends were calling out to one another. Some were laughing. Some sounded like they were about to panic. Others were squinting, trying to discern who was standing right next to them in the darkened huddled throng. We could barely move. Ben-G saw the anxious look on my face and laughed loudly. "This is awesome!," he yelled heavenward. Seth Isenberg, a short Jewish kid I knew, and one of the six male members of "The Seventh

Heaven," looked up at me, unable to move in the crush of bodies, and mumbled nervously, trying his hand at gallows humor. "Is this Buchenwald Junior High?"

39

Get Off Your Aaahh and Dance

"*HELLLOOOO* seventh graders! It's time to *DANCE*!" Ms. Herriman cried with an eardrum-splitting shrill. A group of girls shrieked in approval.

"Let's make the most of these next fifty minutes! To get this started, we have our ninth-grade cheerleaders and the ladies of our ninth-grade student council here to help get us going!" An obligatory cheer arose from the peppiest of the seventh-grade girls.

Instantaneously, soft mood lights came on, and everyone made a desperate dash from the tightly packed center and stampeded toward a smattering of now-visible plastic orange chairs that lined the cafeteria walls. They had purposely not set up enough chairs. Those not fast enough to reach the safe harbor of the chairs or an empty nook along the wall were left with the cruel consequence of nervously wandering the perimeter between the safe zone of the chairs and the uninhabited dance floor, like gazelles pacing and watching for any sign of a sprinting cheetah bounding through the savannah toward them.

On cue, the ninth-grade student council girls and the cheerleaders came bursting through the double doors from outside. Framed by the bright intensity of the sunlight from outside, only their silhouettes were visible. The peppy student council girls were wearing their white-and-red-sleeved student council "spirit" T-shirts, and the cheerleaders were wearing their pleated white cheerleading skirts and their form-fitting white-and-red, short-sleeved sweater tops. They walked briskly toward my group of meandering, seatless refugees and grabbed our wrists, dragging us into heavy clomping steps of resistance that evolved into a brief trot until we arrived in the eye of the hurricane, directly beneath the disco ball. The peanut gallery clinging tightly to the walls of the cafeteria cheered and laughed in sheer, ecstatic relief that they were not us.

There were about fourteen of us. The cheerleaders and student council girls started bobbing and shaking enthusiastically. Some of them even gyrated suggestively and spun themselves around. Some were trying to make up for their own embarrassment by overcompensating with ridiculously fast hand and body shaking, or jumping in place.

I had no idea what to do. I couldn't mimic the girl that asked me to dance—a short, muscular blonde who appeared to be a gymnast. Her dancing was an eclectic and harried mix of a floor exercise routine, football cheers, and hula dancing.

She leaned forward and said loudly, trying to overcome the din of the fast-paced, thumping music, "I'm Stacy! What's your name?"

"Todd."

"*What?!*" she yelled, cupping one of her ears and shrugging while she bobbed back and forth, signaling that she couldn't hear me.

"Todd! Todd Whitman!" I yelled.

"You Gregory's brother?" she yelled back.

"Yeah!"

She nodded and laughed. I couldn't tell if it was a good laugh, like, "Ha, ha, Gregory is so cute and cool!" or a bad laugh, like, "Ha, ha, I can't believe I picked that dork Gregory Whitman's brother." I thought it was a good laugh, but I couldn't be sure.

"Well, c'mon! You have to actually *dance* before I can let you go!"

I felt all four hundred and fifty-six eyeballs of the Mangas Coloradas Junior High seventh grade burning a hole in the back of my terrycloth Kensington shirt. There could be nothing worse than this, I thought. This was way worse than Rawlings, I would happily relive Rusty the Rattlesnake or flunk the Woodshop safety test or sing a solo rather than do this. I was practically *dancing* a solo, which was a million times worse. As I shifted my weight, I realized that the stickiness of the Band-Aids had begun to wear off. I could feel them both half peeled back and flapping, while my tender welts and bare butt cheeks rubbed on the interior of my stiff jeans. Each back-and-forth rock of my weight—left-right, right-left, left-right, right-left—shot a sting through each butt cheek. Left-right, right-left, I continued, not moving my feet.

"C'mon!" Stacy yelled. "Like this!" She slowed down the loop of her now familiar routine and simplified. Small simple steps. She stepped left and clapped. She stepped right and clapped. Left again. Clap. Right again. Clap.

"Got it!?"

I tried it and stepped to the left. I stepped back to the right. I stepped back to the left. *Passable,* I thought. Back to the right. I missed my own hand on the clap. Soon I was shuffling and clapping with her in unison.

Now I got it. Gregory was a goofball. All of us boys that had been captured, we were all twelve years old, or nearly twelve years old—deacons. I was shuffling. I looked around at the other unlucky guys who were being humiliated and, sure enough, they were each similarly shuffling back and forth. It was practically instinctual. It was the deacon shuffle Gregory had foretold.

Although none of us was necessarily sticking out, we all looked equally, collectively idiotic. After several minutes of humiliatingly confirming to myself that I had no contemporary dancing skills whatsoever and convincing myself that I was probably even slightly retarded, Stacy released me back to the other minnows, but only after extracting a solemn promise from me.

"Good job!" she yelled, inching closer. I could feel her hot breath darting toward my ear as I cocked my head to the side to make sure I could hear.

"Now, here's the deal. I'm gonna let you go now, but you have to come *right back* with another girl and dance the *whole next song*. If you don't, I'll make sure that you do a spotlight dance for everyone at the end of the dance!"

She stepped back and looked at me. We were still shuffling.

"Deal?!" she asked. She wasn't really asking. She was telling.

"Deal!" I said nodding—and lying. There was no possible way I was asking anyone to dance.

She smiled, stepped forward, and gave me a courtesy hug. Then she gave me a gentle push toward the perimeter of the cafeteria.

"Have *fu—unn!*" she yelled and walked off to the other side of the cafeteria, prowling for more victims.

40

Last Dance

Stacy did not return. She had no idea that I had disobeyed and didn't return to the dance floor. At first, I hid in the shadows, hoping she wouldn't see me and pull me back out to the dance floor. But, to their credit, the cheerleaders and student council girls had been wildly successful. They had terrorized a few in order to calm the masses. Their successful catch-and-release program had, in less than forty-five minutes, spawned a healthy population of awkwardly writhing seventh graders.

Eventually, many of the chairs became empty, so I left the dark nook I had been occupying and found a seat with a panoramic view of both the dance floor and the DJ's makeshift stage. I spotted Ben-G. He had been pulled out by one of the cheerleaders and had obediently stayed out there the whole time, completely worry free, in his own Ben-G world, talking up girls and dancing with any girl he happened to cross paths with. Ben-G was abnormal. *It's unnatural to be that way,* I consoled myself. He was my best friend, but I hated him as much as I admired him at that moment. It was good old-fashioned envy.

The throb of my welts pulsated with the bass thumping from the huge black speakers facing the dance floor. I couldn't sit for long, so I stood up and observed from the sidelines—dejected. I secretly—almost desperately—wanted to dance, but I would unequivocally deny any such thing if teased or pressed by Ben-G, Gregory, or anyone else.

I stood and watched the bobbing and swaying mob. I found Jenny and watched her get asked to dance over and over. She could never even make it out of the crowd at the epicenter of the dance floor. She was so busy, so in demand, that she was sweating. She smiled. She laughed. She smirked. She was having fun. She danced near friends, and they cupped their hands over one another's ears and yelled secrets back and forth during the middle of songs. She gave a polite parting hug to each boy—mostly William Lloyd Garrison dweebs—at the end of each song. I hated each one of them. Every so often she would lift her left hand to gather and brush her butterfly-winged bangs back into perfect feathered recline.

I stood and continued watching. I didn't really want to, but I couldn't force myself *not* to watch what I was missing. I had to watch. I had to monitor. I couldn't stop myself. I was envious. I was angry. I hated Todd Whitman. I could throw a rotten orange at a car and run for fear of life and limb, I could fake like I was dead on the side of the road and try to talk my way out of harm, I could sit at the dinner table and act like the first day of seventh grade was great and fine and that Coach Rawlings's psychosis was no big deal, but I could not find the courage ("the mettle," Grandma Carter would say) to do the thing I wanted to do more than anything—ask Jenny to dance.

I was jealous of her—her confidence, her smile, her questlike determination to have fun. I was jealous of every single one of the guys that asked her to dance. I lumped them together as a bunch of dorks and goofballs, retards that couldn't even dance anyway. For the first time in my life I learned what real jealousy was. This wasn't a fleeting whine and pout about being denied a new Atari system or special edition red-white-and-blue Adidas Superstars, or not getting the nod to go to a Suns game with Dad when Gregory did. This was a sticky, churning, and gnawing business.

I looked up at the clock. 3:47. Only six more minutes until the last bell of the day. I wished that I could speed up time or that someone would call in a bomb threat to end the dance right that very second. I stood and shifted my weight back and forth in my brand-new Wally Waffle Trainers, royal blue with the gold

Nike swoosh. A wad of grape Hubba Bubba was plastered among four waffle treads, slightly sticking to the acrylic cafeteria floor, annoying me with every movement.

Another song ended, and instead of the usual instantaneous transition to another upbeat disco song, the rent-a-DJ proclaimed that he had some good news and some bad news. He was cheesy and perky, and the synthetic silkiness of his unnatural DJ voice made me hope he would get beat up at a night club someday very soon.

He announced that the good news was that the next song would, "at long last," be the first slow song of the afternoon. But, the bad news, he said, was that the next song would also be the last dance.

A new sense of tension and urgency filled the room. Guys began scanning the cafeteria, trying to find where certain girls were, like parents looking for a lost child at a playground. All the girls hushed, concentrating—waiting to hear the first chords of the song. A collective silent game of Name That Tune was about to be played.

"My name is DJ Anthony," the guy continued. "I've had a great time with you today here at Mangas Coloradas Junior High! I hope you have too! Get ready! Here we go! All you Red Sleeves, have a *great year*! All right, guys, it's time to go find that special *Laaaa-ddddyy*!"

The music started. Soft, slow piano notes. Then Kenny Rogers began crooning about being some lady's knight in shining armor. In unison, all of the girls screamed with delight, rose on tippy toes, and began scouring the back reaches of the cafeteria for a glimpse of any approaching suitors.

I saw Jenny turn and look around, and then I lost her. This couldn't end soon enough. I didn't want to watch her slow dance. Me and the other boys who wouldn't be slow dancing instinctively fell back into a loose circle, unintentionally forming a deep half ring around the dance floor, trying our hardest to look either uninterested or irritated. Girls without dance partners formed small circles and tried to make small talk. As cover, some became unusually preoccupied with trying to read the informational banners posted on the cafeteria walls. The caloric value of a cheeseburger, green-chile burrito, and onion rings never looked so interesting. I pretended to scan with interest the white banners with red letters and red silhouette of a warrior on horseback that hung high on the cafeteria wall—"MCJHS Red Sleeves, Football City Champs '74, '77, '79."

As I glanced up again and took note that Mangas Coloradas had won the city championship for girls' tennis ten years in a row, I saw Jenny swimming upstream, dodging the downstream current of couples heading to the dance floor. She was done with this nonsense. I was grateful. I looked up at the volleyball banner, trying to avoid eye contact with her, like I had no idea she was even in the vicinity. *Four city championships in the last seven years. Not bad.*

I frowned. Here she came.

I squinted ceiling-ward, as if I were really concentrating on the boys' baseball banner. *Be cool, she'll be passing soon! She's approaching. Hold steady. Hold steady. She'll be passing any second. 5, 4, 3, 2 . . .* I squinted intently. The last boys' baseball city championship was in 1974. Fake fascination. *Be cool, man.*

She didn't pass. She stopped right in front of me. I looked down from the rafters. She was not smiling.

"You're the only boy I know that didn't ask me to dance."

I was too shocked to say anything. I had nothing witty or smart or charming or indifferent to say. I was embarrassed and awkward and wished that the circuit breaker would blow, that the place would go dark, and that Kenny Rogers would shut up so I could sneak out in the chaos that would follow.

She just stood there, staring pregnantly.

The only thing I could think to say, the only way to bail myself out, was to blurt out Grandma's instructions. A desperate move—"Excuse me, Jenny, may I have the pleasure of your hand in this dance?" But before I could convince my brain to summon the throaty vibrations from my vocal chords and to tell my mouth to shape the words to say it, to say *anything*, she grabbed my hand impatiently and said, "C'mon Todd. Let's dance."

I followed behind her, willingly, dizzily. There were no clomping steps of resistance this time. Adrenaline spiked through my veins. My heart raced and my mouth turned to cotton. My lips and gums were instantly covered in a salival mortar that made my lips stick to my teeth. I furiously licked under my upper lip counterclockwise, over my front teeth and my bottom teeth, like a numb-mouthed coke addict. My thigh muscles were taut and quivering, like I had just finished three sets of twenty on the squatting machine. I was in disbelief. I, Todd Whitman, was being led to the dance floor by none other than Jenny Gillette. To dance the only slow song. The last song.

I surveyed the room and nodded confidently to friends as I strutted behind her, holding her hand. I even winked at Danny, the stoner kid, as I passed by him. Several boys frowned as I meandered past them, giving away their disappointment that I had found her first. But it was even better than that. What they didn't know was that *she* had come for *me*. *She* had searched and sought. For *me*. She had taken my hand. She had led me. It was a breathtaking triumph. I was miraculously cured of the smoldering step-by-step friction created by denim rubbing on blood blisters. Suddenly, seventh grade became doable, easy, a piece of cake, even. In my mind I conducted my own quiet celebration of ecstasy and conquest while nascent squirms struggled against the suffocating shrink-wrap of Gregory's jockstrap. Containment in action.

She hustled us through a maze of awkwardly bear-hugging couples rocking back and forth in tight circles. We passed T. J. and Curtis and Ben-G and even Seth Isenberg, who was dancing with an obviously post-pubescent girl twice his height, until we finally arrived at ground zero, directly beneath the disco ball.

She let go of my hand and stood in front of me, facing me. A white spotlight had replaced the blue spotlight. A fresh coat of bubble gum–scented lip gloss recently lacquered on her full red lips glistened beneath the intermittent patches of white light twirling clockwise around us. I stood still, unsure what to do. She raised her eyebrows and sighed.

Finally, I realized she was waiting on me. I got the message. Not sure exactly what to do next, I extended my left hand too stiffly and too formally. She looked confused. But she quickly figured out what I meant. She clumsily put her right hand in mine. I brought her closer to me, but not too close. There had been so many late night tutorials with Grandma, that some inexplicable built-in program took over.

I fluidly placed my right hand under her left shoulder blade, extended my right elbow at a sharp angle, and brought her even closer. I raised our clasped hands—my left and her right—to eye level, and took one step forward with my left foot. Then I began gently pushing, sliding, tugging, and gliding through the steps of the Fox Trot. This was dancing, I thought. I knew exactly what I was doing. The others clearly did not. They danced with expressionless faces, like Frankenstein and his bride—he with rigormortised arms stiffly extending to cup her hips, and she with arms just as stiffly extended and hands just as uncomfortably clutching his shoulders—rocking to and fro rhythmlessly in a joyless tight circle.

Jenny looked at me strangely and giggled nervously. *I'm actually pretty good at this,* I thought to myself. *I have this down.* I was moving with uncharacteristic poise, dignity, and grace. A well-trained athlete taking over in crunch time. *She will never forget this. She will never want to dance with anyone else again, ever.*

Pretty soon, the tight circles of the bear huggers began to slow down whenever their goofy orbits came within view of us. Some even stopped to observe. This was real dancing. They were taking notice. The girls smiled. The boys stared in disbelief. Jenny blushed and came closer, burying her head in my shoulder. *I love seventh grade,* I thought. There is nothing better. Rawlings was a distant memory. Directed numbers were meaningless. No algebraic equation would be too difficult. Bring them on. I looked forward to dissecting pig fetuses. I would fearlessly confront any towel-snapping, cursing ninth grader. I would gladly go solo and sing my lungs out in front of the entire school. Sign me up.

I tried to make small talk with Jenny, but she was too impressed to speak. So I continued with confidence, leading and guiding our trot underneath the glimmering disco ball. And after another moment, I decided it was time to deploy Grandma's H-E-R-O method.

H. Health and hobbies first.

"So, what do you do to keep in such good shape?"

She took her head from my shoulder and looked at me, confused.

"What are your hobbies? What do you do for fun?" I continued sincerely.

She looked around and put her head back down, snuggling closer to my shoulder. *She is completely content,* I thought and smiled to myself.

E. Education, I thought. Try Education.

"So, what's your favorite class so far, Jenny? Mr. Laughlin's pretty weird, huh?"

She didn't raise her head. She didn't answer.

She doesn't want to talk. She's like Grandma Carter—she just wants to enjoy the dancing, the pageantry, the artistry, the ambience. It made perfect sense. *Maybe she's just so into me that she just wants to savor this one, final dance. The only slow dance for seventh graders for the entire year.*

R. Relatives. *I'll give relatives one last try,* I determined.

"So, how's your mom? How's Gus? He's a cool little guy."

Nothing. No response.

Maybe Kenny Rogers was crying too loudly about that lady named "Lady" and Jenny couldn't hear me, I thought, just as she lifted her head and looked at me. She was blushing and seemed ready to cry.

Before I could say, "What's wrong?" she turned to look at the couples slow-dancing beside us. I followed suit. We had five times as much room as any other couple. *Maybe they all aren't so bad after all,* I thought. At least they had acknowledged that our need for space was greater than what their Neanderthal dancing required. They had all slowed to a near halt and were looking at us and then whispering to one another.

And then it hit me with crushing force. Their smiles and giggles weren't out of admiration for my skill and refinement or an acknowledgment of my grace and chivalry. They were mocking me. And Jenny knew it. She had known it the whole time. She hadn't been resting her head on my shoulder imagining that I was her knight in shining armor and that she was my lady. She had been ducking for cover. She was embarrassed, but she was too polite to take over and tell me to stop.

Some of the onlookers nudged their partners and nodded in our direction. Others blatantly pointed. Some of the guys whispered to their girls, impressing them with extra background material by reporting that I was Rawlings's infamous swat victim in PE. The girls opened their mouths and nodded as if to say, "*Oh yeah*, I heard about him."

They thought I was the purest, most unadulterated species of capital "D" Dork in the entire junior high ecosystem. There was a saying Gregory liked to repeat at breakfast every morning the week before school started: "If you don't know who the class dork is after the first week of school, it's you."

No one was wondering. They could all breathe healthy sighs of relief. They had their answer. It was none of them. The Dork's name was Todd Whitman.

I ground our Fox Trot to an abrupt halt. Thankfully, Kenny had just sung his last words, and a melancholy, final tinkle of piano keys was fading to silence. The song was over. The dance was over. Jenny gave me one of the customary hugs that had ended each of her previous dances, smiled bravely, and said, "Thanks, Todd. You're a good dancer." Then she walked off toward her giggling friends.

Just as I dropped my head, Ben-G came up from behind and

grabbed my shoulders. "What the heck got into you out there—what *was that*?" he said, and then playfully gave me a violent smack on the butt. I yelped in pain and crumpled to my knees. My puffy blood blisters were squashed flat and oozed like small pieces of Freshen Up gum after the first bite.

Everyone turned around and saw me kneeling on the ground, head bowed and closing my scrunched up eyes in pain. An undeniable second witness that, the promised class Dork had, in fact, appeared in their midst.

Ben-G bent down to see if I was okay. "I totally forgot! Sorry, man!" he profusely and repeatedly apologized. He extended his hand to pull me up, but I shook him off, stood up, and then navigated solo through the maze of lingering flirty and gossipy cliques, past jostling groups of guys raunchily discussing body parts they knew nothing about, past the wall flowers who were sighing in relief that the dance was finally over, through a loose group of stoner kids lamenting about how pop music and D.J. Anthony sucked, and past Jenny and her pack of chosen ones. They stopped talking and uncomfortably looked at their shoes as I passed. I brushed past their outer ring and pushed open the heavy metal doors with an angry heave of my shoulder. Then I stepped into a blinding, blistering burst of afternoon light.

41

The Death of a Disco Dancer

I got home from school. Everything was "fine."

"How was school, bud?" Mom asked when I came in the door. The answer was, "Fine."

"Stacy Ferguson told me she danced with you. Nice work. How did my baby bro do?" Gregory asked. The answer was, "Fine."

Gregory continued. "See, what did I tell you? The jock was brilliant. Was I right?" The answer was, "Yeah. It was fine."

"Wait, what happened?" he asked, noticing that my answers were insincere, a cover to some kind of incident. "Melancholy I detect, young Jedi," he said, trying to imitate Yoda in voice and grammar. It was funny, but I was in no mood to laugh. My response was a plaintive, "I'm fine."

At dinner, there were more questions, but my answers remained the same. Everything was fine. School was fine. PE was fine. Coach Rawlings was fine. No there had not been any more swats. Everything was fine. How many times did I have to say it? Couldn't they all just get it—everything was FINE.

After dinner, I lied and said I had a bunch of homework.

"Do you need help, sweetie?" Mom asked kindly. She could tell something was wrong.

"No, thanks. I'm fine," I lied.

I went upstairs to my room and closed the door. I mindlessly watched my fan move back and forth across the room. Sweet D was still smiling in the pile of candy. Paul Westphal was still tossing a basketball in the air, going home. And George Gervin was still sitting on ice blocks. I wished I could sit up there next to him.

I glanced over at my bookshelf and randomly pulled *Fortress Rock* off the second row and began to reread the story of the three hundred Navajos that hid out while under siege on the top of the promontory at the junction of Canyon del Muerto and Canyon de Chelly. The siege took place during the winter of 1864, and Kit Carson's men chopped down the Navajos' centuries-old peach orchards and pillaged below, trying everything they could think of to starve them off the impenetrable butte. The small band of Navajos outlasted them, though, in part by a creating a daring nighttime human chain down the toeholds carved into the sheer face of Fortress Rock, while American troops slept below. On a ledge overhanging Tsaile Creek, Navajo warriors dangled gourds from yucca ropes and scooped up desperately needed water, then passed the gourds up the human chain to the top of Fortress Rock, hundreds of feet above, all through the night, replenishing their water supplies. After a few chapters, I flipped to the middle of the book, examining the maps of Carson's bifurcated route to the mouth of the combined canyon, the noble poses of Chiefs Manuelito and Barboncito, and aerial photos of Spider Rock, Fortress Rock, and the Chuska Mountains.

After I had been reading for a while, I started nodding off then intermittently dozing until I finally fell asleep, much earlier than my normal bed time. Mom must have come in and checked on me, because when Grandma came in later that night and turned on the light, I was still in my school clothes, but my shoes were off, my sheet was up over me, and *Fortress Rock* was back on my book shelf.

"Good evening, young man," she announced cheerfully, setting the book of remembrance and the album cover in their familiar spots on my desk. "Shall we dance?"

I wondered if I was having a dream. It took me only a second to realize that I was still in my school clothes and that, unfortunately, I was not dreaming.

"I'm not dancing tonight, Grandma."

"Suit yourself," she said suspiciously.

She hummed and twirled for a few minutes. I lay on my side and watched her, hoping I would quickly fall back asleep. She stepped toward my bed again and asked, "Are you ready to dance?"

"I already told you, I'm not dancing tonight, Grandma."

"You need to practice for your love, Jenny. You must be ready for your school dance."

"I had *too much* practice. The dance is already over. You made me look like a weirdo."

"You can never have too much practice, young man," she replied, obviously not getting it, not understanding that the Hello Dance was history. That there was nothing to practice for.

"I already told you—I'm not dancing. The dancing is *over*," I said angrily. She was hugging the stupid album cover against her chest now, but I went on, unable to stop myself. "I will *never* dance again. I'm just like your stupid *Dancer*," I said, angrily pointing to John Travolta in his ridiculous white suit and black shirt peeking out from under her arms. "He said *he* was never going to dance again. Well, *I'm* never gonna dance again.*"

I meant for it to sting. I said it like the idiot eleven-year-old boy that I was.

It was a tone that she was not accustomed to hearing. She bent her head to one side, quizzically and lucidly studying me. I knew I had been too harsh, and I instantly regretted it. I rolled over onto my other side and stared at the wall. I fully expected her to match my orneriness, to say something mean or hurtful. To accuse me of some made-up travesty that had been imposed upon her, to jump on the dog pile of mockery that I felt suffocating me, to tell me I was nothing compared to the Dancer and that I never deserved to dance again, and then pack up her book of remembrance and storm out of the room. But she didn't.

She said nothing for a few long moments, but I could feel her hovering over my bed.

I didn't know if she was going to spank me, slap me, or lecture me. I deserved all three. I convinced myself that she was getting ready to unleash. I preemptively clinched my butt cheeks in self-defense.

Nothing happened. The silence was awkward. Finally, she sat down on my bed.

"Today was your Hello Dance, wasn't it?" she asked tenderly. This was Grandma Carter speaking.

The pent-up angst and embarrassment of the last couple of days, my complete frustration with seventh grade, my utter lack of courage, the painful self-awareness of my own naïveté, my hatred of Rawlings, my fear of math and solos and group showers, my total lack of interest in dissecting pigs and grammar, all of it, everything, gave way.

It was *her* voice. *Her* tone.

I crumbled.

I buried my face in my pillow. She bent down and touched her forehead on the back of my head. "I'm sorry it didn't turn out the way you hoped," she whispered softly.

I tried to regain control, struggled to inhale normally, but the intake sounded like an engine with a bad case of the knocks. She silently stroked my hair.

After a few moments I regained my composure and turned over again, to her side, facing her. She asked if I asked Jenny to dance. I told her I chickened out. I told her Jenny asked *me* to dance. I expected her to frown and go on about shamelessness, hussies, and etiquette, to take the opportunity to opine about what nice girls ought to do and what nice girls should never do. But she didn't. She did the opposite. She smiled approvingly. "I like this Jenny. She's not afraid. She knows what she wants."

I told her I danced the Fox Trot. She was proud. I told her I was mocked. She was flabbergasted. I told her I was angry. She was sympathetic. I told her I hated school. She told me I was smart and talented and kind. She assured me it would get better.

I turned over again on my side. I was exhausted. I stopped talking. So did she. She silently stroked my hair for a few more minutes and then stood up and stepped away. The light turned off and my door closed. It was dark. Sleep came quickly.

In the morning, as I dressed, I noticed that Grandma had forgotten the album cover. It was in its familiar nighttime parking place in the upper left corner of my desk. I left it there. *She'll get it tonight,* I thought. It stayed there for three days.

I wasn't sure if Grandma came in my room those nights; it was certainly possible, but if she did, I didn't wake up, and she kept on forgetting to take the album cover with her. I didn't touch it. John Travolta and Peter, James, and John stayed put, gathering dust and staring at the ceiling.

When I got home from school that Thursday, Mom had the album cover in her hand. "Why is this in your room?" she asked. "I don't know," I said. I really didn't. I went upstairs and she followed me, carrying a basket full of folded laundry and the album cover balanced on top. I went into my room and watched her walk into Grandma's room. She placed the album cover on top of the book of remembrance then walked down farther to Maggie's room with the laundry.

The next morning I woke up and saw that the album cover was back on my desk, sitting face-up, in the upper left-hand corner. I stayed up that night—past the Roger Staubach (QB, #12) hour and nearly all the way through the Rafael Septien (K, #1) hour. She never came. In the morning, I took the album to Grandma's room and put it under her book of remembrance myself. When I got home from school, it was back on my desk. I tucked the album cover in my book shelf, between *Amazing Sports Stories* and *Great American Indian Chiefs,* next to the "Articles of Faith" pamphlet.

I stayed up that night, too, even later this time. I pulled out *Great American Indian Chiefs* and studied the photo of Chief Joseph, his confident, stubborn gaze and unmatched bouffant bangs and braided pigtails. I read about the flight of his seven hundred Nez Perce in the fall of 1877, their fifteen-hundred-mile circuitous sprint over backbreaking terrain through four states while two thousand American soldiers nipped at their heels and finally overtook them just forty miles from the Canadian border.

She didn't come that night. And, as far as I know, she never came again.

XII

I open the back door of D. Boettcher & Sons and hold it for Sheila and the other woman. They carry the vases. I hold two banker's boxes. As we leave the mahogany paneled, dimly lit office and step onto the sidewalk, we squint into the brightness of the October afternoon sun.

We walk out into the simple black-topped parking lot. I open the back door of my rental car, and we place two vases in each banker's box and securely place each box in the foot wells of each side of the backseat. As Sheila and the other woman offer their final, well-practiced and well-worn condolences, I turn the ignition and politely wave good-bye. As I leave the parking lot, I twist in my seat for a moment and look down at the daisies brimming over the top of their box and resist the urge to pluck my card from the vase.

I slowly pull out of the lot and head for Mom and Dad's house, where the others are waiting. The adults will be sitting in the family room talking and dozing, and the grandkids will be running around the backyard throwing ripening oranges, pulling the rusting red Radio Flyer wagons on the sidewalk out front, or shooting baskets on the old basketball hoop that still hangs above the garage.

My thoughts drift to that house and what we will do with it. The thought of selling it, of strangers living in it, seems wrong.

The light ahead turns red, and I roll to a stop. I turn again in my seat and look down at the daisies. I can't resist any longer. I reach back and take the card from the base of the crystal vase. I open the envelope and toss it on the empty front passenger's seat and unfold a single piece of paper, her monogrammed stationery:

LWC

My Dearest Todd,

Wild daisies—my mother's favorite. You know that better than anyone. You are more like her than any of the others—beautiful but feisty, cultured but untamed, loyal but demanding, solid and reliable, but tender. You were more of a comfort to her than you will ever know, and more than any of us were. She loved you even as I do and as Dad and I always will. You were her favorite (it will be our little secret).

She somehow knew, and I now know, that when we get old and get over the "getting" that sometimes suffocates life, all that really matters are the simple bonds that tie family. When you read this, I'll be with Dad—and Grandma and Grandpa Carter—and many others, too. There's no question.

I will never forget watching Dad hold you for the first time in his arms, looking into your big brown eyes. I think we somehow hoped you would never grow old. I am overwhelmed to be your mother and to have been entrusted with your earthly care. You have become a great man and great father. I'm so proud of you.

Although life is sometimes filled with discouragement, starts and stops, and difficulty, promise me now that you will be *you* and that you will never stop searching for the beautiful and feisty wild daisies that spring through the cracks and crevices of life.

I love you,
Mom

I close the card, deeply exhale, and look up just as the light turns green.

I see her for a moment with my toddler eyes. Her and that auburn bob. She tucks a loose strand behind her right ear and crouches down next to me, at my eye level. I reach forward wobbly and unsteady. She gives me a gentle nudge, tapping my diaper-cushioned behind, and whispers.

"Go. Move forward. It's safe."

Appendix

Unofficial Glossary of Selected Mormon Terminology

Ammon—A famous Paul-like missionary from the *Book of Mormon* who dared travel into hostile "Lamanite" country, volunteered to be the Lamanite King's servant, saved the King's flocks by chopping off the arms of a band of Lamanite hoodlums, and impressed the king so much that the king repented of his murderous ways and joined the "Nephite" church.

Articles of Faith—Thirteen concise statements describing the fundamental beliefs of members of The Church of Jesus Christ of Latter-day Saints. The Articles of Faith were first formally articulated by Church founder Joseph Smith in 1842 in a letter to John Wentworth, the editor of the *Chicago Democrat,* who had asked Joseph Smith to summarize the Church's tenets. Young members of the Church are expected to memorize the Articles of Faith before their twelfth birthday. The actual "Articles of Faith" are as follows:

1. We believe in God, the Eternal Father, and in His Son, Jesus Christ, and in the Holy Ghost.

2. We believe that men will be punished for their own sins, and not for Adam's transgression.

3. We believe that through the Atonement of Christ, all mankind may be saved, by obedience to the laws and ordinances of the Gospel.

4. We believe that the first principles and ordinances of the Gospel are: first, Faith in the Lord Jesus Christ; second, Repentance; third,

Baptism by immersion for the remission of sins; fourth, Laying on of hands for the gift of the Holy Ghost.

5. We believe that a man must be called of God, by prophecy, and by the laying on of hands by those who are in authority, to preach the Gospel and administer in the ordinances thereof.

6. We believe in the same organization that existed in the Primitive Church, namely, apostles, prophets, pastors, teachers, evangelists, and so forth.

7. We believe in the gift of tongues, prophecy, revelation, visions, healing, interpretation of tongues, and so forth.

8. We believe the Bible to be the word of God as far as it is translated correctly; we also believe the Book of Mormon to be the word of God.

9. We believe all that God has revealed, all that He does now reveal, and we believe that He will yet reveal many great and important things pertaining to the Kingdom of God.

10. We believe in the literal gathering of Israel and in the restoration of the Ten Tribes; that Zion (the New Jerusalem) will be built upon the American continent; that Christ will reign personally upon the earth; and, that the earth will be renewed and receive its paradisiacal glory.

11. We claim the privilege of worshiping Almighty God according to the dictates of our own conscience, and allow all men the same privilege, let them worship how, where, or what they may.

12. We believe in being subject to kings, presidents, rulers, and magistrates, in obeying, honoring, and sustaining the law.

13. We believe in being honest, true, chaste, benevolent, virtuous, and in doing good to all men; indeed, we may say that we follow the admonition of Paul—We believe all things, we hope all things, we have endured many things, and hope to be able to endure all things. If there is anything virtuous, lovely, or of good report or praiseworthy, we seek after these things.

Bishop—The spiritual leader of a local Mormon congregation (known as a geographical "ward"). A bishop has comprehensive administrative responsibility for the Church within his designated geographical ward boundaries. Bishops are "called" through inspiration by Church authorities to serve for an indefinite period of time, usually five to seven years, and are unpaid volunteers. Bishops spend roughly twenty to forty hours per week performing their ecclesiastical duties in addition to their unrelated "day jobs."

Bishop's Storehouse—A network of Church-owned storehouses that stock basic foodstuffs and essentials that are largely produced from Church-owned farms and canneries and financed by Church member contributions. All storehouse work is performed by Church volunteers, and foodstuffs are distributed to Church members and community members in need.

Blessing—Men holding the "Melchizedek Priesthood" are authorized to give priesthood blessings to those who request them. A blessing may be for the purpose of healing the sick or afflicted or for general purposes (e.g., providing comfort). A blessing given for the purpose of relieving the sick or afflicted has two parts: First, a priesthood holder anoints the head of the recipient with a drop of consecrated olive oil; and second, one or more additional priesthood holders place their hands upon the head of the recipient, call the recipient by his or her full name, seal the anointing of oil, and pronounce a blessing as dictated by inspiration from the Holy Ghost. Consecrated olive oil is not used unless the blessing is for the purpose of healing the sick or afflicted. Consecrated oil is not used when giving a blessing for general purposes.

Book of Remembrance—Many Mormons keep an individual book of remembrance that may contain family histories, genealogies, photographs, and other personal mementos and family memorabilia. Judging by the size of her book of remembrance, it's entirely possible that Grandma Carter is a hoarder.

Brother and Sister—Mormons refer to fellow adult Church

members as "Brother" and "Sister" rather than "Mr." and "Mrs." (e.g., "Brother Croshaw" rather than "Mr. Croshaw").

The Church – The Church of Jesus Christ of Latter-day Saints. Also known as the "Mormon" Church or the "LDS" Church.

Deacon—At the age of twelve, if found "morally worthy" by his bishop, a young man is ordained to the office of a deacon in the "Aaronic Priesthood" and becomes a member of his ward's deacons quorum until his fourteenth birthday. The deacons have the responsibility to pass the sacrament of bread and water to the ward congregation during the weekly sabbath sacrament meeting. The deacons quorum meets together weekly for church instruction and other activities, including as a Boy Scout troop. Volunteer adult advisers and Scoutmasters are "called" by the bishop to help oversee the deacons quorum and the Boy Scout troop.

Fast Sunday—The first Sunday of each month. Members of the Church abstain from eating food and drinking liquids for two consecutive meals and donate a cash fast offering (usually the approximate value of what was saved by not eating for two meals) to the Church to be used by the bishop to care for the temporal affairs of needy Church members and nonmembers within his geographical ward boundary. As members fast, they are encouraged to prayerfully concentrate their fast upon some higher personal or spiritual purpose (e.g., the health of a sick friend or relative, as an expression of gratitude, etc.).

Fast and Testimony Meeting—The sacrament meeting held on the first Sunday of every month. The meeting is like any other sacrament meeting except that there are no assigned speakers. Any attendee of the meeting may stand and "bear testimony" of gospel truths and faith-promoting personal experiences in an "open mic" format. The wild-card factor always makes it interesting.

Family Home Evening—Members of the Church are strongly encouraged to set aside Monday night as a "family home evening." Members are encouraged to participate as families in prayer, gospel instruction, singing, and wholesome activities and recreation.

Father's and Son's Outing—An annual overnight campout held by most wards to commemorate the restoration of the priesthood to the earth through Joseph Smith, eat s'mores, scare the crap out of young boys with ghost stories, and eat a campfire breakfast of invariably half-cooked bacon and doughy pancakes.

Mission—A two-year, pay-your-own-way, volunteer, proselyting mission for the Church. All worthy single young men are strongly encouraged to go on a mission when they turn nineteen years old. The "call to serve" is given by the Church's missionary committee at its worldwide headquarters in Salt Lake City. Prospective missionaries submit their application "papers" to Salt Lake City and a few weeks later a letter with the missionary's assignment is sent. A missionary could be called virtually anywhere the Church has permission to proselyte—anywhere from Boise to Bangkok, Albuquerque to Armenia or Tallinn to Tegucigalpa. Currently, there are approximately fifty thousand full-time missionaries around the world riding bikes, wearing dark suits, white shirts and conservative ties, knocking on doors, and passing out free Books of Mormon.

Primary—The Church's principal religious education program for children aged eighteen months to twelve years old. Every Sunday, after sacrament meeting concludes, children attend Primary for two hours to sing songs and hear gospel lessons.

Relief Society—The official women's organization of the Church. The organization provides educational and service opportunities for its members. Each ward has a Relief Society and a Relief Society president.

Sacrament Meeting—The principal weekly worship service of the Church. The sacrament of bread and water, representing the body and blood of Jesus Christ, is reverently administered to members of the Church in remembrance of the Atonement and Resurrection of Jesus Christ. The sacrament meeting service also contains hymns, talks, or sermons given by pre-assigned members of the congregation, special musical numbers, and the administration of "ward business" by the bishop.

Stake—An intermediate unit of organization between worldwide Church headquarters and the local wards. A stake may contain up to twelve individual wards, totaling roughly three thousand members or more.

Stake Center—A church building that includes a chapel, classrooms, a "cultural hall" (which is just a fancy name for a "gym"), and the offices of the stake presidency. The stake center is the weekly meeting place for three to four wards.

Stake Dance—Periodic dances for Mormon youths aged fourteen to eighteen who live within a particular stake's geographical boundaries.

Teachers Quorum—At the age of fourteen, if found "morally worthy" by his bishop, a young man is ordained to the office of a teacher in the Aaronic Priesthood and becomes a member of his ward's teachers quorum until his sixteenth birthday. The teachers have the responsibility to prepare the sacrament for the weekly sacrament meeting service. The teachers quorum meets together weekly for church instruction and other activities. Volunteer adult advisers are "called" by the bishop to help oversee the teachers quorum.

Temples—The Church of Jesus Christ of Latter-day Saints operates approximately one hundred and fifty temples throughout the world—everywhere from Anchorage to Accra and Helsinki to Hong Kong. Only the most devout Mormons—those who obtain a temple recommend after being interviewed by their bishop and stake president—are allowed to enter the temple. Sacred ordinances, including eternal marriage, are performed, and covenants are made both by the individual members on their own behalf and as proxies on behalf of others who have died (Mormons believe those who have died have the choice in the hereafter to accept or reject vicarious ordinances and covenants like baptism). After making personal covenants, Church members who hold temple recommends are encouraged to return often to reexperience the same ordinances as proxies on behalf of persons who have died without receiving them. The following three temples are mentioned in the novel: Provo, Utah; Manti, Utah; and Washington, D.C.

Ward—see "bishop," above.

Acknowledgments

There are three "R.C.s" without whom this novel never would have been written: My tireless and patient wife, Robin Cash Clark, the glue of our family, who has put up with my weirdness and general idiocy on a daily basis for the past two decades and who first encouraged me to write during the then "Blizzard of the Century" in the Spring of 1992 in Washington, D.C.; the man who first introduced me to the literature of the American West, Mark Twain's "belch in the parlour," and Mormon literature—the erudite, always generous and ever positive Richard Cracroft; and my maternal grandmother, Ruth Cluff Meldrum, who, though not a dancer, did leave a legacy for her children and grandchildren of quiet, determined dedication and deep love of forebearers.

I will always be grateful for the encouragement of my parents, Tom and Virginia Clark (even though my writing makes them squirm sometimes); my in-laws, Butch and Judy Cash; my siblings, Alison Brown, E. T. Clark, Ruth Ann Snow and Elizabeth Estes and their spouses; my siblings-in-law, Jeri Colton, Lori Richards, David Cash, and Kris McBrady and their spouses; one of my oldest friends, my principal "cheese" detector and the first nonfamily member I shared the manuscript with—Eldon Thomas; Bridget Verhaaren for her comments, insights, and outreach on my behalf; Johnny Gardner for suggesting that Todd Whitman attend Mangas Coloradas Junior High, the "Home of the Red Sleeves"; and for the many other friends too numerous to mention by name who took the time to read, opine, and encourage, and were nice enough to hold back otherwise legitimate commentary about my sanity.

The chapters, each named for titles of actual pre-1982 disco songs (with one exception), would have been nameless were it not for "Disco Saavy." I don't know who you are, Disco Saavy, but as far as I can tell, there is no better compilation of disco songs than those found at www.discosaavy.com.

And last, but not least, I owe deep, heartfelt thanks to those who helped this novel make it to print: Angela Eschler and her editing prowess, Jason Robinson for designing an unforgettable cover, and Chris Bigelow and Zarahemla for filling a gaping void in the growing world of Mormon literature and making room in it for Todd Whitman and his family.

About the Author

David Clark is a terrible dancer, former fake fighter, and recovering oranger. His oranging career effectively ended when he was intercepted and physically detained in a dark alley by a victimized college football player and was then forced to either rat out his friends or have his arm broken. His friends have still not forgiven him. He is now engaged in much safer pursuits as a corporate lawyer and formerly served as the general counsel of a major international media company and has practiced law and lived in New York City and San Diego. He now resides with his family in his hometown, Mesa, Arizona. His short story, "Candle," appeared in *Irreantum,* and his short story, "Rock, Squeak, Wheeze," excerpts of which appear in this novel, won the Moonstone award in the D. K. Brown Memorial Fiction Contest and later appeared in *Sunstone.* This is his first novel.

CPSIA information can be obtained at www.ICGtesting.com
Printed in the USA
LVOW080830081211

258416LV00003B/277/P